****

Battlefield Taiwan

Book Three of the Red Storm Series

By
James Rosone & Miranda Watson
****

Published in conjunction with Front Line Publishing, Inc.

Copyright Information

ISBN: 978-1-957634-11-1
Sun City Center, Florida, USA
Library of Congress Control Number: 2022904108

Disclaimer

This is a fictional story. All characters in this book are imagined, and any opinions that they express are simply that, fictional thoughts of literary characters. Although policies mentioned in the book may be similar to reality, they are by no means a factual representation of the news. Please enjoy this work as it is, a story to escape the part of life that can sometimes weigh us down in mundaneness or busyness.

Table of Contents

Foreword

The first chapter of *Battlefield Taiwan* picks up where *Battlefield Korea* left off. Then, in the following chapter, we look back to a couple of months prior to the start of hostilities in Korea, looping in what was happening in Taiwan during the lead-up to the invasion. This allows us to focus more of each book on the theater it is named after.

Chapter 1
Devil Dogs

Kimhyonggwon, North Korea
Thirty Miles Southeast of the Chinese Border

A light dusting of snow began to fall as the sun started to rise above the mountains. The valley below basked in the first glimpse of the new day. Staff Sergeant Tim Long of the 3rd Battalion, 5th Marines, saw the rays of sunlight penetrate one of the windows in the tent and knew it was time to get up. Even though the tent had a heater, Tim had spent the last few hours shivering in his sleep.

Forget it. I'm too cold to lie here another second, Staff Sergeant Tim Long thought to himself as he climbed out of his sleeping bag and hurriedly shoved his winter boots on.

Long had voluntarily chosen to sleep on the colder section of the tent, on the opposite side of the lone heater. Part of being a staff sergeant was making sure the young Marines in his platoon were taken care of, and if that meant he had to be a little cold while he slept so they could stay warm, then so be it.

A couple of the other Marines in the tent also stirred as more sunlight crept into their moderately heated accommodations. Private Tilley rubbed the sleep crusts from his eyes and groggily inquired, "What day is it, Staff Sergeant Long?"

Long had to think about that for a moment. Although he'd shivered most of the night, the last six hours was the longest stretch of consecutive sleep he'd had since their battalion had hit the beach a few weeks ago. His mind flashed back through the series of chaotic events he had just lived through with the rest of the 5th Marines.

After securing the city of Hamhung, Long's regiment had fought their way to a North Korean Air Force base at Hwangsuwon. They had received some intel from an Army Special Forces team that the 39th People's Liberation Army was setting up shop there so that they could threaten the Marines' newly established beachhead. Sure enough, as Long and his fellow Marines had arrived, they'd encountered quite a bit of resistance. At first, the 5th Marines were effectively beating back the enemy brigade at the airport, but then it had become clear that the rest of the Chinese army group was not far behind them. A desperate fight in the surrounding ridges had ensued until the rest of the 1st Marine Division had arrived, and the tide of the battle had finally turned back in favor of the Allies.

Staff Sergeant Long jolted himself from his memories. "It's November fifth, Private Tilley," he answered as he fastened his helmet on and then reached down for his rifle.

One of the young private's friends punched Tilley in the arm. "Happy Birthday, Tilley! You're finally old enough to buy cigarettes and join the Army," he said to a chorus of laughs and cat calls from the others in the tent.

Tilley had gotten his parents to sign his enlistment papers so that he could join the Marines at seventeen. He was the youngest Marine in the regiment, but despite his age, he was liked by everyone and was already turning into a great leader.

"Wow, I can't believe I almost forgot about my own birthday," he shot back, to the jeers of his friends.

While everyone finished getting ready, they heard the racket of the artillery guns resuming their barrage on the Chinese positions.

I'm glad they pulled our company from the line yesterday so that we could get some sleep, thought Staff Sergeant Long. This was going to be an absolutely critical day for his division. *We've got to push those Chinese soldiers back across the border.*

"Everyone, get your gear on and weapons ready," Long announced. "I want everyone to go grab some hot chow and get to the vehicles in thirty minutes." He looked down at his watch.

"Yes, Staff Sergeant," came the reply in chorus. His men scrambled to grab their remaining gear and move out as quickly as possible.

Though Long had struggled to stay warm enough to sleep, he knew these Marines were lucky that someone had studied the lessons of the first Korean War. With the temperatures dropping to subzero, the Marine commander had made the decision that units would only spend two nights on the frontline before being pulled back for an evening of rest in heated tents. Once the air base had been secured, an engineering unit had quickly come in and made a space that was livable enough for the units who were pulled away from the front to have a place to rest before returning back to the battle a few kilometers away.

As Long stood in line to get breakfast, he spotted a few dozen Super Cobra attack helicopters.

They must have gotten here while we were asleep, he thought. Seeing the helicopters so close to the frontlines was comforting. *We're going to have steady support with us for the coming offensive*, he realized with a smile.

He wondered if there was any truth to the rumor that the Air Force was going to move a squadron of Warthogs to the base once the frontline moved further north and they could better protect the critical aircraft.

A couple of Air Force C-17 cargo planes began to offload what looked like several companies' worth of soldiers. Looking more closely at the uniforms, he noticed these were not American soldiers, or Japanese. A smile spread across his face as he realized they were Australians.

It was good to see the Aussies were getting in the fight. Long had trained with the Australian Army in the past and knew them to be excellent soldiers.

A mere ten minutes later, Staff Sergeant Long had scarfed down a plate of creamed beef, grits, four strips of bacon and a cup of piping-hot coffee, and he felt like a human again.

As he stood to walk out of the chow hall, Second Lieutenant Chet Culley caught up to him. "Staff Sergeant Long—hold up a second."

"What can I do for you this fine morning, sir?" Long asked cheerfully, hoping he hadn't just had his last warm meal for a while.

Culley had been their platoon leader for the past eight months. He was a pretty decent officer and liked by the men thus far. His brother was currently a captain with the 3rd Marines, not too far away from there, and his father was a Marine brigadier general back at Camp Pendleton.

"Staff Sergeant Long, we're going to start pulling out for the front in about an hour. I wanted to go over our primary objectives with you and also pass along some good news." He pulled out a folded map and placed it on the hood of their joint light tactical vehicle.

"First, I wanted to let you know that Master Gunnery Sergeant Nopel is going to make it. I spoke with the battalion surgeon, and he said Nopel may still lose his leg, but he'll live," Lieutenant Culley announced with obvious relief on his face. Master Gunnery Sergeant Nopel had served with Culley's father many years ago and had taken him under his wing when he was assigned to the company as the Third Platoon leader. Nopel was also well-liked by everyone and respected for his off-duty work with the Toys for Tots program.

Smiling, Staff Sergeant Long responded, "That's great news, sir. I'll make sure to pass that on to the rest of the guys. Have you heard anything about Captain Millet or Lieutenant Patel?" He hoped their company commander and XO were also OK. Just before they had been pulled off the line, an RPG had hit their vehicle, injuring everyone inside. So far, their fellow Marines had received no updates about the extent of their wounds.

Lieutenant Culley's face darkened, and he suddenly looked like he had aged a few years. "Unfortunately, neither of them made it. I don't know how bad their injuries were or why they didn't survive. The battalion surgeon only told me they were in pretty bad shape when they were medevacked out."

The two men stood there in silence for a moment as they reflected on the loss. They had experienced so much grief since the start of this war—not just here in Korea, but they also had friends that had died fighting in Europe, and so many had perished in California.

Finally, Staff Sergeant Long nodded. "I'm sorry, sir. I know Captain Millet had become one of your first friends here." He put his hand on Lieutenant Culley's shoulder.

Culley wiped a tear from his eye. "You're right, Staff Sergeant. Unfortunately, they probably won't be the last friends I lose today, or before this war is over…but enough of that. The battalion commander told me I'm going to be taking over as the company commander. He didn't have any captain bars to give me this morning but assured me I'll have them before the end of the day. He also told me I had to replace Master Gunnery Sergeant Nopel." He reached down into a cargo pocket on his trousers and pulled out a new set of chevrons.

"The company and the battalion are desperately short on officers and senior NCOs. As such, you're getting another promotion. You're going to be taking over as the platoon leader for Third Platoon until a new officer is assigned," Captain Culley announced with a smile. "These are for you, Staff Sergeant Long. You're now Master Sergeant Long," he declared as he handed Long his new set of stripes.

Long almost took a step back. He hadn't expected this. He'd gone from being an E-5 sergeant at the start of the war to a staff sergeant two days later, and now a mere five days after that, he was a master sergeant.

Realizing there would be time to process everything later, he shook Captain Culley's hand and accepted the new rank. *Right now, we need to get ready for the fight that's coming*, he realized.

"All right, what's our objective and when do we hit it?" Master Sergeant Long asked.

Looking back at the map, Captain Culley pointed to the city of Kimhyonggwon. "Second Battalion secured the city yesterday afternoon and has pushed the PLA to these positions here and this hilltop here." He pointed out the locations on the map. "Our battalion is going to be assaulting this ridgeline. The vehicles will drive us up to this spot and then drop us off, and we'll advance on foot from there. They want us to secure the ridge by nightfall and then be prepared to hold it for the next couple of days. This entire ridgeline is less than twelve kilometers from the Chinese border. I was told the division commander wants to be the first American unit to cross into China." The rest of the platoon started to gather around them.

Not wanting to linger too long, Captain Culley quickly folded the map. "All right, Master Sergeant, I'll let you get your platoon ready. We roll out in ten minutes," he announced, and then he rushed off to go find the next person he needed to speak with before they left.

An hour later, Master Sergeant Long's vehicle joined a long line of medium tactical vehicle replacements intermixed with the more traditional 8X8 marine light-armored vehicles. While the convoy continued to snake its way through the valley, the thudding sound of artillery rounds impacting against the earth steadily grew louder. On occasion, they could hear aircraft somewhere high above them, blasting additional targets. Slowly, the convoy made it through the last major North Korean city before they reached the Chinese border. After several days of fighting, the city was mostly a smoking ruin of charred vehicles with dead bodies scattered everywhere. The Chinese had fought hard in the city, slowing the Marines' advance considerably. Ultimately, the Marines had had to resort to leveling most of the city with airstrikes and artillery before the Chinese finally withdrew to the surrounding ridgelines and hilltops to start the process all over again.

As the sun neared its apex, the convoy finally came to a halt along a small dirt road that jutted off from the main highway. "Looks like we're here," Master Sergeant Long said to his driver.

Turning to the Marines around him, he yelled, "Everyone out! Grab your gear and let's get ready to move out."

The men immediately complied with his request and hopped out onto solid ground. With the vehicles now emptied of their human cargo, they began their trek back to the airport to bring up the next battalion.

"Listen up, Marines," Master Sergeant Long barked. "We're going to advance to contact and secure that ridgeline." He pointed to their objective a couple of kilometers away, an imposing range of hills that ran for many kilometers in either direction. The ridge was currently covered in thick pine trees that had received a light dusting of snow. Had there not been enemy soldiers hunkered down under the trees waiting to kill them, this hike might have been a beautiful walk through nature. However, this was going to be anything but a leisurely stroll.

While at the airport, they received a forward observer from the artillery battalion that would be supporting their attack. The FO quickly called in a series of artillery strikes across the top of the ridge to prep the enemy position. After he made his call, the various platoons and companies fanned out and started the trek up the ridge. As the Marines moved into the woods, the friendly artillery fire lifted, leaving the ridge in momentary silence. Then all hell broke loose.

Dozens of enemy machine guns opened fire on the advancing Marines. "Everyone down!" yelled Master Sergeant Long as he hit the dirt, bullets ripping through the air where he had just been. Tree splinters and chunks of branches sprinkled down on Long like snow as hundreds of bullets cut down everything in their path.

Seconds later, the Marines returned fire, throwing just as many bullets back at the enemy. Long raised his head up to survey the scene before him. In the distance he saw several machine gun bunkers near a plateau, just below the top of the ridge. There was also a series of either foxholes or loosely connected trenches filled with enemy defenders. Despite the artillery barrage, the enemy was well entrenched.

As the bullets continued to whip over his head, he knew they needed to silence those machine guns. "Second Squad, advance. Everyone else, lay down covering fire!" he shouted to the soldiers of his platoon. With one squad pressing forward, the other three fired at anything that moved in front of them. Once Second Squad had advanced maybe fifteen or twenty meters, the next squad began to run forward with the help of covering fire. This continued until their entire frontline had proceeded towards the enemy lines.

While Master Sergeant Long's platoon was bounding their way up the ridge, the other platoons in their company were doing likewise. As the Marines moved steadily up the hill under fire, the artillery FO once again called in for more rounds to hammer the top of the ridge to help provide additional cover for the ground troops.

The Chinese had made the mistake of opening fire too soon on the Marines. While they were getting lucky and hitting a few Marines at the outset, they had given away their position, and the Allied soldiers were still far enough away that they could call in artillery support. Had the Chinese waited until the Marines had gotten within 200 or 300 meters of them, they would have been helpless.

"Third Platoon!" Captain Culley yelled over the cacophony of the barrage through the platoon net. "When that artillery stops, I need you guys to hustle as quickly as you can to the top before those guys start back up again. How copy?"

"That's a good copy!" Master Sergeant Long shouted over the roar of the explosions. The constant whistling followed by the concussions of the explosions was deafening.

The artillery scouts had changed the orders so that the new incoming rounds would explode in the air rather than on impact with the ground. This small distinction was having a devastating effect on the enemy. Dozens of 105mm rounds were detonating at treetop level, splintering the tops of the trees and throwing shrapnel down on the Chinese soldiers.

Long heard shrieks of agony from wounded men. *It has to be pure murder, what's going on at the top of the hill*, he thought.

After maybe five minutes of intense artillery fire, the barrage lifted. Master Sergeant Long yelled to his platoon, "Charge!"

In that instant, the intense physical and mental training the Marines put their people through took over as the forty-three members of Long's platoon jumped to their feet, screaming like men possessed as they charged towards the Chinese lines.

Long dashed forward, lifting his rifle to his shoulder. He fired a few rounds in the direction of the enemy before returning his focus to the task of reaching the top of the ridge. The Marines probably had twenty seconds to advance before the remaining Chinese soldiers opened fire on them once again.

As he was running, Master Sergeant Long spotted a Chinese soldier manning a machine gun. He dove to his right and placed his body behind a large pine tree and boulder. He heard several bullets impact against the tree and ricochet of the rock next to him.

That was way too close for comfort, Long thought. *We need to take that guy out*.

Master Sergeant Long inched around the tree to see the gunner. He brought his rifle to his shoulder, closing his nondominant eye as he looked through his Trijicon 4x ACOG sight and placed the red dot on the enemy soldier's face. It was then he realized with disgust that the man before him was actually laughing as he gunned down his comrades. Master Sergeant Long gently pulled the trigger, and the man's head exploded in a mist of red, his body slumping to the ground.

With one of the enemy machine guns down, the rate of fire being directed at the Marines slackened considerably. Then, sure enough, another enemy soldier ran up to the now-silent machine gun and resumed fire on Long's men. Master Sergeant Long took careful aim at the new gunner and fired another shot, silencing him as well.

A scream pierced the air not very far from Master Sergeant Long. He paused his advance as he leaned against a tree and looked to see who was calling out for help.

"I'm hit! Corpsman!" screamed the wounded Marine. Long was probably only ten meters away. He ran to the aid of his wounded comrade as bullets continued to whip through the air all around him, slapping trees and ricocheting off nearby rocks. As he got to the wounded man, he saw a pool of blood all around him. The Marine had been hit in the thigh and the bullet must have nicked an artery. Dark blood that was almost purple oozed through the young Marine's fingers with each pulse.

Master Sergeant Long glanced at the young man's name tape. "Hang in there, Tarpin!" he yelled above the constant din of machine guns and explosions going off all around them. Tim reached over and grabbed the field tourniquet all Marines carried with them and began to apply it just above the wound. He needed to stop the bleeding or Corporal Tarpin would bleed out. Master Sergeant Long got nervous as he observed that Tarpin's face was already starting to turn pale and he was sweating profusely despite the cold temperature.

He's going into shock, Long thought.

"Am I going to die?" Tarpin asked, fear written all over his face.

"No, Corporal. You're not going to die," Long replied with conviction in his voice. "I got a tourniquet on your leg and the bleeding has stopped. You'll be fine, just hang in there. I see one of the corpsmen heading towards you now…I need to keep moving. Hang in there, Marine!"

Tarpin just nodded in response. He knew Master Sergeant Long had to get back to leading the platoon.

Long looked up the hill and saw most of his platoon had advanced without him. They had probably moved sixty or seventy meters ahead of him while continuing to lay down heavy fire at the Chinese positions. A few of his men had been hit as they charged up the hill, and he heard them calling out for help. Master Sergeant Long desperately wanted to stop and check on each of them, but he knew he also needed to be leading and guiding his platoon to the top of the ridge. His men needed him, and he needed to trust the corpsmen to handle the wounded. Darting from one covered position to another, he quickly caught up to the rest of his guys. They were nearly in range of their hand grenades and would soon overrun the enemy positions.

"Come on, Marines! We're almost there. Let's go!" he yelled.

He moved with speed even he didn't realize he had from one covered position to the next, all while bullets zipped and snapped all around him. As he took cover behind a decent-sized rock and some shrubs, Master Sergeant Long grabbed one of his hand grenades and shouted, "Frag out!"

He threw that grenade for all he was worth at the enemy position. A couple of seconds later, it exploded while still airborne, over one of the enemy machine gun positions. The two Chinese soldiers operating the gun screamed out in pain, temporarily stopping their murderous rampage.

"Charge!" Master Sergeant Long shouted for what felt like the tenth time that day. He jumped to his feet again and raced towards the enemy lines.

As he came within ten meters of the PLA soldiers, he saw the fear in their eyes as he leveled his rifle at them and fired multiple times

14

into their positions. He kept charging, screaming like a banshee and firing his rifle rapidly until he ran out of bullets.

At that moment, Long realized that he didn't have enough time to reload his weapon before the PLA soldiers in front of him would start to fire back at him. So, he leaped right towards one of the shallow slit trenches the enemy had dug and plowed into three of the soldiers, knocking them all off balance. Quickly, Master Sergeant Long rocked back on his heels, raised his rifle up high into the air and then slammed the butt of it into the cheekbone of one of the enemy soldiers. He felt the bone crack and give slightly from the sheer force of his hit, and the man groaned as he slumped down from the shock and pain.

Long shifted his weight and swung the butt of his rifle at the next soldier, slamming it into the man's mouth and nose, crushing several of the man's front teeth in and breaking his nose in an instant. Quite a bit of blood sprayed into the air with that last hit. The man screamed, dropping his rifle as his hands went to his face.

The third soldier swung his AK-74 like a baseball bat at Master Sergeant Long's head and landed a solid blow on the side of his helmet. The shock of the hit caused Long to see stars as his head snapped back. Still reeling, Master Sergeant Long reached down with his right hand, grabbed his M17 SIG Sauer handgun and shot the enemy soldier three times in the face, exploding the man's head. Blood, bone, and brain matter splashed back on Long and the dead man's two comrades.

Master Sergeant Long twisted slightly to the right and fired several more rounds into the chest of the first soldier he had struck in the cheekbone. Then he rocked back on his left leg and prepared to fire at the last remaining soldier, the man with the broken nose. As he took aim, a three-round burst from the man's AK-74 slammed into the front ballistic plate of Long's body armor, causing him to stumble backwards out of the trench.

As he fell, Master Sergeant Long raised his SIG and fired four rounds at his attacker. All of the bullets missed, with the exception of his final round, which briefly caught the man's helmet and caused him to lose his balance as he fell backwards while firing a string of bullets into the air, just barely missing Long.

I've got to recover or I'm a goner, Master Sergeant Long realized. He threw his body to the ground, then re-aimed his pistol at the enemy soldier and fired three more rounds into the center mass of the man before he felt that sickening click that let him know that his pistol was empty.

I hope that guy's dead because I'm out of bullets, he thought. He lifted himself up slightly and grabbed for his next SIG magazine.

To his relief, he saw the enemy soldier clutch his chest and fall backwards, presumably deceased. The battle wasn't over, however, because in the next instant, Master Sergeant Long involuntarily dropped his head to the ground. His lungs desperately tried to fill with air, and his chest hurt something fierce—it was almost impossible to get the oxygen his body was screaming for.

A moment or two passed, and then his body recovered from the impact of the bullets against his body armor. His lungs filled, and he rolled over on his side, taking in several large gulps of air as he immediately began to fiddle with his pistol to get it reloaded. All around him, his Marines moved past him and continued to take out the remaining enemy soldiers. It was pure chaos, with multiple groups of Allied and enemy soldiers grappling with each other in desperately fought hand-to-hand combat involving knives, brass knuckles and pistols.

More enemy soldiers appeared from atop the ridge and charged down to join the melee. Master Sergeant Long saw an enemy soldier rushing towards him and aimed his pistol at the man, firing three times before the soldier's body crumpled to the ground.

The fighting continued for another five more minutes, with each side desperately trying to kill the other. It was only the superior combat training of the Marines that let them prevail; they had been badly outnumbered when the second wave of Chinese soldiers had joined the fray.

Slapping his third magazine into his SIG pistol, Long found his rifle lying next to one of the dead enemy soldiers and grabbed it. He dropped the empty magazine, slammed a full one in its place and slapped the bolt closed, loading a fresh round in the chamber.

"Master Sergeant Long, are you OK?" asked a voice that seemed far away. At first Long couldn't place where he knew that voice from. It sounded like it was coming from a tunnel. "Tim, are you OK?" asked the voice, a bit closer to him now.

He turned to his left and saw Captain Culley as he jumped into the trench with him and the dead enemy soldiers. Two other Marines jumped in with them as well.

16

"I, uh, yeah…I think I'm OK," stammered Master Sergeant Long, still trying to collect himself. Captain Culley looked him over for a second before nodding. "Good. I saw you jump into this trench here and fight those guys off. I swear I thought you were dead when that guy shot you at point-blank range. I'm glad you're all right. Maybe we should have one of the corpsmen check you just to make sure," he offered.

"No, sir. I'll be OK. I can get my ribs checked after we've secured the objective," Long replied. However, when he went to stand up, he saw a spinning red haze. Then he involuntarily doubled over in pain and threw up. In the midst of the vomit, Master Sergeant Long spotted a fair bit of blood, and he knew then that he must really be in a bit of trouble.

"Corpsman!" yelled Captain Culley, flagging down one of the medics.

"Are you hit?" the medic asked as he approached.

Culley explained what he saw happen to Master Sergeant Long.

The corpsman said, "He probably has a punctured lung. He's going to need to be medevacked out, along with the rest of the seriously injured guys."

Master Sergeant Long tried to protest but nearly passed out from the pain in his ribs. Reluctantly, he consented to being evacuated out with the other wounded. As he made his way down the ridge, helping a few other wounded Marines along the way, he felt angry that he couldn't continue to be there for his platoon. They had been together since the start of the war, and now he was going to be out of the action for at least a few weeks, maybe a month or two, until his ribs and punctured lung were all healed up.

It took nearly an hour to get to the base of the ridge where they had originally started the day. Once down there, all the wounded were loaded into a number of trucks, waiting to be driven back to the airport they had been at in the morning. The more seriously wounded Marines were being picked up by chopper and immediately flown off to receive a higher level of care.

Six hours after being wounded, Master Sergeant Long found himself at a trauma center on one of the amphibious assault ships, getting an x-ray. Sure enough, it was quickly determined that he had five broken ribs and a punctured left lung. The doctors there told him that he'd be flown to Japan the following morning. From there, Long would recover in a military hospital until he was able to return to his unit.

Chapter 2
Two Months Prior

The Republic of China
Taiwan

Following the surrender of the Japanese to the Allies in 1945, the Chinese Civil War heated up again. The communists were eager to pick up their fight against the Chinese Nationalist Party for control of the country and waged a successful campaign. Between 1946 and 1950, the communists had been able to gain control of the country, forcing the nationalist party to flee to the island of Formosa, now known as Taiwan. Although the new foothold in mainland China was firmly established, no armistice or peace deal was ever reached between the two warring factions. It was not until 1971 that the United Nations officially recognized the People's Republic of China (PRC) as a separate state from the Chinese nationalists who had set up a government in exile on the island of Taiwan, and that declaration was only achieved through a warming of relations between the United States and China when US President Richard Nixon visited Mao in China in 1971.

Despite sixty-seven years of relative peace between the Chinese mainland and Taiwan, the communist government never gave up their territorial claim to Formosa or stopped denouncing what they claimed to be an illegitimate government. These tensions had nearly boiled over into renewed fighting on multiple occasions. The only thing keeping the communists in check was the knowledge that Taiwan had fallen under the protective umbrella of the United States. In the 1990s and throughout the 2000s, the United States not only increased its military aid to Taiwan, it began to sell the Taiwanese more and more advanced weapon systems to negate any technological or numerical advantage the PRC might try to leverage.
****

It was another hot, muggy August morning at the Hsinchu Kansai military training base as Colonel Wang finished his tea. Today was the final day of his brigade's training exercise, and he was determined to see them do better than they had the day before. His armor brigade had just been outfitted with a series of upgrades by the American

19

defense firm Raytheon, giving their M60A3 Patton tanks new life. With a shiny coat of brand-new reactive armor and a seriously improved fire support system, they felt like completely different machines. The main gun had been switched out from the old 105mm to a new 120mm cannon, giving them a lot more power.

Colonel Wang smiled. *These upgraded tanks are on par with anything the communist mainland can throw at us*, he thought with satisfaction.

Looking through his binoculars, Wang could see his battalions were still working out the kinks in the new equipment and getting their crews up to speed. Today was the final day of their annual training and unit certification, so they had to make the most of it.

Putting the specs away, he walked up the stairs to the observation and control room of the tank range. It was a beautiful day. Birds were chirping, the sun was out and there wasn't a cloud in the sky—perfect range weather. A private who had been guarding the door stood to attention, snapping off a sharp salute. The colonel returned the gesture. Then, the door was held open for him to walk into the control room.

Once inside, Colonel Wang saw several officers with headsets on, directing the various units that were approaching the three tank trails that made up the exercise. A tank would head down one of the lanes and then move at different speeds from one point to another. At certain times, an enemy tank would appear, and the crew would have seconds to identify the target and engage it before they would be deemed killed. Some of the engagements were shoot-on-the-move exercises meant to test their ability to use the new targeting system, while others would have them come to a complete stop and fire at the target.

While this was happening, the crews in their tanks would hear the explosions of artillery landing nearby and have dirt and fake shrapnel thrown at them, courtesy of some sophisticated pyrotechnics. A couple of light machine gun crews would stitch the tanks up with some training bullets that would harmlessly ricochet off their armor. This simulation was meant to put the tank crews under the most realistic training exercise possible. If they handled themselves well in this situation, then chances were, they would handle them well in combat. If they failed, then they could focus on why they'd failed and work to correct those deficiencies before their lives were at stake.

Looking to his executive officer, Colonel Wang inquired, "How are the units shaping up today?"

His XO, Major Chin, smiled and nodded. "Much better than yesterday. The First Battalion did an exceptional job. Everyone passed. Second battalion had three crews fail. We're going to run them through again for a second try. Third battalion is going through the exercise as we speak. It looks like only one of them is going to fail, so I would say this is a marked improvement over the past week," he replied with a look of satisfaction on his face.

A ninety-three percent pass rate for the brigade is nothing to sneeze at, thought Chin. They could work with the few crews who struggled to help them improve.

The colonel smiled and nodded in agreement. This was a marked improvement indeed.

Major Chin, who was still rather excited by the new upgrades, asked, "Are they still going to outfit us with the American Abrams battle tanks in a few years?"

Colonel Wang turned to look at his XO. "That is what I've been told, but sadly I will not be the brigade commander if and when that happens. It will be you younger officers who will have that distinction." Explosions rumbled in the distance as the tankers that were running through the exercise engaged fictitious targets.

Wang's expression hardened. "Major Chin, I'm not sure if a conflict will arise with the mainland soon or not, but we need to make sure the brigade is ready in case it happens. The air force and navy are not going to be able to prevent the mainland from landing a ground force. It will be incumbent on brigades like ours to push them back into the sea. Do you understand?"

His face also somber, Major Chin responded, "Yes, sir. I understand, and so do the battalion commanders. If the mainland does attack, we'll be ready to push them back to the water."
****

Sergeant Lin was in a bit of a foul mood. His company had just arrived at the training range for a week of intense training on marksmanship and small-unit tactics, and the five new recruits that had joined his platoon out of basic training had rifle skills that were, to put it mildly, terrible.

The first couple of days at the range were spent going over the basics of their T91 assault rifle, which was essentially an American M4 rifle that used the standard NATO 5.56 x 45mm round. It was important for soldiers on the coastal defensive line to become excellent shots and learn how to fire accurately under immense stress. They also had to learn a myriad of other weapon systems, from the various heavy machine guns used in the bunkers to the anti-armor missiles that would be used against the amphibious assault crafts the mainlanders would use. This two-week annual exercise was meant to refamiliarize everyone with all the weapon systems, should they need to be used. While there was no indication the Chinese mainland was looking to start hostilities, their recent acquisition of Mongolia and the movement of a large number of soldiers towards their southern border meant there was definitely a larger plan afoot.

Sergeant Lin gritted his teeth as he saw another new soldier making stupid mistakes. It was as though they had suddenly developed amnesia under the pressure of their new platoon sergeant.

"No, Private!" he yelled, loud enough to gain the attention of the other soldiers nearby. "You hold the rifle tight into your shoulder, and then you lean your cheek into the stock of the rifle with your nose gently touching the charging handle." Sergeant Lin demonstrated the proper posture for holding the assault weapon, making sure the other soldiers also saw what he was doing.

"Then you close one eye and look through the scope with your dominant eye, placing the red dot on the target you intend to hit. Next, you gently squeeze the trigger, making sure not to jerk it. The rifle will kick once you fire it, but keep your cheek tucked in tight to the stock, re-aim and repeat. You do this over and over again, until you run out of ammo, and then restart the entire process again. Understood?" he shouted, surveying the nearby soldiers like prey.

"Yes, Sergeant!" they all yelled in unison, hastily retrieving their rifles to resume practicing what they had originally been shown in basic training. They loaded their first thirty-round magazines, took aim at the targets down range and began to fire. Most of their shots were now hitting the mark, and their aim was steadily improving.

The company commander, Captain Kuo, walked up to Lin. "How are the new guys coming along, Sergeant?" he inquired.

Sergeant Lin smiled wryly as he turned to face the captain. "They are green, but they will learn. I'll have them ready in a couple of days. Any word on whether we are moving to the beach or staying in garrison for a while?" he asked.

"Once our training is complete here, the orders from the brigade are to move to the beaches to begin a series of fortification improvements. It looks like the mainland may be making a move on Vietnam again, and if that happens, they may also choose to attack us," he replied in a voice that lacked conviction.

"You don't sound like you fully agree with that sentiment, sir," Sergeant Lin observed, the left side of his mouth curling up in a mischievous smile.

Captain Kuo laughed, knowing that he had been caught. "Unless the Americans become bogged down in a new war in Asia, we can count on them to prevent the mainland from doing anything stupid. Should that situation change, then we'll have something to be worried about. In the meantime, headquarters wants us to make sure the beach defenses are as ready as possible."

The two of them talked for a few minutes longer before the captain headed off to inspect the next platoon and Sergeant Lin turned his attention back to his new recruits. They both hoped that all of the work they were currently doing would turn out to be completely unnecessary, but Murphy's Law could come back to bite them at any time, so it was best to be safe.

****

People's Republic of China
Wanzihu, Hunan Province

The weather was starting to turn cool as the young men from the small village of Wanzihu filed into the school auditorium to listen to the political commissar from their province speak. As Lei Wei entered the auditorium, he was surprised to see how full it was.

They must be offering something special to have gotten this many people to attend the meeting tonight, Lei thought as he slid past one of his friends who had saved a seat for him. Just as he was about to say something to his friend, the evening's speaker walked onto the stage and tapped the mic to capture everyone's attention.

As Colonel Li Qiang, the political commissar for the city of Yuanjiang, looked out at the faces of roughly two hundred young men

23

from this small village, he saw a softness that concerned him. He realized that he was going to have to train these men hard if he was going to secure the necessary military victories that would allow him to advance his career. Li Qiang was determined to use the coming war to move up the ranks, and he was fortunate that his militia regiment had been chosen to be a part of the invasion of Formosa. However, as he surveyed the gentlehearted men before him, he realized that although he was still confident he could lead his regiment to victory, most of those sitting in tonight's crowd would likely be killed in the process.

Colonel Li cleared his throat. "Good evening, everyone. Thank you for coming tonight," he began.

As if we had a choice, thought Lei Wei.

"I am here to inform everyone that the Yuanjiang's militia has been officially called up for duty," Li Qiang announced to audible groans and gasps, a highly unusual display of emotion. "All young men between the ages of eighteen and twenty-eight are to report to this auditorium in two days to start military training. We will be formed up as the 27th Infantry Regiment."

Lei Wei sat in stunned silence. As he surveyed the room around him, he was surprised to find that some of the others actually appeared to be excited by the news.

Colonel Li lifted his hand to signal for everyone to be quiet, then signaled to a man nearby, Major Zhang Jun, to come up to the podium. Major Zhang was a regular army major in the People's Liberation Army, and he would be responsible for the bulk of this regiment's military training.

Everyone in the room settled down as Zhang walked up. Calmly and methodically, the major went over what they would need to bring with them when they returned to the auditorium in two days. He also informed everyone that they would be given some forms they would need to sign before they would be allowed to leave.

Two hours later, Lei Wei walked back to his family's small home at the edge of town. He told his parents what had transpired during that evening's dinner. While his father beamed with pride, his mother's face fell. She was clearly scared for his safety. Like many families in China, Lei was an only child. His family relied on him to help manage the family's small farm, and more importantly, they would rely on him to take care of them in their retirement years.

Seeing the concern his mother harbored, Lei promised, "I will send my military pay home to you each month to help you with managing the farm. I only want you to save a small portion of it for when I return home with my medals and become the village hero."

His mother wiped away a tear, filled not with sadness but with pride.

Chapter 3
The Coming Storm

Guangzhou, China
Southern Theater of Operations Headquarters

General Yang Yin was hot, dirty and exhausted as he walked into the briefing room of his headquarters building. His army group had led the invasion of Vietnam and secured their primary objectives with lightning speed. They were now being replaced by secondary units and relocated back to their primary bases to rest, rearm and begin training for their next operation, the invasion of Formosa.

As Yang approached the head of the briefing table, he saw his division commanders all standing behind their chairs, ready to sit once he gave the order. He signaled with his hand for them to be seated. Almost in unison, they dropped into their chairs.

Yang surveyed his generals, eying each of them carefully. He had spent the last couple of days going over each division's war reports from the generals' staff and the political officers. Overall, he was satisfied with their performance. However, this next theater of war would prove to be a true challenge.

"Generals," Yang began, "while the war in Vietnam has not yet been fully won, our army group has accomplished our major objectives and has been ordered back to garrison to prepare for our next mission."

"As you know, the Americans appear to be preparing for war with our communist brothers in North Korea. As if attacking the peace-loving people of Ukraine and Russia was not enough, the Americans and NATO invaded Belarus yesterday. Now it appears that they are going to bring their war to the doorstep of the Korean Peninsula," he announced. Yang could see that his generals were not happy about the Americans sticking their noses into the affairs of China. None of them agreed with what was happening in Europe, but Europe was a long way from China.

General Yang continued, "Army Group North will be handling the situation in North Korea if the President directs the PLA to intercede on behalf of our communist brothers. However, *our* army group has been selected for a much greater honor."

At this announcement, everyone sat a little straighter in their chairs.

"We have been chosen to be the lead army group to reclaim the renegade province of Formosa," Yang announced in a triumphant voice. The generals and officers at the table all smiled. This was great news indeed.

Yang continued, "When I was in Beijing, I was personally congratulated by President Xi and the Minister of Defense himself for our superb handling of the invasion of Vietnam. They both said they could think of no army group better than ours to lead this invasion. I assured them that I have the best division officers and generals in China and made sure that every one of you will receive a special award for your leadership in Vietnam." Some light murmuring of excitement and chatter spread through the room before General Yang raised his hand to regain their attention.

"Now, this next operation is going to be much tougher than Vietnam. I have been assured that all our lost equipment and troops will be replaced by the end of the week to bring us back up to one hundred percent strength. We are also going to be augmented with additional soldiers from the People's Liberation Army Militia for the invasion."

One of Yang's division commanders immediately raised his hand, wanting to ask a question. Seeing that it was General Wong, one of his best commanders, he nodded for him to go ahead and speak.

"General Yang, I do not mean any disrespect towards our brothers in the militia, but how do you envision us using them with our divisions and how many militia forces are we being given?" he asked, lowering his head slightly in a soft bow to indicate that he meant no impertinence.

Yang had known his officers would ask about this, and he had prepared for the question. Clearing his throat, he responded, "It is true that the militia forces are not nearly as trained or prepared for war as our active duty divisions, but the Ministry of Defense wants to get them ready for a larger potential conflict, should one arise with the Americans. To that end, our army group has been assigned 350,000 PLAM units to get prepared for combat and to use in the upcoming invasion. A group of similar size has been assigned to General Sheng's Army Group B, which is still continuing the war in Vietnam."

Surveying his generals, Yang could see in their eyes that they were excited, even eager, to get the invasion started. "I have not been given a timetable for the invasion of Formosa, other than I've been told to be prepared for hostilities in as little as thirty days. I want to break our militia groups down into three segments. One will focus solely on logistics and will be critical to keeping our army group supplied and supported once the invasion starts. The second group will focus primarily on occupation duty and will be integrated with our military police units. The third militia group will be given a lot of additional training and focus on the invasion. I am going to assign 200,000 militiamen to General Wong, to prepare them for the invasion. I want seventy percent of the first wave of soldiers to be militia. I know that means a lot of them will be killed, but they will identify enemy strongpoints in their deaths, which we can then destroy through the air force or navy's resources. Following the first wave, I want the militia forces to make up no more than thirty percent of the troops involved until we have secured the beachheads."

Yang paused for a moment, lifting his glass of water to his lips and proceeding to take several long gulps before he went on. "When we have secured the landing zones, I want the militia units to be largely used in clearing out some of the heavy lines of enemy resistance. We do not have a lot of time to get them battle-ready, but the ones that do survive are going to become the nucleus of a much stronger militia unit going forward. These units will then be heavily integrated within our own units."

Turning to General Wong, Yang explained, "I want your units to spend a lot of time training the militiamen on marksmanship, small-unit tactics and weapons. Make sure they know basic first aid and how to effectively call in air support or artillery. Train them just as hard as you would soldiers in your own division. The more enemy soldiers they are able to kill, the fewer enemy soldiers will be left to kill your own men. Do you understand, General Wong?"

Wong nodded. "You can count on me, General. I will not let you or our army group down. They will be as ready as I can get them in thirty days," he replied with a serious look on his face.

The group continued to discuss the invasion plans, where the various divisions would land, and their objectives once on shore. Paratroopers were also going to be used for the invasion, along with the People's Liberation Army Naval Infantry, who had proven they could effectively carry out multiple amphibious invasions during the Vietnam campaign. This was going to be a truly combined-arms effort by the Chinese military.

Chapter 4
Sail Away

Hainan Island, China
Yulin Naval Base

Vice Admiral Shen Shengli yawned as he looked over the deployment plan for what felt like the fifth time in the last twelve hours. His entire fleet was nearly ready to set sail for Formosa and begin their part of the invasion. His 15,000 marines had just finished loading into their various troop transports and assault ships for the voyage. While the PLA hit the rebel army from across the straits, his forces would assault Orchid Island, which was controlled by Taiwan. After that, the plan called for his men to attack the Itbayat and Batanes island chains controlled by the Philippines, and the Miyako Islands in Japan's southern Okinawa Prefecture. This would cut off any naval passageways to Formosa and enable the PLA to extend its anti-ship missile perimeter.

Once these islands had been secured, waves of engineers would be flown in to build up the fortifications and anti-ship missile bunkers. The key to his plan's success would be getting his submarine force in position to neutralize any potential threats to his flotilla. As his subs moved into position, they would wait for the attack order to be given. It was an audacious plan that Chairman Zhang had developed many months ago, and if it succeeded, China might truly be able to achieve its goal of controlling Asia.

Admiral Shen heard a soft knock on his door as his aide stuck his head into his office. "Is everything all right, Admiral? Do you need me to do anything before we leave?" he asked.

Shen smiled pleasantly. "Yes, everything is in order. I was just reviewing the plans one last time. Have all of the captains reported in that they are ready to set sail?"

"Yes, sir. When the sun rises in a couple of hours, the fleet will pull anchor and start to head to Formosa," his aide replied confidently. He was proud to be serving Admiral Shen. This coveted position would make him privy to some of the most closely-guarded information and allow him to be a part of making history. Since the end of 1949, the rebel government on Formosa had asserted themselves as the true government of China. Soon, that government would be removed, and the stain of the

PLA's failure to finish the rebel government off would finally be wiped clean.

"Excellent, then let the pilots know I am ready to fly out to the *Mao*."

His assistant nodded and bowed in respect as he exited the room.

Admiral Shen suddenly felt more awake. It energized him to see how excited his aide was about this mission.

He continued to review the plans one last time. *Even though the war with Vietnam hasn't been fully concluded, it has already served several purposes*, he thought. It had definitely allowed his planners and operations groups to work out the kinks in coordinating the marines, air and naval support. They'd also been able to figure out which cruise missiles work best for the types of enemy ships they were most likely to encounter.

He reviewed the supplies. Already, the majority of his ships and aircraft had been replenished with the new anti-ship missiles and ground attack cruise missiles.

Admiral Shen sat back in his chair, satisfied. His ships and aircraft were as ready as possible for this coming fight. *Now it's time to execute*.

Chapter 5
At the Gates

Shaxian, China

The sound of planes rumbling in the air was nearly constant as a new flight of Xian Y-20 transport craft landed on the runway at this once-quiet airport. Several weeks ago, a battalion of engineers had arrived at Shaxian and constructed a second runway, additional hangars and a massive tent city for several battalions of paratroopers from the 43rd Airborne Division's arrival. When Captain Ma Qiliang's company arrived in the middle of this hustle and bustle, he knew something big was being planned. His best guess was that they were going to invade Formosa.

Ma lit a cigarette as he watched the two new transports taxi up to a hangar. The ground crew immediately went to work on getting the aircraft shut down and ready for whatever might happen next. They shuttled back and forth in a predetermined pattern, like bees navigating a hive.

The roar of engines drew Captain Ma's attention, and he turned to look at the main gate of the airport. Another convoy of transport trucks arrived under heavy guard. They were either transporting additional paratroopers or bringing in a lot of ammunition. While Ma suspected he knew what their next mission would be, he did not want to openly speculate or offer up his own opinions in front of his men. He'd wait, just like everyone else, until he was briefed on what they were going to do.

I just hope we don't have to stay at this airport for too long, he thought. There wasn't a lot of room for his troops to do anything more than basic exercises and runs around the perimeter. If they were going to be there for a while, he really wanted his men to be able to spend some additional time at the rifle range and practice patrolling through the surrounding hills.

Ma took one last pull on his cigarette before flicking it to the ground and stomping on it with his boot. Then he turned away from the runway and headed back to the officers' tent to catch some shut-eye.

Maybe tomorrow at the briefing, I'll at least be able to find out how long we're supposed to be here, he hoped.

****

The hangar at the far side of the airport was nearly full of officers and senior sergeants as Captain Ma and his senior sergeant and platoon leaders sat waiting for their brigade commander to begin the briefing. Eventually, the commander finished his conversation with someone over to the side and walked up to the lectern to begin the brief. The lights in the hangar dimmed, and a PowerPoint image covered a white sheet someone had hung against the wall to act as a screen.

A hush came over the room as the paratroopers examined the image. Once the reality of what they were looking at began to settle in, the mood turned very serious. On the screen was a picture of the renegade province of Formosa, or "Taiwan," as the West called it.

I knew it, Captain Ma thought with satisfaction.

The colonel started talking, and a new image appeared, this one showing images around Taipei. The Shanshuilu Ecological Park was highlighted, along with several key parks on the east side of the city and the major road junctions that linked the eastern half of the country with the western half.

"Gentlemen, this is going to be our greatest hour as paratroopers," the colonel announced, beaming with pride. "Our brigade has been given the task of securing a series of major road junctions and tunnels that connect the eastern and western halves of the country. Our objective is to block these major traffic routes from being used by the nationalist army here, here and here." He used a laser pointer to indicate the major intersections leading to the city.

"Our actions will block additional reinforcements from coming to the capital and stop any possible retreat to the western side of the island. We will box them in and hold the enemy in place for the main PLA ground forces to smash them. The rest of the division will be hitting objectives in other parts of the city, to include the international airport. We are being ordered to hold our positions until we are relieved by the ground forces, which will be making multiple landings across the island."

The crowd was a very eager audience. The colonel continued the briefing for another hour as each battalion was given their specific assignments. Once the battalion commanders had their orders, they'd discuss with their company commanders how best to execute the missions.

As Captain Ma walked out of the room after the meeting, he realized this was going to be one tough mission. *Most of my men and I may not make it back from this one.*

Chapter 6
The Calm Before the Storm

Taiwan
West Coast Expressway, Hill 137

It was a cold and gloomy morning. Sergeant Lin, from the 269th Mechanized Infantry Brigade, roused his platoon from their sleep to begin the morning work of strengthening the coastal position that their unit had just been assigned to the day before. After setting up their camp, they had immediately gone to work identifying where they wanted to build the various machine gun positions, lay concertina wire, and dig positions for their armored vehicles to lie in wait for what they all hoped would not happen.

On top of Hill 137 was a Buddhist temple, large and beautiful, with ornate designs and manicured gardens all around it. It would have been a monument to preserve for the ages, if the same hill hadn't also boasted an incredible view of the coastline for several miles in either direction. With a 500-foot incline from the main highway and beach below, it provided them with an exceptional field of fire to prevent the communists from landing any of their larger transport crafts at the nearby port. Any ships wanting to dock there would have to pass right in front of their position, which was also why they had several missile trucks with them, equipped with anti-ship missiles.

Sergeant Lin was a bit cranky at how slowly his men were moving. "Get in formation!" he yelled.

Just as he was getting ready to start handing down the day's work assignments to the squads, a captain walked up to him and signaled to get his attention.

"Sergeant Lin, I am Captain Qwang from the 53rd Engineer Group. I was told by your captain that you had identified a series of positions you wanted to turn into reinforced machine gun and missile bunkers," he explained.

As he spoke, the roar of engines grew louder and louder, and several construction vehicles arrived.

Lin smiled broadly. Having an engineering company show up was the best news he'd had in days. This would make their work a lot easier and most likely get them ready to deal with any potential communist incursion.

"Thank you for your help, Captain. Let me issue a few work orders to my soldiers, and then I'll walk you through what we're thinking of doing on the map. I'd like to show you a few positions in person to get your take on them," he replied.

The captain nodded and stood back to let Sergeant Lin get his men organized.

After he had finished issuing the day's orders, Lin turned back to the captain and guided him over to the hood of one of the company vehicles. The sergeant pulled out his map and showed where they wanted each fortified position. The two men discussed matters for roughly twenty minutes before they began to walk the line, going over each location in detail. They were going to build a series of cement-reinforced pillboxes and missile bunkers, overlooking the sea and the port.

As they identified what each bunker would be used for, one of the captain's senior sergeants made some notes and then began to get some of their own soldiers to start marking out the positions. The engineers would dig out the bases of the bunkers and then build the molds needed to create eighteen-inch-thick rebar-reinforced walls with a series of gun slits. In between the bunkers, they would also construct a series of trenches to connect the strongholds.

Mixed emotions filled Sergeant Lin as they finished their planning. It was tragic that much of the manicured gardens around the temple would have to be torn up to turn Hill 137 into the stronghold it needed to become. He was grateful that the Venerable Dhammananda allowed for soldiers to defend their country from outside aggressors when there was no other option.

The next several days were abuzz with activity as the engineers used their backhoes and trench diggers to turn the hill into a modern-day fortress. Cement trucks were constantly climbing the winding road up the hill to fill in the molds of the various gun positions. For decades, the Taiwanese military had avoided turning the coastline of the country into a military fortress, but as the situation with the communist mainland continued to deteriorate, they felt it imperative to prepare for the worst. When the People's Liberation Army invaded Vietnam and annexed Myanmar and Laos, they knew Taiwan would be next.
****

Taipei, Taiwan
Presidential Building

President Hung Hui-ju was the first female president of Taiwan, ushering in a woman as the most powerful person in the island's politics since its inception. Hung had a lot of dreams and visions for what she wanted to accomplish during her first term as president. She had been an ardent supporter of increasing wages for workers, and while Taiwan had an exceptional trading relationship with the US and Japan, she wanted to work to increase trade with India, the second-most-populous nation on earth. Her hope was that increased trade with India would lead to an economic boom for Taiwan and possibly even enable her to win a second term.

Today, however, she was in a somber mood. She had just met with the US representative to Taiwan the day before, and it had not gone well.

"Madam President," the representative began, "I am here to share some of our recent intelligence with you. We have confirmed reports that Russia and China are both encouraging North Korea to attack the South Koreans and the US Forces that are stationed in the region."

The representative cleared her throat and then took a big sip of water, unhappy with what she had to say next. "Madam President, as you are already aware, the United States is already engaged in war in Europe, and we fully anticipate hostilities in the Korean Peninsula. Because we are stretched so thin, we will be very limited in the type and amount of assistance that we will be able to provide to Taiwan should the People's Republic of China attack."

The Taiwanese Minister of Defense, who had been sitting quietly beside the President, asserted, "I understand that it is highly unlikely that we will have any American boots on the ground here, but I would like to formally request an emergency shipment of vital munitions. In addition, we would sincerely appreciate any and all available intelligence that the US has right now on the Chinese military movements near Taiwan."

The US defense official nodded. "I can definitely promise that we will share our intelligence with you, and I believe we will be able to assist you with munitions. However, this will be the extent of the assistance that we can provide at this time."

When the Americans left her office, the Minister of Defense tapped the desk nervously. "Madam President, I recommend that we set up an emergency meeting with the senior defense officials, intelligence officials and the foreign secretary. We have a lot to discuss, and from the sound of it, not a lot of time, so I recommend we meet within 24 hours."

****

As President Hung walked into the briefing room, everyone stood and waited for her signal. She saw the concerned looks on their faces and knew this would be one of those pivotal meetings that would define her presidency. She motioned for the Minister of Defense to begin his brief and get herself and everyone else up to speed.

Clearing his throat, Minister Lu began. "Madam President, after reviewing the latest intelligence and satellite imagery from the Americans, and reviewing the intelligence sent by our sources on the mainland, we are certain the PRC intends to launch an invasion of our country soon. We have not been able to determine an exact date yet, but looking at the troop movements, the redeployment of aircraft, and the location of the communist navy, we anticipate hostilities starting within the next seven to ten days at most."

The military members present in the room all nodding in agreement.

President Hung looked around at the other faces of her national security team. "Is there any dissent in this assessment? Is there any reason to believe the mainland may not attack us?" she asked, hoping, almost pleading that this nightmare scenario might just be another training exercise by the mainland designed to intimidate them.

The Foreign Minister, Chang, spoke up. "Madam President, as you know, this morning the Americans launched a preemptive attack against the North Koreans. One thing is certain—the mainland will use that conflict to their advantage, knowing full well that America will not be able to intervene and come to our aid. With the Americans out of the equation, it is extremely likely that the communists will launch an attack against us."

Lowering her head and sighing softly, the president remained quiet for a minute, trying to determine what to say next.

She had had such high hopes for her administration. *To think that I might be the last democratically elected leader of Taiwan*, she bemoaned as chills went down her spine. *I can't let that happen.* She had to continue to fight for what all of her countrymen believed in…freedom.

She looked up at her Minister of Defense. "What should we do now to prepare for what may be coming our way?" she asked him, leaning on his years of military experience for guidance.

Minister Lu nodded and replied, "Madam President, I recommend that we immediately activate the reserves and place the military on alert. We should have the army deploy to the possible invasion positions and prepare as strong a defense as possible. Should all of this prove to be nothing more than Chinese posturing, then we can recall the army and stand down. But should this be the real deal, then at least our forces will have had time to prepare a layered defense to repel the invaders before they are able to secure a beachhead. I also recommend that we be prepared to move you and the other essential government leaders to our underground command bunkers, should it become necessary."

President Hung agreed. "Begin the call-up of the reserves and prepare to repel an amphibious assault. Make sure our navy and air force are also dispersed and ready. The last thing we need is for them to get caught by surprise and lose our only forward defensive capabilities," she said.

Hung knew once the fighting started, she would have little control of anything; management of the country would essentially fall to the military. If they were lucky, they would be able to bloody the communists badly enough that they could keep them from landing any substantial ground forces on the island. If they could achieve that, then chances were they could stalemate the war.
****

President Hung would not have to wait long in anticipation. Later that day, her special red phone rang.

"Hello?" she answered.

"Madam President, we need to move you to the underground bunkers." Hung immediately recognized the voice as that of Defense Minister Lu.

"What's going on, Lu?" she queried nervously.

"The North Koreans have used nuclear weapons, ma'am. The American city of Oakland, California, has been destroyed by a nuclear missile, along with most of San Francisco."

"My God…"

"Madam President, it's very likely that the United States will respond with nuclear weapons. Whether or not that will cause the Chinese to retaliate with nuclear weapons is another question. We have to get you underground."

****

Golf Course, Taoyuan City

It had taken nearly eight hours, but Colonel Wang Xing-Wei's armored brigade had finally deployed to their marshaling area. His tank brigade was going to be acting as a quick-reaction force. They would either support the infantry at the coastline or repel an airborne attempt on the Taiwan Taoyuan International Airport.

"Are the camouflage nets secured yet?" Colonel Wang asked his tank gunner.

"Yes, sir. From what I can see, it looks like the rest of the tanks around us have their nettings up as well," his gunner replied with a crooked smile that implied that the colonel should know better than to ask a question like that.

Colonel Wang just smiled and nodded in reply.

"Is it true the North Koreans used nuclear weapons on the Americans?" asked his gunner, becoming suddenly serious.

"Yes, it is true. They did. The city of Oakland, California, was devastated," Wang responded. He scratched his chin as if pondering whether or not to continue speaking. "Not everyone knows yet, but the mainlanders provided the Koreans with the ICBMs that hit the US mainland—the Americans responded by dropping a nuclear bomb on Shengyang in retaliation. From what I've heard, they believe the bomb killed more than five million people." He spoke in a hushed tone, almost as if this was some sort of national secret.

Colonel Wang could see the look of surprise and then horror written all over his gunner's face at the realization that multiple nuclear weapons had been used by the North Koreans, the Americans, and apparently the mainlanders as well.

"When do you think the communists will attack us?" his gunner asked nervously.

"Soon. Just be ready. It could be today, or it could be tomorrow, or the next day. But I believe it will be by the end of the week, and so does the general," Colonel Wang replied. He had always been honest with his gunner. Sometimes he told him too much, but he found the sergeant to be a good listener, and he never went around blabbing to others what he heard.

Now all they could do was sit and wait, pray, and hope that somehow this war could be avoided. It was just a matter of when, and if they would live through it.

****

Hunan Province, China

"Aim small, miss small!" yelled one of the sergeants from the 27th Militia Infantry Regiment as they took aim at the paper targets roughly 100 meters in front of them.

Lei Wei closed his left eye and looked through the sights, lining up the top post with the black silhouette of the target and gently squeezing the trigger as he had been taught. He immediately felt the butt of the rifle recoil into his shoulder as his ears registered the sound of the rifle firing.

"Excellent shot!" exclaimed his sergeant. "Now, just keep doing that over and over again. We'll make a marksman out of you yet, Lei."

Two hours later, Private Lei and the rest of his platoon began their ruck march back to the barracks, where they would disassemble and clean their rifles. It was the final day of range practice and qualification. The following day, they would board a convoy of trucks that would take them to an encampment outside of Fuzhou, where they would await further orders. Rumor had it they would be invading Formosa before the end of the month.

"Private Lei, what are you going to do when the militia disbands?" asked one of the young farmers from Lei's small village.

Lei thought about that for a moment. Prior to his militia being mobilized, he had never ventured further than ten kilometers from his village. Now he had seen several large cities and met numerous people from beyond his hometown. He suddenly felt like there was a large new world to explore, and he desperately wanted to see it.

"Well, I had planned to take over my family's farm and try to acquire some additional land. Now, I'm not sure," Lei replied.

It was hard for him to talk about it. He knew his family was counting on him to take care of them when they got older. *But how do I stay in this small little corner when there is so much out there I have yet to discover?*

His friend chuckled at Lei's comment and saw the perplexed look on his face. "First, we have to live through whatever they're going to use our militia unit for before we can plan our futures, I guess."

Just as Lei was about to add something, their sergeant came along and yelled, "Lights out! Everyone get some sleep. We move out at dawn."

Everyone finished packing their rucksacks and climbed into bed.
****

Four days later, Lei and the rest of his platoon found themselves at a small encampment near Changle, adjacent to the coast and only a few kilometers away from the Matsue Islands, which were currently under the control of Formosa. Their commander had briefed them earlier in the morning that their regiment would be leading the assault of the Juguang Township—two small islands that needed to be secured prior to the invasion of Formosa. Their colonel had assured them this would be an easy assault given how small the islands were and the amount of artillery fire that would be hitting it prior to their arrival. While no specific date had been given for when the attack would take place, they had been told it would be soon. In the meantime, the regiment began training on how to use the amphibious assault crafts that would ferry them the few kilometers it would take to reach the two small islands.
****

Lüneburg Heath, Northern Germany
Bergen-Hohne Training Area

After nearly three months recovering from a bullet wound he'd sustained in the opening hours of the war at NATO's alternate command center, Castlegate, Captain Hermann Wulf was promoted to Oberstleutnant, the equivalent of lieutenant colonel. As the German government moved to increase the size of the army by more than tenfold, they needed officers to fill the new units being created. Oberstleutnant Wulf suddenly found himself in command of the newly created 35th Mechanized Infantry Battalion. His battalion had forty-four Puma infantry fighting vehicles and a little over eight hundred soldiers. As a maneuver element, their job was to help screen for the armor units and protect the more vulnerable tanks from enemy missile teams. They would also be responsible for the holding of ground secured by the tanks until the light infantry units arrived and they could once again take to their armored chariots.

Seeing a few of his officers listening to a portable radio, Wulf yelled, "What's so important that you all have stopped to listen to the radio instead of seeing to the men's training?!"

His officers startled as they suddenly realized he had been standing next to them.

One of the officers stiffened. "Herr Oberstleutnant, the American president just announced that they had dropped a nuclear bomb on the Chinese city of Shenyang."

Wulf's eyebrows rose, and he paused for a second as the news commentator continued, "The world waits with bated breath to see how the Chinese will respond to the loss of one of their largest cities and millions of its citizens—"

Wulf grunted and interrupted, "Turn off the radio and get back to work. Whatever happens between China and the US will happen a long way from us. We have the Russians to worry about, and unless the Russians use nuclear weapons here in Europe, we have nothing to concern ourselves with."

"Yes, sir," responded the chorus of chastised officers. They quickly scurried away to implement the next few days' assignments.

It would not be long now before their unit, largely made up of draftees and green soldiers who had yet to see combat, would be facing off against the Russians. Wulf wanted them as ready as possible for what awaited them, and that meant spending a lot of time at the range.

Chapter 7
The Red Storm

Twenty Miles East of Hong Kong

It had taken the People's Liberation Army Navy's Southern Fleet several days to arrive on station not far from Hong Kong. Now the fleet would begin a 30-mile-wide circle around one of their man-made islands and Hong Kong as they prepared themselves for the opening salvos of the invasion of Taiwan.

Nearly three dozen submarines had moved forward to begin identifying and then engaging the Taiwanese navy and other surface ships that could pose a threat to the fleet. They had already identified one Australian and two American submarines that were monitoring their positions. Once the final order was given to attack Taiwan, Vice Admiral Shen would also issue the order to sink those three submarines. He was not about to let an American or Australian submarine get close enough to his fleet to do any damage.

Today was the second day since the Americans had nuked Shenyang, and Vice Admiral Shen was still reeling with anger. *The death of over five million people screams for vengeance*, he thought. His countrymen would be marching in the streets if he didn't balance the scales of justice after America's disproportional response to the attack on Oakland. *But in a couple of hours, I will sink this Yankee fleet.*

As the *Mao* plowed through the calm waters of the South China Sea, Admiral Shen grew more and more impatient as he waited to receive the orders for his fleet to initiate their attack. He had been told their cyber-warfare groups were going to cause some problems for the Taiwanese, and the air force and navy needed to wait for confirmation that their attack had succeeded.

Shen reached down and picked up the glass of tea one of his aides had just poured for him. He raised the glass to his lips and took in the hot liquid, letting it warm him. After taking several more sips, Shen turned to his communications officer.

"Have we received the final orders from Beijing yet?" he asked for probably the fifth time in the last hour. His forces had a hard fix on these hostile submarines, and he wanted to sink them now, before his forces could lose track of them.

The officer was just about to say no when the printer warmed up and spat out a single sheet of paper. The officer pulled it off the printer, briefly reading it before passing it to the admiral.

The orders have finally come, Admiral Shen thought as he allowed a smile to spread across his face.

He stood up and made his way to the combat information center. As he briskly walked into the room, he tapped his knuckles on the wall to get his officers' attention. "Send a flash message to our submarines and destroyers to immediately engage the Australian and American submarines. I want them sunk *now*," he announced emphatically.

One of his officers asked, "Shall I send the order to the cruisers and other ships to begin firing their cruise missiles at their assigned targets?"

Admiral Shen turned to the commander who had asked the question and nodded while smiling. "Yes, tell the fleet to begin engaging our assigned targets. The air wings should stand by for orders. We are not going to launch our aircraft until the mainland has at least hit the Taiwanese airfields with a barrage of cruise missiles. They can absorb aircraft losses; we cannot," he responded.

A flurry of activity began as his operations officers issued the myriad of orders for the fleet to begin combat operations. Within minutes of the orders being given, the *Renhai* destroyers in the fleet began to fire off their land-attack cruise missiles at their designated targets. The *Luyang III* destroyers let loose with a string of anti-ship missiles at the Taiwanese naval ships they had been monitoring, and the *Jiangdao* corvettes joined the fray, going after the American, Australian, and Taiwanese submarines they had been tracking. The air filled with anti-ship and land-attack cruise missiles, and the war officially started.
****

Twenty-Five Thousand Feet Above Nanping, China

The sky was clear, with not a cloud to be seen, and the air was relatively smooth as Major Wu's H-20 stealth bomber flew steadily towards its launch point. Wu and his copilot watched with delight as the radar screen filled up with short-range missiles being fired from their homeland of mainland China to Formosa. A moment later, their radar began to pick up the hundreds of People's Liberation Army Air Force fighters and fighter-bombers lifting off to head for their targets. By the time the Chinese fighters arrived over the island, all the Taiwanese air bases would have already been hit multiple times by air- and submarine-launched cruise missiles, cratering their runways and preventing the Taiwanese aircraft from being used to defend the island.

As they approached their launch points, dozens of the older H-6 bombers rose up to meet them and fell into formation with the stealth bombers. When their newer H-20 bombers fired off their Dong Hai-10 cruise missiles, they hoped to distract the US Air Force and make them believe that the older bombers had fired the shots.

I hope this plan works and deceives the Americans, Wu thought.

While the Americans knew of the development of the H-20, Chinese intelligence officials believed that so far, the US was still unaware that the bombers were combat-operational and being actively used. The PLAAF generals really hoped that once Formosa was secured, the H-20s would be unleashed on the American Pacific Fleet in Japan and once and for all cripple the American Navy.

As Major Wu checked and double-checked the weapon systems, the voice of their commander came over the radio. "All bombers, prepare to launch missiles on my command."

Wu tensed up as he heard the order. His heart raced and beads of sweat formed on his forehead. As the tension grew, the minutes felt like hours. Finally, the voice of their commander broke the silence. "Fire all missiles and return to base."

Wu toggled the safety switch off on his missiles and then depressed the red button on the side of his flight stick, firing off a missile each time he depressed it until he had expended his payload. One by one, the missiles dropped from the internal bomb bay from the rotary systems of each bomber, igniting and then flying off to hit their targets.

Each H-20 carried a total of eight cruise missiles, all of which whizzed through the air towards major Army installations and other key strategic strong points that Chinese intelligence had identified. Once the stealth bombers had fired off their missiles, they collectively turned and headed back to their base to rearm. The H-6 squadron that had joined them for the ruse also returned to base and waited to be called upon if a further deceptive plan required their services.

Chapter 8
Declaration

Beijing, China
U.S. Embassy, Chancellery Building

Vincent Jones was feeling incredibly nervous, almost queasy as he and the ambassador's senior leadership team waited for the Chinese Foreign Minister, Wang Yi, to meet with them. The reports they had received from the Defense Intelligence Agency, CIA and the Diplomatic Security Service had all said that war between the United States and the People's Republic of China was all but inevitable. It was now a question of when conflict would begin and if any warning would be given prior to hostilities.

It had been nearly two days since President Gates had authorized the nuclear strike against Shenyang, and everyone at the embassy had been caught by surprise. They knew there was a chance the President would respond with nuclear weapons when Oakland and San Francisco had been destroyed, but they had not anticipated that Gates would nuke one of the largest cities in China.

Could this really be the end? Are we at the cusp of a nuclear war with China? Vincent thought as he stared out the window. It was starting to rain, adding further gloom to the already dreary situation.

A phone vibrated on the table. The regional security officer had received a message from someone.

"The foreign minister has arrived," the RSO announced. "He's being led up to the room now."

The ambassador, Max Bryant, sighed. He was not looking forward to this meeting. He had done everything he could to try and calm the tension between President Gates and President Xi the past few months.

When Bryant had confronted the Chinese about the intelligence they had of their support of North Korea, they had just shrugged it off like it didn't matter. When the DPRK launched a nuke at the US, he tried to warn them that President Gates would hold them accountable if they had any involvement, and there were crickets. *Maybe now that the President has retaliated, they won't ignore my warnings anymore.*

The others in the room fiddled with their coffee cups, exchanging nervous glances as they waited for the foreign minister to be led to their room. The senior DIA representative jolted to attention as his government-issued Blackberry buzzed on the table. He read the alert, then cleared his throat anxiously.

"Before the foreign minister arrives, I wanted to let everyone know the war has officially started. The US 7th Fleet is reporting an attack underway by the Chinese," he said to the shock of everyone in the room.

At that moment, a knock at the door interrupted their thoughts, and all eyes turned to the noise.

Foreign Minister Wang entered the room with one of his deputies, surveying everyone's faces briefly as they stood. Then he walked towards the ambassador to deliver his message in person. Without saying a word, the two men shook hands and bowed slightly, which was the customary thing to do.

Minister Wang presented the ambassador with a formal leather-bound folder with ornate lettering on it. "It is with great sorrow that I have to present to you, Ambassador Bryant, the People's Republic of China's formal declaration of war against the United States of America."

"As I am sure you have just been informed, hostilities between our two nations have already begun. During this period of conflict between our two nations, we request that you send all nonessential personnel back to the United States and leave only those individuals whom you absolutely need to carry on the diplomatic mission between our two nations."

"We will work with your embassy to allow American citizens to safely exit China to India, a neutral third-party nation. From there, they can travel freely. As a government, we are working to inform all US citizens currently in China that they are hereby ordered to leave the country within the next seven days. Any failure to leave beyond that point will result in immediate arrest and deportation."

The Foreign Minister paused for a second, looking beyond the ambassador out the window behind him as the rain beat down, harder now than when he had first entered the building. After a few tense seconds, he returned his attention to the ambassador.

"I am sorry that it has come to this. Some disagreements cannot be settled through diplomatic talk but must be resolved through military force. The US can no longer dictate to China what we can and cannot do. With that, I wish everyone safety through these troubling times, and a quick end to the hostilities our two nations now face."

Foreign Minister Wang unceremoniously turned around and left the room with his deputy in tow.

Everyone in the room stood there, not saying anything for a moment. The rain beat loudly against the window as they replayed the conversation over again in their own heads. It was quite a surreal scene to take in.

The ambassador finally sat down to look over the formal document. He signaled to the Deputy Chief of Mission.

"Send a verified copy back to the State Department and inform the Secretary of State and the President of what just transpired," he ordered.

"Also," said the ambassador, "we need to figure out how many American citizens are presently in China and might need assistance being flown out to India."

"Yes, sir," responded one of the aides.

It was going to be a long day.

Chapter 9
Like Sardines in a Can

Changle, China
Fourteen Kilometers from Juguang Island, Taiwan

It was 0300 hours and the smells of seawater and fish were strong in the air as the wind provided a gentle breeze for the 46 soldiers of Private Lei's platoon. While it was still dark, the soldiers of the 27th Infantry Regiment were standing in platoon-sized formations, waiting for the dozens upon dozens of Type 067 utility landing craft to finish pulling up to the beach.

As each landing craft aligned itself to the beach, it slid forward in the water until the flat bottom of the boat eventually ran aground and it stopped moving. The crews immediately lowered the ramps and signaled to the soldiers on shore to load up the ammunition and supplies that were waiting on the shore. Each of the landing craft was 28.6 meters in length, large enough to carry one light tank or two small vehicles, or a company of soldiers. Three-quarters of the landing craft assaulting Juguang would be carrying soldiers and their supplies, while the remaining ships would be landing several light tanks.

Despite the early hour, there was plenty of light as dozens of portable floodlights had been set up along the beach. Thousands of soldiers formed up into lines that stretched from the supply trucks on the beach to the numerous landing craft and hovercraft. While the men loaded the small ships, the thunderous roar of dozens of artillery guns and missile trucks broke the morning silence. The bombardment of Juguang Island, fourteen kilometers away, had begun.

As Private Lei passed another crate of ammunition to the soldier next to him, he paused long enough to look off to the horizon and saw hundreds of smoke trails from the rocket artillery heading to the small island they would themselves assault in a few more hours.

I hope the artillery wipes the enemy out and we don't encounter any serious resistance, he thought as the soldier next to him nudged him to take the next crate of ammo.

Ten minutes later, their sergeant yelled at them, "It's time to load up! Everyone, get on the landing crafts. We're going to push off shortly to head towards Juguang Island," he shouted.

The soldiers obediently headed towards the water, wading up to their ankles before walking up the ramps to line up in the ships. Because the island itself was not very large, their assault force would not be landing with a lot of armor support. The goal was for them to quickly capture the islands and then be prepared to join the other units assaulting Formosa.

Private Lei waited anxiously in the dark, surrounded by the smell of nervous sweat. Thirty minutes went by before his landing craft finally backed off the beach and headed out into the channel that would lead them to Juguang Island. Once in the channel, their landing craft picked up speed until it reached ten knots, falling in line with the waves of other landing craft, all headed towards the same objective. From time to time, a wave would crash against the side of the craft, splashing seawater over the men sandwiched inside.

A soldier standing next to Lei nudged him. "How long do you think it'll take us to get to the island? I think I'm going to get sick if we stay on this boat any longer."

Another large wave hit their boat, rocking it hard to one side, and the young soldier proceeded to throw up all over Private Lei's boots.

Lei was about to yell at him when the unmistakable scream of an artillery round rushed nearby.

That was close! Lei thought, panicked.

Another scream pierced the air, then another. Lei poked his head above the metal lip of the boat just in time to see a lucky round land in the center of the landing craft next to them. It exploded in a ball of flames, throwing burning soldiers into the air like ragdolls.

Just as Lei thought it couldn't get any worse, a long object that was on fire landed in his craft, falling mere feet away from him. Upon closer inspection, he saw it was the leg of one of the soldiers from the landing craft that had just blown up. As he screamed at the sight of it, he heard, *ping, ping, boom, ping!* His ears were assaulted as dozens of machine gun rounds bounced off the front ramp of their landing craft.

"We're almost to the beach! Prepare to leave the landing craft!" their platoon sergeant shouted above the overwhelming percussion of machine gun fire. Lei looked up just in time to see a geyser of water splash down on them from a nearby explosion.

I can't take this anymore! I need to get off this boat before we all die! Lei thought.

He didn't have long to wait before the front ramp of the landing craft dropped into the water. The first row of soldiers ran off the landing craft into the water and then up the beach, quickly followed by the second and then the third row.

Private Lei clutched his rifle as he shuffled towards the front of the landing craft. As he neared the exit, an enemy machine gun fired directly into their craft, cutting down row after row of soldiers in front of him. Without thinking, Lei hurled himself over the metal edge of the landing craft, plopping into waist-deep water. Dozens of other soldiers did the same, trying to escape the certain death that would have met them if they had stood still.

"Get to the beach! Grab cover!" Private Lei heard himself yelling to the soldiers around him.

He clutched his rifle firmly in his hands and trudged through the water to get to the beach. The soldiers around him rallied to him and followed his lead. Within a minute, he had broken free of the water that was slowing him down and he ran up the pebbled beach.

Lei charged at the closest enemy position he could see. He had spotted a cement machine gun bunker, pitted with scars and missing chunks of cement from the hundreds of bullets and artillery fragments that had already hit it. The position was roughly 200 meters inland from the beach, and the gun position continued to rake the beach with relentless fire, cutting down the invading soldiers like a scythe. It had to be taken out or they would all die on this beach.

Yelling at the top of his lungs, Private Lei charged the gun position, waving with his right arm for everyone to follow him forward. In that instant, anyone who was still alive around him lurched to their feet and yelled at the top of their lungs with him, rushing forward towards the enemy position.

As Lei neared the bunker, he fired his entire magazine into the gun slit, desperate to kill the occupants before they killed him or his remaining friends. Just as he made it to within ten meters of the bunker, Private Lei saw several soldiers running out of a back entrance. He stopped momentarily, raising his weapon and firing into the backs of the retreating soldiers, killing them instantly as he emptied his thirty-round magazine. His fellow soldiers began ran past him and overran the bunker. A couple of soldiers threw some grenades into it to ensure no one else was in there.

The fight for Juguang Island lasted another hour before the entire island had been completely overrun. Not a single defender surrendered, inflicting horrific losses on the militia forces that had assaulted this small plot of land. However, with the capture of Juguang, the PLA and the militia forces could now shift their focus towards their primary objective, the island of Formosa.

Chapter 10
Battle of the Hill

Island of Formosa
West Coast Expressway, Hill 137

Sergeant Lin yawned as he stretched his arms and shoulders. His body felt sore from the physical work of turning this hilltop and ridge area into the stronghold it had become. After stretching his aching muscles, he bent down and picked up his body armor, sliding it on over his head. Lin tightened up the vest a bit, making sure it fit nice and snug against his body.

It was 0600 hours and time to get the day started. With a lot of help from the engineers, his unit had turned Hill 137 into a formidable fortress. They had also built a series of bunkers over the past ten days to help ride out any potential enemy bombardments the mainlanders might try to throw at them.

Lin shrugged. *I really hope the politicians are able to sort things out*, he thought. *We need more time to prepare if we're really going to go to war.*

While outwardly, he would never show any emotion except strength and resolve in front of his soldiers and officers, inwardly, he was just as nervous and uncertain about the future as everyone else.

Sergeant Lin pulled a pack of Pall Mall cigarettes out of one of the pockets on his body armor. He slapped the pack a couple of times against his hand, pulled a cigarette out and lit it. Lin held it to his lips and took a long pull, lifting his head slightly to face the sky and then slowly releasing the smoke. The nicotine began to calm his nerves.

I just hope my family will be OK if war does break out," he thought.

He looked over to the mess tent and saw the line was starting to form.

I better get some food, he realized. *Today is going to be another long day of work while we put all the finishing touches on our fortifications.*

As the line steadily moved along, Lin was given his breakfast, and he found a seat near several of the junior sergeants. Lin had just taken his first bite when the first siren blared. Everyone paused mid-bite as the wailing sound pierced the morning air. The noise echoed and grew in volume, spreading across the nearby cities and destroying the solemn silence of the morning.

Lin jumped to his feet and shouted, "Everyone to the bunkers, *now*!"

The soldiers immediately grabbed the weapons that had been sitting on the ground next to their chairs, leaving their breakfasts where they were. They all raced to the underground bunkers that had essentially just been completed the day before. The engineers had just finished placing a couple feet of dirt on the roofs, and they had all spent the better part of the previous day moving crates of additional ammunition and other supplies into the bunkers before turning in for bed.

While the soldiers rushed into the bunkers, a couple of men chose to remain in the reinforced machine gun positions to spot for possible enemy ships. These men would alert the others to leave the bunker and man their battle stations when the time came.

In less than three minutes, the rest of the 200 soldiers stationed on Hill 137 had reached the four designated bunkers. Each bunker could hold around 50 men and acted as the supply depot for the portion of the defensive line and fortress it was near.

The soldiers in the bunker with Sergeant Lin looked to him with scared looks on their faces, almost pleading for him to tell them that this was just some sort of drill and not the real thing. Lin, for his part, tried to look strong and stoic. Inwardly, he was both excited and scared. He had spent his whole life in the army up to this point training for this very scenario.

Just as he was about to say something to try and calm everyone's nerves, the first missile landed on their little hill. The bunker shook violently. Everyone looked up at the ceiling, unsure if it would hold. The ground shook again, violently, then again and again. The thunderous booms of explosions filled the air.

Sergeant Lin looked at the faces of his men, most of whom were casting glances at the ceiling between each violent shake of the earth. Where before he had seen fear in their eyes, he now saw anger and a determined resolve to do their jobs and defend their country. At that moment, he felt immensely proud of his soldiers. Their training was now starting to replace the fear and trepidation they had once felt with grit and a force of will.

The bombardment lasted for nearly three hours, though the intensity ebbed and flowed. At times, they thought it had ended when five minutes would go by and they heard nothing, but then a few more rockets or missiles would land nearby and remind them that the mainlanders had not forgotten about them.

Suddenly, the field phone sitting near Sergeant Lin rang. He looked at it in surprise, almost having forgotten that it was there. Then he remembered that he needed to pick it up.

"This is Sergeant Lin," he said formally, unsure of who was calling them.

"This is Corporal Cho in Bunker Three. Bunker Four is reporting enemy landing craft in sight and said they are going to engage them with their anti-ship missiles."

Lin thought for a moment. *The mainlanders must have skipped Kinmen Island altogether if they are landing here so quickly*, he realized.

He acknowledged the soldier's message and hung up. Everyone in the bunker was now staring at him, waiting to learn what had just transpired. Lin smiled and stood, which made everyone else stand as well.

"Bunker Four is starting to engage communist landing craft. The mainlanders will be here shortly. I want everyone to man their battle stations and prepare to repel this dastardly invasion of our homeland. Remember, our families and country are depending on us to hold our ground. Let's go show them what we're made of!" he shouted.

Sergeant Lin led the way out of the bunker, through the network of trenches to their fighting positions. His company had two heavy machine gun positions and two antitank bunkers to defend, with one of the antitank bunkers also acting as the command center. Just behind their position were a couple of trucks, which had several anti-ship missiles on them. A couple of soldiers in two of his bunkers had laser designators, which would help guide the missiles to their intended targets.

As he arrived in the command bunker, he saw the captain there, along with the couple of radio operators that would help to coordinate the defense of the hill. The command bunker would essentially direct the various bunkers' fields of fire, depending on where the heaviest concentration of enemy soldiers was.

One of the soldiers in the bunker was using the laser designators to paint one of the large Yuting III-class landing ship tanks that could carry multiple amphibious assault crafts and hovercraft ashore. The ship was still several miles off the coast, but clearly taking up position to begin disgorging their troops. While the soldier was lasing the target, an anti-ship missile flew over their bunker and raced out to sea, skimming just above the water at nearly Mach speed. It took only a few seconds for the missile to travel the distance and plow into the rear of the LST, just above the waterline.

For a brief moment, nothing seemed to happen as the missile's semi-armor-piercing tip punctured the hull of the LST and plowed deeper inside. Then the warhead exploded, sending flame and shrapnel out the hole it had just punched through. The LST shook violently from the explosion and listed heavily to the side, with the rear of the ship filling up quickly with water. Only two ZBD2000 amphibious armored fighting vehicles made it out of the ship before its entire rear half slipped beneath the waves.

Any sense of victory was blunted when the smoke began to clear in the ocean before them, and they saw dozens of LSTs of all sizes had moved into position, along with a number of smaller patrol boats and corvettes.

The soldier who had lased the first LST and sunk it quickly moved his targeting laser to the next ship and began the process all over again. He would continue to work with the missile trucks, guiding anti-ship missiles into the LSTs until either they ran out of missiles or the trucks themselves were destroyed.

While the ocean was now starting to fill up with ZBD2000s and hovercrafts heading towards the shore, the antitank bunkers fired their guided missiles at the armored vehicles quickly approaching. Each of these vehicles typically carried eight soldiers, so taking them out at sea would save them a lot of trouble.

Sergeant Lin called over to one of the antitank bunkers. "Hey, we need to focus on those hovercrafts! Just one of them can carry as many as two hundred soldiers. If we don't take them out, it won't be long before a few thousand soldiers arrive on the beach. We can focus on the ZBDs when they make landfall."

Lin knew they had armor support units being held in reserve; their captain would call upon them once the enemy tanks landed. The infantry, though, could cause them all kinds of problems if they established a foothold.

Just as the soldiers were responding to the changing orders, Lin's bunker shook violently from an explosion. One of the patrol boats had darted in closer to the shore and had fired a round from its turret at them, and it had nearly succeeded in landing the round right through the gun slits in the bunker. There was no time to dwell on the near-death they had all just experienced; everyone shook off the effects of the explosion and went back to the business of repelling the invasion.

It didn't take long before the first wave of amphibious vehicles made it to the shore and began to speed up the beach, trying to rush up the highway and reach the base of their little fortress on Hill 137. Fortunately for Lin and his men, as the vehicles moved up the beach, the series of mines that the engineers had planted began to explode, ripping the ZBDs and light tanks apart with no effort.

Lin looked to his right. A hovercraft glided right up on the beach, dropping its front ramp. In seconds, dozens upon dozens of soldiers rushed forward, firing their weapons in the direction of his men. As quickly as the hovercraft had arrived and unloaded its human cargo, it moved back to sea to pick up another load to bring to the beach.

It's already starting to happen, thought Sergeant Lin with dread. The very thing he'd feared—the human wave of communist amphibious vehicle and hovercrafts would overrun them with more troops than they could ever possibly kill.

One of the soldiers who had been manning a T74 machine gun died violently as his head exploded. He had been hit by a heavy-caliber bullet, leaving his machine gun silent at a critical moment.

Lin immediately rushed to the soldier and grabbed the machine gun, placing the butt of it firmly in his shoulder. He proceeded to let loose a controlled burst at a group of People's Liberation Army soldiers who were charging one of the gun bunkers less than two hundred meters away from him.

He turned to one of the privates nearby and yelled, "Ammo! Keep me stocked with ammo!"

The private immediately grabbed one of the crates next to the dead soldier and pulled out several 100-round belts. He attached one of the belts to the current one Sergeant Lin was burning through, so he wouldn't have to stop and reload.

Lin nodded to the private, which was the only thanks he had the time to give out. Then he pointed to the gun before making his next request. "Pour some water on the barrel. Keep pouring water on the barrel and keep the belts linked, OK?"

The young soldier nodded and grabbed one of the nearby water bottles, emptying it over the barrel of the gun, which was starting to steam and smoke from the heat of the constant use.

Sergeant Lin heard the captain yelling on the radio for artillery support and additional reinforcements.

Good, he's calling in the artillery, he thought. *We just might be able to stop this first wave.*

Sergeant Lin spotted another hovercraft coming in quickly, almost directly in front of his machine gun, so he turned and aimed right for the landing ramps, waiting for them to drop so he could begin the process of mowing down the enemy soldiers that would emerge. The private next him had just linked another belt to the one he was currently using and poured another bottle of water over the barrel, since Lin had stopped shooting for a few seconds. They desperately needed to change the barrel, but there just wasn't time. They needed to keep firing if they had any hope of survival.

Just as the hovercraft was moving onto the beach, an explosion hit the front of their bunker, knocking nearly everyone inside to the floor. Sergeant Lin smacked the ground hard. Something hit him, searing his left arm. He shook off the effects of the explosion and immediately climbed back to the machine gun. He didn't even take a moment to look around the bunker to see if anyone else had been injured or killed.

He trained the machine gun back to the hovercraft just in time to see the front ramp drop. He immediately squeezed the trigger, pouring dozens of controlled bursts right into the nearly 200 PLA soldiers charging off the hovercraft. Lin just kept firing and firing until the barrel of his machine gun was glowing red and he ran out of ammo.

The sergeant turned to yell at the private to load more ammo and pour additional water on the barrel, only to see the private had bled out on the floor behind him from a shrapnel wound to his neck. Then he surveyed the rest of the bunker and realized he was the only one left alive.

Lin moved away from the machine gun as dozens of bullets peppered the face of his bunker. He grabbed the radio the captain had just been using and called to one of the other bunkers. "I need you to send a few soldiers over here. Everyone else at this bunker was killed, including the captain."

The voice on the other end acknowledged his request. As Lin waited for additional soldiers to arrive, he grabbed a different radio and called for the quick-reaction force to be rushed forward, along with the tanks that were being held in reserve.

He heard a voice yelling over one of the other radio handsets, so he rushed over and grabbed the receiver. "This is Sergeant Lin, Bunker One, go ahead with your message," he said in as calm a voice as he could muster. The incessant pounding of gunfire, explosions and men shouting was overwhelming. Just then, eight of his soldiers rushed into the bunker, pausing only long enough to survey the carnage of dead bodies on the floor.

"Change the barrels on the machine guns and get them operational!" he yelled at them before turning his attention back to the radio.

"Sergeant Lin, I was just talking to your captain. I was letting him know that nearly half of our artillery guns have been destroyed. We are just now shifting our fire to your sector. We are sending the first wave of six rounds right now. Please let us know if we need to adjust fire or just keep firing on the current positions," the voice on the other end of the radio demanded.

"Yes, send the artillery," Lin acknowledged. "I will radio back once I have seen them impact to let you know where to adjust fire," he responded before placing the handset down on the crate near the other handsets and walking towards one of the gun slits.

His soldiers had gotten the two main machine guns working again and were already tearing into the PLA soldiers on the beach and the ones rushing across the highway to the base of their hill. Once the enemy soldiers made it to the base of the hill, it was up to the soldiers manning the various trenches and fighting positions to deal with them. The bunkers could really only focus on the beach and provide covering fire in support of each other's positions.

Surveying the beach before him, Sergeant Lin grabbed his rifle and took careful aim at the soldiers trying to advance up the hill near one of their trench lines. His rifle barked with each carefully aimed shot. Each time, an enemy soldier collapsed.

He had fired off maybe five rounds when he heard the whistling sound of artillery coming in. *Boom, boom, boom!* Geysers of water, dirt, and sand sprouted into the air from the impacts of the 155mm high-explosive rounds. Dozens of PLA soldiers were thrown into the air from the concussions of the blasts. The six rounds had met their marks. Now Sergeant Lin had to ensure they kept coming.

He ran to the back of the bunker and grabbed the handset to the artillery. "Those rounds hit right on the money. Fire for effect, six rounds HE if you can. The PLA is starting to overrun our positions and we need that artillery," he yelled over the concussions of gunfire and explosions going on all around him.

"Copy that, the rounds are on the way. Once these rounds are complete, we have to shift fire to the next sector. You'll be on your own for a little while," the voice from the artillery battalion responded.

This is it, Lin thought. *We won't get another fire mission.* His life began to flash before his eyes.

It took a little less than five minutes before the artillery barrage began to land throughout the beach, killing hundreds of PLA soldiers in the process of landing, along with those still trying to make it across the highway to the base of Hill 137.

Just as Sergeant Lin had hope that the enemy might actually be on the ropes, the bunker not more than 200 meters away from them exploded in spectacular fashion.

Lin surveyed the scene and spotted a Xian JH-7 fighter bomber flying low and fast across their bunkers and trench lines. Several oblong objects tumbled through the air towards them.

"Incoming! Everyone, drop to the ground!" Sergeant Lin yelled.

Seconds later, a thunderous explosion ripped through the air. Searing heat rushed across the hill as flames of napalm began to expand. The jellied liquid was thrown across the trench line and bunkers of Hill 137, marking everything it touched with devastation. Fortunately for Sergeant Lin and the soldiers next to him, the dangerous fuel did not fly through the gun slits of their bunker as it had one of the others. However, nearly the entire trench line had been saturated with the napalm.

Dozens of his soldiers screamed in agonizing pain as the material stuck to their clothes and burned through to their skin, then melted through their flesh to their bones, killing them in one of the most horrifying ways imaginable.

"Get back to the guns! Keep firing at the enemy. We have to keep them from overrunning our positions!" Sergeant Lin yelled, trying to get his soldiers to focus on the task at hand and not the burning carnage of their comrades. There was nothing they could do for them anyway; they needed to hold out long enough for their reinforcements to arrive and throw the invaders back into the ocean.

With several of their machine gun bunkers down and most of the soldiers in the trench line killed, the PLA ground forces were steadily advancing to the base of Hill 137 and working their way through the concertina wire Lin's men had placed at various intervals to slow them down. Light and medium tanks were also starting to land at the beach.

The level of resistance they could provide had dwindled significantly since that fighter bomber had paid them a visit. Sergeant Lin grabbed one of the radio handsets and tried to raise their brigade headquarters. On the first couple of tries, he was unsuccessful. Once he was able to get through to someone, the colonel on the other end seemed very surprised that Hill 137 was still holding the line.

"All of the other beach strongpoints in your sector have fallen," he explained. "What is left of the brigade is falling back to their secondary position."

"Can you send additional reinforcements?" Lin asked. "We can continue to hold the hill if we get immediate support."

There was a pause. The colonel was probably conferring with his counterparts on the other end. "Have what is left of your company fall back to the secondary position and rejoin the brigade. We have prepared additional fortifications, but we need all the soldiers we can get to man them."

"Acknowledged," Lin replied.

He set about doing his best to get word to the remaining soldiers to fall back. Once he had fired off the green flare and contacted the bunkers that were still able to answer his radio calls, he and four of the remaining soldiers in his bunker ran for their lives.

As they ran through the trench towards the back of the hill, they saw the charred bodies of their comrades, twisted, contorted, and still smoldering. The smell of burnt flesh hung in the air as the remaining survivors did their best to escape. One of the soldiers, who had been doing his best to keep up with Sergeant Lin, suddenly stopped and began to throw up from the sights and smells that were overwhelming him. After emptying the contents of his stomach, he shook off the horror and resumed running after his comrades.

When they reached the bottom of the hill, they found nearly two dozen other survivors, and collectively they moved as quickly as their feet would take them to the secondary position, roughly three kilometers away on another ridgeline. For the time being, their fight was over. They had done their duty to the best of their ability and had paid dearly for it. They had started the day with 220 soldiers. Now they were down to just twenty-eight.

Chapter 11
Roadblocks

Taipei, Taiwan
Jinhe Sports Park

Captain Ma's aircraft buffeted a bit as the transport craft started its final approach to the drop zone. The air force and navy had been hammering the Taiwanese air force and air defenses for the past six hours. In that short amount of time, they had already effectively destroyed the Taiwanese air force, and now they were working on taking out the island's remaining air defenses. With heavy fighter and ground attack aircraft support, the airborne forces were being sent in to capture their objectives.

Like the other paratroopers from the PLAAF 43rd Airborne Division, anxiously waiting in the cargo hold of the aircraft, Captain Ma was both excited and terrified at the same time. The transport bounced up and down, weaving around more than he was used to. There were a few extreme evasive maneuvers as Taiwanese anti-aircraft artillery narrowly missed them; the closer they got to the capital and their primary objectives, the more danger they were in.

Their flight plan evened out, then one of the crew chiefs yelled out to everyone, "We are almost to the objective, so get ready to jump!"

The pilots had no intention of staying in the area any longer than they needed to. Ma stood up and began to shuffle towards the door lining up for the big leap.

Remember, this is just like Mongolia and Vietnam, he thought, trying to calm his nerves. *No big deal. Just get on the ground and take it from there.*

The small red light near the exit of the aircraft switched from red to green, and the jump master standing at the door yelled, "Go, go, go!"

One by one they walked through the door. Before Captain Ma knew it, he had reached the door and stepped out, just as he had done in training and his previous jumps. As planned, his rip cord caught, and in a second, his freefall ended. His main chute deployed, jerking him hard as his descent to earth slowed. Ma looked up at the transport he had just jumped out of and saw the rest of his men making their way out of the aircraft.

Nearby, another Chinese aircraft was also unloading a group of paratroopers. He watched as the men floated down through the sky. All of a sudden, the engine of that lumbering plane took a direct hit and exploded. The fire spread to the fuel bladders in the wing, and the entire right wing of the aircraft collapsed, sending the plane into a terrible tumbling circle as men continued to try and jump out.

He didn't have time to dwell on the loss of his comrades; he was steadily floating towards the earth below. He looked down. Below his feet he identified the park that was their designated drop zone, and he guided his parachute towards it.

Despite the loss of the nearby plane, there were now thousands of parachutes in the sky, hovering towards the ground. In a way it was strangely beautiful to watch the thousands of paratroopers descending from the sky with Taipei in the background and the lights of tracer rounds reaching up from the ground like a giant laser show.

Before Ma knew it, the ground was quickly approaching, and he prepared to tuck and roll and engage any enemy soldiers he might encounter. His feet hit the ground, and he bent his knees in perfect form before he disconnected from his parachute. Captain Ma grabbed for his drop bag and placed his pack on his back, calling out to the soldiers nearby. Several of them came running towards him, ready for any orders he might issue.

Ma's first step was getting his company collected and organized. They would be responsible for securing Highway 3, preventing any Taiwanese reinforcements from entering the city. Their sister company was going to secure Expressway 64 near the Jinhe Sports Park, further blocking another major road running through the city. Their goal was not to try and secure the city, just prevent enemy reinforcements from traveling freely while the ground forces arrived at the shore.

As his group of men gathered around him, Captain Ma issued his orders. "Lieutenant Zang, get your platoon moving to the tunnel entrance. Find whatever civilian vehicles you can and set up a road block. We need to make sure no enemy soldiers are able to get through."

"Yes, sir," Zang replied.

Ma turned and repeated his order to the other platoon commanders, asking them set up road blocks at different sections of

Highway 3. He kept one platoon in reserve with him, in case he needed them to reinforce one road block or another.

The first thirty minutes on the ground was rather chaotic. Heavy machine gun fire rattled loudly through the city. Somewhere overhead, jet aircraft screamed as they whizzed along. At unexpected intervals, explosions rang out.

Captain Ma's soldiers did not encounter a lot of regular Taiwanese army soldiers, but they definitely met some initial resistance from the local military police units that had been deployed throughout the city. As Ma listened to the scene around him, it sounded like most of the fighting in the city was taking place where the rest of Ma's brigade had landed.

One problem his soldiers were starting to encounter was the immense number of people trying to flee the city. While his platoons were trying to set up the roadblocks, they were also dealing with an overwhelming number of frightened civilian refugees trying desperately to flee the fighting. Ma had given explicit orders to his soldiers not to shoot at or kill any civilians unless absolutely necessary. If people were trying to flee the city, they were to let them flee.

There was actually a larger strategy at play than a display of mercy. As the refugees clogged up the major roads and paths leading to the fighting, this would prevent the Taiwanese army from being able to move their forces where they were needed. Mainland China also did not want to intentionally alienate the population. The end goal was to bring Formosa back into the fold, and they couldn't do that if they turned the civilians there even further against them.

Just as Captain Ma thought his sector was being safely secured with little resistance, the radio crackled to life, letting him know that one of the platoons was reporting the sight of Taiwanese heavy tanks.

Crap, he thought. *I don't know that we have enough antitank missiles with us if they are any larger than a platoon-sized element.*

Ma turned to his company sergeant. "Make sure our Hongjian-12s are deployed to that road block immediately," he ordered. While they had plenty of RPG-7s with them, they only had fourteen of the HJ-12 Red Arrows, which could lock on a target before launch.

Boom! Everyone turned in the direction of the second platoon. A billowing cloud of black smoke rose into the air. Another explosion rocked the earth, and then frantic calls came in over the radio.

"We have tanks to our front. They are punching a hole through the road block!" a frantic voice cried out.

Ma turned to the platoon leader he had kept in reserve. "Get your platoon moving to reinforce them *now*. Report back how many tanks there are and if you guys are going to be able to hold the line. If not, I need to know ASAP, so we can fall back into the surrounding area," he ordered.

The young lieutenant, who had just joined his unit a week ago as part of the replacements they had received, quickly responded, "Yes, sir." Then he rushed off to mobilize his platoon to the endangered roadblock.

When Li's platoon got within 100 meters of the roadblock, they spotted soldiers from one of their sister platoons, who were starting to fall back. Immediately behind them was a Taiwanese M-60 Patton tank, hell-bent on killing them.

"Sergeant, get that missile set up and take out that tank!" yelled Li, loud enough to be heard over the roar of the machine guns firing all around him.

The sergeant yelled back, "Copy that, sir!" and set to work. A couple of his soldiers had been lugging around several Red Arrow 12 "fire and forget" antitank launchers. The shoulder-fired weapons were still relatively new, but in their limited use thus far, they had proven to be extremely effective at taking out enemy tanks.

Whoosshhh...BAM! The explosion reverberated through the air as the paratroopers watched the missile leap from the launcher, traveling the short distance to the tank in less than a second. Once it was hit, the tank came to a halt. One of the hatches on the turret blew open and a small geyser of fire shot up into the sky.

Lieutenant Li stopped to look back at the soldier who had launched the missile to congratulate him on the hit, when a second tank rammed the now-burning wreck, pushing it to the side. The commander of this new tank was standing outside the turret and used his M2 .50-caliber machine gun to rake the paratroopers' positions. The soldier who had successfully destroyed the first tank was cut down in a hail of bullets as the large caliber rounds tore his body apart.

"Someone, take that tank out!" yelled Li to any of the soldiers left who still had another missile.

There was no response. Seeing everyone ducking for cover, Lieutenant Li immediately scanned the area for options. He spotted a dead paratrooper lying on the ground next to a small delivery van that had been torn to ribbons by the tank's heavy machine gun. Lying next to the soldier was another Red Arrow missile.

Not thinking about his own safety, Li jumped up and ran across the street to the missile launcher. He ran past several of his solders writhing on the ground, calling for help.

If I don't take down that tank, there's nothing I can do to help them, Li realized.

Reaching down, Lieutenant Li grabbed the missile and pulled it back behind the van. He was startled as a tank round hit the front of a building not more than thirty meters to his left, sending debris flying in all directions.

That was way too close, he thought.

Li looked down at the missile launcher, toggled the safety on the missile and then raised it to his shoulder. The ground below him was starting to vibrate now as the tank continued to move closer to him. The creaking of the tanks treads and the clanking sound it made as the metal and rubber tracks hit the asphalt sent shivers down his spine.

In that moment, he knew it was now or never.

Taking a deep breath and steeling his nerves, Li jumped out from behind his covered position, aimed the missile at the tank and squeezed the trigger. In a fraction of a second, the missile leapt from the launcher and streaked across the short distance to the enemy tank that had been bearing down on them.

The missile scored a direct hit, and for a second, Li was elated at having taken the enemy tank out. Then his world went black; suddenly he didn't feel or see anything as his lifeless body collapsed to the ground, riddled with bullets. Taiwanese soldiers who had been using the tank's armored body as a shield had rushed forward, and Lieutenant Li was their first target.

The battle for control of this major road interchange lasted for nearly an hour, until the Taiwanese tanks pushed Captain Ma's forces back into the city, opening the roads back up. Ma's company retreated and took up residence in a nearby elementary school and several surrounding buildings. They moved eight different RPG teams to the roofs and windows of their shelters. If those tanks or infantry decided to try to head in their direction, they'd be in for a rude awakening. Since they were unable to hold their primary objective, they moved to their secondary mission, which was to attack as many enemy vehicles and cause as much chaos in the city as possible.

I hope the other companies are having better luck in their sectors than we are, Ma thought.

What Captain Ma did not know was that one of the Chinese battalions had been cornered shortly after landing by a much larger armored force. They had been compelled to surrender after taking heavy losses. Only two of the battalions from their mainland brigade were still actively fighting.

Chapter 12
Out of the Darkness

Taoyuan, Taiwan
Taiwan Taoyuan International Airport

The ground surrounding Colonel Wang shook and vibrated with the force of constant explosions. He looked nervously at the walls of the bunker around him, hoping they would hold.

Two days before the invasion, the tanks in his 542nd Armored Brigade had been moved to a series of underground tunnels. They were being held in reserve for when the PLA began to land their heavy tanks at the beaches. When the air raid sirens had first blared, they had all thought this was another drill. False alarms were common on Formosa. However, as the first series of explosions rocked the earth, it was clear that the threat was very real.

The next hour brought a nearly constant barrage of explosions, some near, some far, but all violent in the destruction they caused to the villages and cities above them. While Colonel Wang was glad he and his men were underground, he felt sorry for the civilian population that was having to ride out the attack in less-fortified bunkers than his tank unit was currently surrounded by.

After being cooped up in the tunnels for nearly three hours, Colonel Wang received a radio call. "This is Iron Mountain. The communist forces have officially landed at the beaches. They are presently being engaged. Get your brigade ready to respond to your assigned targets and prepare to exit the tunnels."

It's about time they get us into the fight, Wang thought. If the PLA could land a large enough force, the Taiwanese wouldn't be able to push them back into the sea.

He turned to his executive officer. "Send word to the other battalion commanders that we are to prepare to leave the tunnels. They are to head to their assigned sectors and begin engaging the PLA ground forces as soon as they encounter them. Also, tell our air defense units to be ready to engage enemy aircraft shortly after exiting the tunnels. I have no idea if the air force has been able to maintain air superiority or not, but we'll need them to cover our advance to the beach. Understood?" he asked.

His XO just nodded, smiling at the thought that they were finally going to get into the action.

Once he had given his XO the green light to move ahead, Wang turned and walked down the line of tanks he would be traveling with, informing each tank commander that they would be leaving shortly. As he stopped to talk to commanders, a group of the tankers gathered around him. He got the sense that they might be a bit nervous.

"This is it, men," he said, getting their attention. "All our training and long days and nights in the field have led us to this point. When we leave the tunnels, you need to head as quickly as possible to the various beach locations we've been assigned. By the time we arrive, the PLA will probably have a substantial amount of armor already landed, so identify your targets quickly and take them out. Keep moving and make yourselves hard targets to hit. We have some mechanized infantry support, but do not rely on them exclusively to keep you safe," Wang said, hoping his speech would give them the reassurance they needed.

After Wang's impromptu speech, his men returned to their tanks with a bit more grit and determination than they had a few minutes before. Almost all at once, the tanks and other armored vehicles began starting up their engines in the tunnels. As Colonel Wang made his way back to his command vehicle, he could hear the sound of the tunnel entrance being opened up, which meant the order to move must have come while he was giving his little pep talk. Wang picked up his pace a bit and trotted quickly back to his vehicle, where he was greeted by his tank gunner.

"Sir, the order came down for everyone to prepare to advance," confirmed his gunner.

The radio in his vehicle suddenly sprang to life. "Striker Six, this is Iron Mountain One. How copy?"

Colonel Wang recognized the voice of his division commander, but it sounded a bit more strained than usual. "This is Striker Six. Good copy, Iron Mountain. What do you have for me?" he asked.

"Striker One, we have lost air superiority. Expect heavy enemy aircraft support when you approach the beach. The international airport has been placed out of commission, and there are currently enemy airborne troops landing across the airport. Your orders are being amended to support the 232nd Infantry Brigade as they attempt to retake the airport. Once that has been accomplished, resume your attacks against the beach landing zones. How copy?"

Shocked by the response, Colonel Wang was lost in thought for a moment before responding. Once his unit left the tunnels, they would be fully exposed and moving as quickly as they could to engage the enemy at the beach. If they redirected to the airport, then chances were a lot of his forces would be destroyed by the enemy aircraft that would undoubtedly be supporting the airborne troopers.

"Iron Mountain, I copy the request. If we do this, my brigade will most likely not be combat effective to engage the beach zones. Do you want me to focus on the airport over the beach zones?" he asked.

There was a pause in the conversation. Clearly the division commander was thinking about that and trying to decide what was more important.

"Striker Six, this is Iron Mountain. Disregard my last order. Continue with your original plans. Hit the beach zones hard. Prepare to fall back to Zone B if air opposition is too high. How copy?" asked the general.

Colonel Wang keyed his mic. "That's a good copy, Iron Mountain. Good luck and happy hunting. Out," he responded before he switched over to the brigade net.

"Listen up," Wang said to his men. "We are a go to attack the beach zones. I want each battalion to hit their objectives and do as much damage as you can. When your units reach seventy percent casualties, I want you to fall back to Zone B and be ready to defend from the entrenched positions the engineers have ready for us. Happy hunting, gentlemen. Let's go kill us some commies!" he shouted.

In minutes, the tanks revved their engines and surged forward out of the tunnels. As Colonel Wang's tank emerged from the tunnel, he stood in the turret so that he could gain a better sense of their surroundings. His jaw dropped; the destruction before them was astounding. While the area around the tunnels was not that bad, black columns of smoke filled the skyline in nearly every direction. As he looked further down to the beach zones, all he could see was explosions and large billowing clouds of black smoke.

Wang's tank followed the others in the lead, heading towards Beach Zone Foxtrot, roughly twelve kilometers away from their current position. As they moved across the roads that were not bombed out, he heard the swooshing sound of several missiles. He craned his neck around to see where the noise had come from and spotted one of his air defense vehicles firing off a third anti-aircraft missile at an unseen target high above them.

As long as his air defense vehicles can keep the enemy aircraft off my tanks, we still have a fighting chance of crushing the landing operations that are underway, Colonel Wang thought, trying to remain optimistic.

Within the next fifteen minutes, Wang had already seen two enemy helicopters blown up, as well as three enemy aircraft that had attempted to attack his armored column. Three of his tanks and two infantry fighting vehicles were also blown up, his first casualties of the war.

When his column came within three kilometers of the beach, they encountered their first enemy armor resistance, a group of Type 96 main battle tanks, the ZTZ-96s. While not as formidable as the T-99s, they were still dangerous, and Colonel Wang was exceptionally lucky that his M60s caught the enemy tanks by surprise. They were able to get off the first shots, destroying the four ZTZ-96s before they knew what hit them. In seconds, his lead company of tanks punched past the burning wreckage and moved aggressively towards the beach, where the PLA was clearly in the process of offloading additional armor.

The lead company soon radioed back to Colonel Wang. "Sir, we are engaging dozens of mainland infantry fighting vehicles and light tanks. Request assistance to take them out. How copy?"

"That's a good copy. Sending reinforcements your way," Wang replied.

Just as the rest of the battalion was moving forward to assist their fellow tankers, nearly two dozen light and heavy tanks emerged from the beach sector two kilometers to their right and charged his units.

"Tank, stop!" Colonel Wang yelled to his driver. "Gunner, turn forty-five degrees and engage enemy tanks!"

The following three minutes were pure chaos as dozens upon dozens of tanks began to engage each other. While projectiles from both sides filled the air like a swarm of killer bees, the Chinese ships added to the fray and shot off quite a few three-inch rounds to try and produce some indirect fire support for their ground forces.

72

Wang's tank was rocked twice by near-misses before his driver began to move the tank to another firing position. As the pandemonium subsided, the Taiwanese battalion broke through the remaining defenders and pushed forward to hit the beach directly.

Colonel Wang's tank followed another vehicle through a cut in the sand that led them straight across the highway to the beach. Just as Wang's tank cleared the cut, the vehicle in front of him exploded in spectacular fashion, showering Colonel Wang's tank with shrapnel. Despite the shock of losing their comrades so violently, they pressed on.

As they cleared the wreckage of the tank, Wang had to do a double take at what he saw. There were dozens of amphibious assault ships in the water and driving up the beach towards his tanks. A hovercraft flew in from the water and drove ten meters up the beach before dropping its forward landing deck to offload two ZTZ-96 main battle tanks.

"Gunner, target the tanks on that hovercraft!" Colonel Wang shouted over the intercom.

In seconds, their turret turned to point right at the enemy tanks less than 500 meters away and fired. The first tank blew up as it began to leave the hovercraft; Wang's gunner had scored a direct hit. A mere second later, the other tank exploded in a blaze of glory—another one of Colonel Wang's tanks had had the same idea.

While they engaged the tanks and amphibious assault vehicles arriving at the beach, Wang's gunner grabbed the coax machine gun and poured fire onto the infantry soldiers who were trying to charge toward them. The other Taiwanese tanks followed suit, splattering the enemy forces with heavy and accurate tank and machine gun fire.

When it looked like they might finally succeed in securing the beach, a sudden series of thunderous explosions rocked their tanks. Colonel Wang peeled himself off the floor of his tank and reoriented himself to reality. Through the daze of what was most likely a mild concussion, he realized that they had just been hit by a series of bombs dropped by enemy aircraft. Several more of his vehicles had been completely obliterated. Wang's only comfort was the thought that those soldiers had not had to suffer in their demise.

"Everyone, fall back to Zone B!" the colonel yelled into the radio. "I say again, everyone fall back to Zone B immediately! We've done all the damage we can do here!" he shouted over the battalion net.

At least we did our best to crush this invasion force right here, Wang thought. *I hope my other battalions had as much luck as we just had.*

As the battalion fell back, Wang heard the telltale sounds of chopper blades approaching as a series of PLA ground attack helicopters flew in. They strafed Wang's tanks with machine gun fire. The colonel held his breath; the armor on their tanks seemed to be holding up well against the incoming bullets. A moment later, Wang heard the unmistakable whistle of antipersonnel rockets and his stomach sank. A couple of the rockets did not connect with their targets as Wang's brigade all performed evasive maneuvers; however, two more tanks were completely destroyed. The losses were adding up.

One of Wang's anti-aircraft gun trucks sprang to life, rapidly firing heavy machine gun rounds into the choppers above them. Within seconds, one of the helicopters was turned into a fireball, descending quickly from the sky. Two more enemy helos were damaged as several of Wang's tank commanders returned fire with the M2 .50 machine guns they had on board. They were able to break free from the aerial attack fairly quickly.

It took nearly forty minutes for his entire brigade to make it back to Zone B and begin to prepare to meet the enemy in their fixed fortification. While Wang hated using his tanks in fixed positions like this, he realized that his tanks should have no problem beating back a PLA ground attack from there. Colonel Wang's main concern was that enemy aircraft and helicopters would still be able to snipe at them with their long-range antitank missiles.

If that happens, what's left of my brigade will be ripped apart before they can even make a difference, he thought with dread.

Chapter 13
Whose Side Are You On?

Outside Taipei, Taiwan
Heng Shan Military Command Center

President Hung glared at General Sheng, her Air Force Commanding General. "Are you working with mainlanders, General?" she asked, her voice dripping with hostility and contempt.

General Sheng, for his part, looked appalled at the mere mention of such an accusation. "My force is doing its best to defend this country, Madam President. Perhaps if your government had not cut our funding so severely, we'd have the aircraft, pilots, and equipment needed to properly defend ourselves against a much larger force," he shot back. Since she had come into power nearly fifteen months ago, President Hung had done what she could to cut the defense budget, shifting that money to education and other social programs; this had not grown any love between her and her senior military leaders.

Minister Feng interrupted the two parties. "Enough. None of this arguing is going to change what has happened. We need to figure out if we are going to be able to stop the invasion."

He turned and looked to the General of the Army and asked, "What is the status of the beaches?"

General Wong, who had been reading something on his tablet, snapped to attention and turn to address the group. "Our forces held the PLA invasion force at the beach for nearly an hour. In some areas they held out for much longer, but overall, we have not been able to stop the PLA from overrunning our positions and establishing multiple beachheads. They have also secured a couple of ports, although we have some underwater divers that will start to sink the transport ships they try to bring in. I have ordered our reserve forces to move forward and attempt to push the PLA ground forces back to the beaches, but unless my guys can get some sort of air support or air defense, our armored units are going to get wiped out."

General Sheng bristled at that last comment. "I cannot guarantee any sort of air support for your forces," he replied. "Just prior to the attack, our advanced warning radar systems came under a sustained cyber-attack. We did not know the mainlanders had launched a cruise missile attack against us until we spotted the missiles as they flew over the island. By then, it was too late to react. Most of our aircraft were caught on the ground. The ones that were in the air were quickly shot down by the sheer number of enemy aircraft being thrown at us. The few remaining aircraft we have left are trying to protect specific areas where we have the strongest air defense systems."

Sighing softly, President Hung was almost in despair as she tried to calculate the next move. The American delegation had already told them the US would not be able to come to their aid should China invade.

"What are our options, generals?" she asked.

General Wang was the first to speak up. "Right now, our options are limited. We cannot hold the beaches, so we are falling back to our second and third lines of defense. We are going to make the PLA pay in blood for every kilometer of ground they take. At some point, we are going to start losing the major cities, and the island is going to get cut in half. At that point, the focus of our defensive effort will shift to the countryside, where we will try to bleed the enemy dry by carrying out insurgency operations. The bigger question is, at what point do we try to evacuate you, Madam President, and the civilian government to set up a government in exile someplace safe?" Wong replied solemnly.

They might only be in the opening hours of the war, but things were happening rapidly, and at some point, it would become impossible to evacuate the civilian government. President Hung lowered her head. This was not the response she had hoped for.

Chapter 14
I'd Trade My Kingdom for a Horse

Washington, D.C.
White House Cabinet Room

The President rubbed his temples. He was feeling immensely overwhelmed by the events swirling around him.

As the Secretary of Labor, Maria Sanchez, finished her brief on the state of the economy and the manufacturing sector, Gates was lost in a sea of thoughts. *I wanted my presidency to be focused on domestic issues—fixing our economy, tax reform, regulation reform, healthcare and immigration.* Now they were embroiled in a global war that just keeps spreading, destroying any hope he had of trying to fix the nation for the little guy. Those wretched war hawks had led the US into this mess. *I'd like to string them all up—especially that Senator McGregor.* How had that man thought sending a carrier strike group into the Black Sea would force the Russians to back down from their threat of force?

He heard the secretary say something more interesting, and it brought his attention back to the task at hand. Sanchez continued, "While the war is certainly taking resources away from our grander infrastructure plans, it has caused an immense boom in the manufacturing sector. Ford, GM, and Chrysler have shifted over seventy percent of their production lines to producing military equipment and their factories are now operating twenty-four hours a day, seven days a week. Shoot, even Boeing has had to shift from producing civilian airliners to nearly one hundred percent military production. They just can't keep up with the demands of the Defense Department."

"You realize they're having to do all this because tens of thousands of military members and their equipment are getting killed and blown up?" the President shot back. "While the economic news is good, let's not forget that we are in the middle of a war—a war that has cost our nation deeply up to this point."

Secretary Sanchez stiffened at the comment. "I meant no disrespect, Mr. President. I'm just stating the facts. I have a daughter who just enlisted in the Air Force, so I'm well aware of the war and its many consequences. The truth is that the economy is still booming as a result of what's going on, and that, Mr. President, is a good thing," she replied matter-of-factly. She then closed her briefing book and sat down.

The president looked at his economic team. They were smart people, all hand-picked based on their ability to get things done, not based on political donations or nepotism. He sighed as he realized his response might have been overly harsh.

"I appreciate everything you guys are doing. I just want everyone to remember that our goal right now is to win the war and bring a lasting peace to our nation and the world. Unfortunately, I need to end this meeting and head down to another briefing. If you will all please excuse me and continue your efforts, that would be greatly appreciated." The President got up and headed for the door.

As the President began to walk the corridor to the elevator that would take them to the basement and the Situation Room, his Chief of Staff, Retired General Liam Greeson, leaned over. "You were a bit harsh with them, don't you think?" he muttered.

The President grunted as the elevator door opened and they got in. "You're right, I was. I'll call Maria later and apologize."

The two of them rode the elevator in silence and walked into the Situation Room. The generals and military advisors had already beaten them to the meeting and stood up once Gates walked in, waiting for him to take his seat before they took theirs, as was customary.

Once everyone had taken their seats, Jim Castle, the Secretary of Defense, cleared his throat. "Mr. President, would you like me to begin with the overall brief of what is going on, and then you can ask more pointed questions of the various generals?" he asked. They had a lot to discuss and needed to make decisions on all the major theaters of conflict: Europe, Korea, and now Taiwan.

The President looked up and simply nodded for him to begin.

The SecDef brought up a map of Europe with various unit markers and symbols written on it. "Our forces in the Belarusian capital of Minsk had to withdraw back to Lithuania. While this is a minor setback, the Polish forces and the rest of III Corps was able to push the Russian 6th Tank Army to the outskirts of Minsk and is now holding the line. The 4th Infantry Division and two battalions of the 82nd Airborne in Lithuania still pose enough of a threat to the Russians' right flank that they haven't tried to push our forces out of Belarus."

The President held up his hand. "What happened with the 4th ID? Why did they have to give up Minsk?" Gates asked.

"The Russians rushed two additional divisions from other parts of the country and a brigade of Special Forces to the capital region. We just were not able to hold the line—the 6th Tank Army fought better than we thought they would. While they didn't have any of the newer T-14 Armata tanks, they were able to maintain a high level of air defenses over most of the country, negating our air power and making this much more of a one-dimensional fight," Jim replied, hoping that his answer would suffice.

Gates nodded in acknowledgement and signaled for him to continue.

"In Ukraine, the Russians have held their current positions and appear to be settling in for the winter. We have a couple of proposals we would like to go over with you, Mr. President, regarding our choices in Europe."

Jim signaled for the Chairman of the Joint Chiefs to proceed with his portion of the brief.

Admiral Peter Meyers stood up. "Mr. President, we're training 6,000 new infantry soldiers each week. That number will rise to 25,000 a week by the end of the year and hit 75,000 a week by April of 2018. With the war going full speed ahead in Europe and Asia, we're stretched incredibly thin right now. Presently, we're training just enough soldiers to replace our casualties. We're still not training enough soldiers to start creating the new divisions needed to win this war. That should start to happen around January if we slow the pace of the war in Europe and Asia down and allow our forces to build back up. What we'd like to propose is pausing the war in Europe while we focus on building up an army to defeat the Russians and looking to launch a new offensive in May or June—"

"If we hold off until essentially the beginning of the summer," the President interrupted, "what exactly is that going to provide us with at that point, and what are we going to do to harass the Russians throughout the winter?"

"Holding off until summer will allow us to build up our forces in Europe and give our allies the time they need to rebuild their own armies. The Germans have said they'll be able to field an army of 300,000 soldiers by June. The French have said they'll make 250,000 soldiers available by that deadline as well. While there is significant political opposition to the war in Britain, the Minister of Defense has assured me that the Prime Minister is going to move forward with a draft to rebuild their military, and they would also contribute 250,000 soldiers to the fight by the June deadline. Italy is drafting 90,000 for their new army group, and the Greeks are drafting 400,000, although we believe that's most likely in response to the Turkish government's announcement that they would be doubling the size of their military."

"Mr. President, by holding off until June, our allies will be able to provide 890,000 soldiers, in addition to the 250,000 new soldiers we'll be sending to Europe when they complete basic infantry training. Mind you, these are infantry soldiers, so our overall troop levels will probably be closer to double that by the time the offensive kicks off," Admiral Meyers explained.

Gates smiled. *Finally, the Europeans are building an army to take ownership of this war*, he thought.

"Admiral, please send my regards to our allies for agreeing to begin a buildup of forces. I will call the various political leaders to thank them as well. From the onset of this war with Russia, I have been adamant that this war cannot be an American war. I'm very relieved to hear that our European allies are finally moving forward and doing something about the state of their militaries. I want you to press them hard in meeting the timelines. Do whatever you need to in order to prod and poke them to make sure they are ready. I've already spoken with the Treasury Secretary, and we are making two percent interest loans available to our allies if they need access to additional funding—so there should be no excuse of them not having enough capital to meet the deadlines," Gates said.

Admiral Meyers leaned forward, pausing for a second. "Mr. President, do you approve of our buildup in Europe and plan for a resumption of offensive operations in June? It means we'll settle in for the winter where our troops are at right now. The Air Force and the Navy will of course continue to carry out operations, but the ground war will remain static until we're ready to move forward," he clarified.

"I'm fine with holding things in place in Europe until June," said the President, resigned to the reality before him. "What I still haven't heard from you guys, and what we need to figure out, is what is going to be our end state? Aside from removing the Russians from Ukraine, we still have to determine what we're going to do with Petrov. If we leave him in power, he will just rebuild his forces and remain a belligerent threat to Europe. I don't think that's the outcome any of us wants."

Those around the table sat back in their chairs, digesting what he had just said. It was a rather profound statement. Until now, the objective had been to remove the Russians from Ukraine, but with the massive buildup of military forces in Europe, they were being presented with an opportunity to do something more.

Tom McMillan, the President's National Security Advisor, leaned forward. "What would *you* like to see happen, Mr. President?"

Gates thought about that for a moment before responding. He had been pondering this question for some time. *The world is at a tipping point*, he realized. These conflicts had been brewing under the table for some time, but now that things had finally boiled over, it might just be time to reassert American dominance as a world power. *We could build ourselves up not only as the military superpower, but also as the leader of a new global alliance so these wars don't happen over and over again.*

He sighed. *Too many people are being killed in these senseless wars, and for what?* he wondered. *So that the defense industry can continually have a boogeyman to create more means of killing each other? To fund a trillion-dollar defense budget? No...this war may have been thrust upon me, but if I have to fight it, then by God, I'm not just going to win it—I will end it!*

When he had fully finished calculating his answer, President Gates cleared his throat. "First, I want us to finalize the creation of this global defense force alliance to replace NATO. This alliance needs to be politically and militarily binding in all respects. Nations will be obligated to maintain three percent of GDP spending on defense, no matter the size of the nation. They will also fall under US military control in times of war. We will integrate their military leaders into the leadership structure of the force carrying out any military operations, so that they are fully vested in the alliance. They will also have to meet whatever force compositions we determine the alliance needs; we don't need the entire alliance to focus on aircraft and not have a ground component or naval component, for instance."

The President paced with excitement. "Second, with regard to Russia—I want Petrov removed. I want us and the Allies to start working on finding a political opposition group we can start to back now, and we should work with them on fomenting resistance to the current government. When we topple the Petrov regime, I want this new opposition government to come into power, fully backed by us. To ensure this new government has a chance to take root and survive, I propose the Allies assert administrative control of Moscow, just as the Allies did to Berlin at the end of World War II. We will work with the new government to assume full control of the government and military within a ten-year period. Unlike Iraq, Germany and Japan, we are not going to demand the dissolution of the military. We will need those troops to assist in maintaining law and order. We are also not going to occupy all of Russia with an occupation force. The new opposition force will handle that with advisors from the Allies until they're fully able to assume control of the country from us."

The President sat down, and there was a brief moment of silence as everyone in the room absorbed the massive amount of information that had just been thrown their way.

NSA McMillan folded his fingers into a temple on the table as he leaned forward, clearly deep in thought. Admiral Meyers, the Chairman of the Joint Chiefs, likewise said nothing, wanting to see what the others had to say. Jim Castle placed his pen down and looked around at the group.

"I like it," Castle began. "I think this is a solid plan to ensure we have peace and stability in Europe for generations to come. We need to find a way to end the hostilities and animosity left over from the Cold War and World War II, and this is probably our best course of action. It may be a hard sell to the Allies, but if they join this new alliance we are going to create, they'll have to go along whether they like it or not," he concluded.

The generals nodded in agreement, all except for Admiral Meyers.

"Mr. President, I like this idea, but let's go over the logistics," Meyers asserted. "We're talking about keeping a substantial number of US forces in Europe for at least five to ten years. We still have to figure out what we're going to do with Korea and China," Meyers said.

McMillan jumped back into the conversation. "Admiral Meyers is right about Asia. That's going to be a long, drawn-out fight. Even if we are able to knock the Russians out of the war by the end of summer or the fall, we're going to have to shift a lot of our combat power from

Europe to Asia. The logistics alone are going to be a challenge. We're also going to have to convince our allies that they will need to shift their forces to help us deal with the Chinese as well. That's going to be its own challenge, to say the least."

The President scratched his chin, deep in thought. They were right, of course. It would be a challenge to get their allies to want to support their fight in Asia. *I don't want this war to still be going on as we enter the 2020 election—then the election would just become a referendum on the war*, thought Gates. *This war needs to be fought clean of politics, if at all possible.*

"You bring up a great point, Admiral. I've been reading up on the Republic of China in Taiwan and the People's Republic of China and their history. I think we can do something similar with China. Taiwan views itself as the rightful government of China, and if this war has shown us anything, it's that communist China is not only a rival superpower. If left unchecked, it will become *the* dominant power in the world. Their version of government and civil society is not something we want to see promulgated across the world."

Gates took a deep breath, letting it out slowly. "What if we look to remove the communist government and replace them with the democratic government of the Republic of China? We could break Beijing down into administrative zones, along with the rest of the country. We could administer the country until elections can be held and then work with the newly elected government to take full control of the country. Over time, we would phase ourselves out of occupation duty and control of the country, just as we would with Russia."

The President paused for a second before continuing. "I know this would be a long-term commitment on the part of the alliance and the United States, but if we don't address these problems now, we're going to be fighting the same war twenty or forty years from now. We need to find a way to end the bloodshed and get our countries focused on economic prosperity for our people," Gates explained.

McMillan understood the President's grander vision but wanted to focus on the short-term issues. "This has been a lot to take in, Mr. President, and you've certainly made your wishes known for how you'd like things to play out in both Europe and Asia. The challenge for us as your military and national security team is to determine how best to implement the vision you have just laid out. While a lot of details need to be hashed out, I'd like to present you with some options for how to handle China and work to contain them in their current positions while we grow the Navy and finish off the Russians," McMillan said, looking to Admiral Meyers for support. The admiral just nodded, as if telling him to run with it.

"With regard to China, we have to acknowledge that Taiwan is lost. Our initial wave of bombers and cruise missiles did hurt the PLA invasion force, but it was never going to be enough to stop it, nor can we sustain any sort of heavy military support to Taiwan with the conflicts in Korea and Russia still going. I know that the attack on Taiwan is less than two days old, but we have no forces we can shift in their direction to help. We can hope their military is able to maintain an effective insurgency operation and keep the dream of freedom alive, but aside from periodic military and strategic bomber support, we just don't have the naval or ground troops available to intervene. The Chinese navy has dispatched so many of its submarines to the Taiwanese sector and the areas around some of the Japanese islands that it's incredibly risky for our ballistic missile submarines to launch continual cruise missile barrages against the Chinese mainland or in support of operations in Taiwan. It's going to take us a few months to hunt these submarines down. Our ballistic missile submarines are too important of a national asset to risk losing them in combat right now. We should have an additional thirty attack submarines in the East China Sea and the South China Sea within the next forty days, but until then, we're being very cautious with what we do with our submarines," McMillan explained.

The President didn't like what he was hearing, but knew he needed a better understanding of the situation on the ground. He gestured for McMillan to continue.

"While we can't do anything about Taiwan, what we can do is fight to win in Korea. The Chinese have sent over 150,000 regular army soldiers across the border. They're also in the process of preparing to send more than 200,000 militia forces to join them. We expect these numbers to more than double over the next couple of months. As of right now, the Republic of South Korea or ROK forces have done a superb job in blunting the Chinese advance. With help from Japan, our Allied forces have been able to secure half of North Korea, and we may have the rest of the country within our grasp before the end of the year. The ROK has fully activated their reserves and is currently rushing them towards the frontlines. Nearly sixty percent of the North Korean Army was either destroyed during the first seventy-two hours of the war or has surrendered. The remainder of the army is poorly equipped and poorly fed. While the Chinese have announced a new leader to take control of North Korea, that new leader has virtually no support with the army or among the civilian population."

Admiral Meyers cut in at this point. "Mr. President, the military recommendation, which I am sure the NSA will agree with, is for us to do whatever is necessary to capture North Korea and then park our forces on the Chinese-North Korean border for the winter and well into the summer months. While the focus is on building up our forces for Europe to finish off the Russians, the Navy and Air Force will look to expand our capabilities in Asia. The Japanese, for their part, are converting their helicopter support ships into modern-day aircraft carriers. Each carrier will be able to hold sixty-two aircraft, making them a potent force considering that the Japanese have three of them that will be ready by spring. They're also announcing a draft of two million men to join their self-defense force and have suspended parts of their constitution that restrict them from operating an army on foreign soil. Like our European allies, they'll be ready to contribute a significant ground force in June."

The President interrupted Meyers before he could continue. "So, what would be the strategy for attacking China and defeating the PLA?

The admiral turned briefly to confer with the Commandant of the Marine Corps before turning back to the President. "We plan on launching a two-pronged attack. The first will be a massive invasion across the North Korean border into China proper. This prong, which will be led by the ROK forces, will be the right flank pincer that will drive towards Beijing. The second pincer will be an amphibious assault on the critical port city of Qingdao. Once the port has been secured, we will be able to offload our heavy armor forces and begin to expand upwards towards Beijing from the left flank. This force will be largely led by the Japanese and the US Army. The US Marines will be accompanying them and securing the beach and port for them, but the JDF will be the bulk of the ground force that will lead the way to Beijing while our forces focus on holding the port and the outer flanks."

Meyers took a swig of water before he continued. "To further complicate the PLA's ability to reinforce their northern military district, we're going to carry out a massive invasion of the ports near Nantong, which is just north of Shanghai. Once our forces have secured the ports and begun landing the bulk of our ground forces and their armor support, they'll drive our forces to the industrial heartland of Hefei, 441 kilometers inland from the coast, essentially dividing northern China from the rest of the country." Admiral Meyers brought up a map of the area and walked the President through the plans and objectives.

Gates nodded in approval. He was partial to the idea of hitting the Chinese from multiple points. "In general, I like the plan you've laid out, but what forces are going to make up this landing force north of Shanghai?"

Marshall Grant, the Commandant of the Marine Corps, answered. "This would be a Marine-led operation. By the time the end of summer rolls around, the Corps will be standing at nearly one million Marines. We'll have 60,000 Marines operating with the ROK in northern China on the right flank, another 60,000 operating with the JDF on the left flank, and then nearly 550,000 leading the charge from Nantong to Hefei. We're going to make central China howl as we look to divide the country," Grant said with a mischievous grin. His devil dogs would be chomping at the bit to be released once they reached full strength.

The President smiled at the confidence his Marine commander was showing, but he still had concerns and questions. "Assuming all of this goes according to plan, what will we do with the Army forces in Europe once they have defeated the Russians? Also, what type of resistance are we potentially looking at?" he asked.

The Marine Commandant replied, "We expect there to be heavy resistance, Mr. President. In addition to the PLA's reserve force, they also maintain a multimillion-man militia force. These soldiers are much less trained and probably equipped with subpar weapons compared to their regular army counterparts, but they have numbers. Their goal will be simple, to try and overwhelm us wherever they can."

He pulled up a map on the PowerPoint. "Our plan, or at least the Marine plan, calls for us to advance in a relatively slow and methodical approach. We'll be establishing firebases with artillery support at set intervals throughout the lines of advance. Every so often, a brigade of soldiers will be left to support the bases as a quick-reaction force. Our goal with this 441-kilometer line here is to prevent any additional reinforcements from arriving up north to where the battle of

Beijing will be taking place. I suspect that as the army units from Europe start to arrive, we'll start to be reinforced by them as well."

Gates sighed for a moment, wishing they had more time to get into the details. But as he thought about it, he felt he had enough information from these guys to feel comfortable in giving them the go-ahead to begin the plans for this major operation. It might still be nine months away, but it would be imperative to get the planning of it underway.

The President briefly stood, signaling for the others to stay seated for the moment. They had been talking for several hours and were probably hungry. "This has been a productive meeting. I'd like to talk privately with McMillan and Jim about some of these options over lunch. I would like to request that you all remain here and continue to flesh out more details on this new alliance we're going to form. Start to identify what countries we should extend an olive branch to and why. Determine what they'll be able to offer the alliance and how much long-term support we should expect from them. I'll have lunch brought in for everyone. We'll reconvene in two hours."
****

NSA McMillian and Jim Castle pulled out their chairs and sat down for an informal lunch with the President. When Gates wanted to have a frank and open discussion, he usually held them over a meal at his personal kitchen table. It was less formal and provided a softer environment for everyone to talk freely, something he greatly valued.

"OK, so what countries do you believe we should include in this new alliance?" asked the President, wanting to get right down to business.

Jim smiled. "I think we want to ensure the UK, Germany, France, Italy, Belgium, the Netherlands, Denmark, Poland, Romania and the Nordic countries stay in the alliance. We should also work with Canada, Australia, New Zealand, Japan, South Korea, Brazil, Argentina, Columbia, Thailand, Israel, and South Africa. These should at least be the charter members of the alliance. We can expand it in the coming years to include other countries, but for the time being, I believe these countries should make up the bulk of the alliance," the SecDef said as he popped open the can of Coke he had grabbed from the counter before he sat down.

"Why not try and include India, Indonesia, Malaysia or any of the other Gulf states?" asked the President.

McMillian responded, "Frankly, sir, while it may not be the PC answer, Indonesia has a large Muslim population, so they would have a huge problem being in an alliance with Israel. The same goes for the rest of the Gulf states. Malaysia is not the most stable government and has issues with Indonesia. That could cause problems if the two of them restarted their border disputes, believing they now have a protective alliance that can bail them out if they get into trouble."

The President nodded. These were the off-the-cuff comments he had been hoping for.

Tom continued, "While it would be ideal to have India as part of the alliance, we're not certain they would join right now, given the open hostilities with China. They *just* signed a nonaggression treaty with them. I suspect that once the war has concluded, they'd be more than open to becoming a member."

Less than thirty minutes later, the White House chefs brought out a five-star lunch fit for a king, and the three men continued to discuss their ideas and plans for how this new military alliance should work and the finer details of actually implementing it.

They determined that a special military and diplomatic emissary should be commissioned and given power to negotiate the establishment of this new alliance. This would allow the existing generals and senior diplomats to stay focused on their current tasks and what they were working on, which was doing whatever was necessary to win this war. Following their lunch, they had plenty to discuss with the rest of the national security team and the military leaders. It would be a busy couple of weeks as the wheels of progress moved forward with lightning speed.

Chapter 15
All's Quiet on the Eastern Front

Landstuhl, Germany
Landstuhl Regional Medical Center

Master Sergeant Luke Childers lay in his bed, looking out his window. As the morning dragged on, the snow began to fall more steadily. It was beautiful watching the white "fluffy cotton balls of love," as his mother used to call them, fall from the sky to blanket the ground below. Luke was grateful that his bed was placed next to the window; at least he had an excellent view of the wintery weather unfolding.

He eventually glanced over to his other side at the row of nine other beds with wounded soldiers in each of them. Some of the soldiers had what appeared to him to be minor injuries—a cast on a foot or an arm, or some minor bandages. Others were in much more serious condition, with obvious amputations or covered head-to-toe in dressings from second- or third-degree burn wounds.

An orderly entered their room with a wheelchair and headed towards Luke. It was time for his physical therapy session. While he hated these sessions, he knew if he wanted to get out of this hospital and back to his unit, he needed to try to push through the pain and regain his strength.

The man wheeled the chair right up to the edge of his bed and locked the wheels before coming around to the side of his bed. "You need me to help you up, Master Sergeant?" the orderly asked with a warm smile.

"No, I can get into the chair myself, Jim. I've been practicing the last couple of days while you've been gone," Luke said with a smile and a wink.

He slowly lifted himself up and turned his legs towards the edge of the bed until they were just above the floor, then used the button on the side of the bed to lower it a bit until his feet were level with the floor. Then with a gentle lift of his arms, he was standing; albeit with a little bit of pain, but he was standing on his own. He took a few steps towards the chair and slowly lowered himself into it, wincing a little as he did.

"It looks like you're starting to heal up nicely, Master Sergeant. The physical therapy must be working," the orderly replied as he unlocked the wheels. He pushed Luke out of the room and down the hall to the elevator that would take them to the floor with the physical therapy rooms.

Jim had been working as an orderly for the hospital for the past two years, enjoying every minute of it. While stationed there at Ramstein Air Force Base, Jim had met a local woman, fallen in love and gotten married. When his enlistment had been up, he'd opted to stay in Germany and found a government civilian job at the hospital as an orderly. The rest was history.

The physical therapy room was busy, but Patricia, Luke's therapist, was waiting for him.

"Hello, Luke," she said with a bright smile and a twinkle in her eye. "How's my favorite patient doing today?"

Luke felt his face flush a bit as her warm brown eyes sparkled at him with that gorgeous smile and bright white teeth. *God, she's gorgeous*, he thought.

"I'm doing good, Patricia. You going to work me hard today?" he joked.

"You know it, soldier boy," she said with a devilish grin on her face, which warmed his spirits.

Jim locked the wheels to Luke's wheelchair and watched in amazement as Luke slowly stood up, then proceeded to take a couple of steps towards the physical therapist. With his work done, Jim left to go get the next patient.

This is the best part of my job, seeing these wounded soldiers recover, he thought as he whistled a soft cheerful tune.

Patricia worked strenuously with Luke's right leg, lower back and left arm for the next two hours. She ran him through a number of different exercises before turning him over to the next therapist, who would guide him through a series of water exercises before he had massage therapy.

Master Sergeant Childers was lucky. The shrapnel he had taken in his lower back, leg, and arm had not caused any serious long-term problems. It hadn't severed any tendons or nerves, and just needed time and physical therapy to heal up. The doctors had told him he would probably be ready to go back to his unit around Christmas or maybe just after the New Year, which was fine by Luke. He hated being separated from the rest of his unit. They had been through so much since the start of the war, and he wanted to hang on to those friendships he had left.

Following an afternoon of physical therapy, Luke was wheeled back to his bed in the room with the other wounded soldiers. As he entered the room, he saw the first lieutenant who had woken up screaming a couple of times last night. He looked rather sedated. At the foot of the lieutenant's bed, he saw the officer's name was Joe Dukes and he apparently hailed from some armor unit.

When he had asked the nurse about him earlier that morning, she'd lowered her voice and said, "He and two other soldiers were the only ones who survived from his battalion. He's taking it hard. To make matters worse, the poor guy lost a brother and his mother, who were visiting San Francisco when it was destroyed by the North Koreans."

The staff was really not supposed to share information on the other soldiers, but it had become somewhat commonplace in these large recovery units to give at least basic information about the people the soldiers were sharing a room with. As Luke rolled past him on the way back to his bed, he could tell that physically, Dukes was nearly healed up, but mentally, the poor guy was a mess.

I should try to talk with him after dinner, see if there's anything I can do to help him, Luke thought.

Childers, who always had his ear to the ground, had heard one of the doctors say that Dukes had been awarded the Distinguished Service Cross, but it had been officially upgraded to the Medal of Honor. It was a big distinction, and clearly, this poor guy had been through the wringer to have been awarded such a medal. A week after arriving at the hospital, Luke had been awarded his third Purple Heart and second Silver Star and had also been put in for the Distinguished Service Cross for his actions in the Kiev breakout. While he felt honored to be awarded these medals, he knew there were others who had done more than him and also deserved to be recognized.

After settling back into his bed, Luke saw one of the orderlies had left him yesterday's copy of the *Wall Street Journal*. He picked it up, skimming through the headlines and trying to decide if he even wanted to read it. *Drafting of New Army Continues…War in Europe on Hold Until Spring…Battle for Taiwan Enters Second Week – Fighting Said to be Fierce…Allied Forces Stop Chinese Offensive in Korea…US Secures North Korean Capital Despite Chinese Counterattack.*

I think I'll skip the paper today, Luke thought as he placed it on the nightstand between him and the soldier in the bed next to him. He reached over and began to read a new book that had been brought to him by one of the hospital volunteers.

As he finished the third chapter, he looked up at a familiar face who had entered his room and begun walking towards him—Lieutenant Jack Taylor, who was now sporting captain's bars. Luke placed his book down and smiled at Captain Taylor as he approached.

"I see congratulations are in order, my friend. How are you doing, sir?" Luke said as he held out his hand to shake Jack's.

"I'm doing good. I should be the one asking how *you* are doing. You're the one still stuck here in the hospital," Captain Taylor responded as he stood next to Luke's bed.

"I'm doing OK. Getting better, slow and steady. They say I should be able to return to the unit around Christmas or New Year's at the latest. How are the other guys in the unit doing?" he asked now out of concern for the soldiers in his unit with whom he had not had a lot of contact since their breakout of Kiev.

Jack looked down at his battered platoon sergeant for a second before responding. He had to admit, Sergeant Childers was looking a lot better now than he had when they'd first left Kiev. He hadn't been sure he was going to make it for a while. "Three of the wounded guys have been flown back to the States, where they'll recover and probably be discharged from the military. Two of our other guys are still here with you, as you know, though they should be discharged within the next week or two and will return back to the unit."

He paused for a second before continuing. "You probably haven't heard yet, but the 2nd Calvary Regiment is being reorganized with Fifth Corps now, so we've been effectively taken off the line for the time being. It's probably best, since we were down to less than forty percent strength. The colonel has our regiment focusing on resting and recovering and writing out as detailed of an account as we can of our various engagements. They want us to break down what went right and wrong with each engagement, so we can develop some training scenarios around them. It's a good idea, and it's taken our minds off the losses we've sustained. We're also getting a ton of new raw recruits fresh from basic training, so we're working hard at getting them as ready for combat as we can," Taylor explained.

Childers had been desperate for information from outside his four walls; Taylor's visit was just what he'd needed.

"Does it look like there will be any fighting in the near future?" Luke asked, not sure if he wanted to be a part of it or miss out on it entirely.

Captain Taylor smiled. "From what we've been told, there won't be any new offensives until sometime in the spring. They want to build up our forces and then go for the jugular when the time is right. Besides, the situation is still very tense with China, and the Pacific is taking a lot of resources away from Europe."

Looking up at Captain Taylor, Luke asked, "Where does the colonel want me when I'm able to return to duty?"

Taylor thought about how to respond before he answered, "I was hoping you'd be assigned back to work with me, but I'm not sure if that's going to happen. We've lost a lot of officers and NCOs. I heard a rumor you may either get promoted to sergeant major and be assigned to one of the battalions or end up being promoted to officer." He wasn't sure if this was what his friend wanted to hear or not.

Luke sighed and then nodded. "I guess I'll see when I report back. As long as I can continue to lead soldiers, I'll be content wherever they place me," he responded, although he felt a bit uncertain about the future now. The two of them talked for a little while longer before Captain Taylor said he needed to get going, but he promised to visit again in a couple of weeks.
****

A couple of days later, Luke worked up the nerve to go talk to Lieutenant Dukes, the tanker who was having a hard time mentally with all that had transpired. He wanted to offer up a few words of encouragement to the guy. It was clear JD (as Childers learned he was usually called) had been an NCO before he had been an officer; he was too old to be a fresh lieutenant. Childers hoped their shared bond as sergeants might help him break through whatever was haunting him.

Luke sat down at JD's table. "I'm Master Sergeant Luke Childers," he said as he extended his hand.

JD paused and then looked up at Childers. He took a moment to focus on who had just introduced himself and looked at Luke's extended hand before shaking it.

"I heard you are being awarded the Medal of Honor for your actions in Kiev," Childers said.

JD looked up at him with sad eyes. "Not like it did a lot of difference. Thousands of soldiers were still trapped in that god-awful city, and nearly everyone in my battalion was killed," he replied, clearly trying to gain control of his emotions.

Luke paused for a moment before responding. "JD, I know it's hard losing a lot of the friends you had in your battalion, but it wasn't you who killed them. That was the Russians. I was one of those soldiers trapped in the Kiev pocket with the 2nd Cav. We broke out with a lot of help from tankers from your battalion who were still trapped with us and a lot of help from a German tank unit. Those guys from your unit that were trapped in Kiev, they helped us break out of the city and saved thousands of other soldiers." He spoke with genuine gratitude.

JD took a deep breath. He had never heard about how some of his trapped comrades had helped the soldiers stuck in Kiev. It was somehow a relief to him that they had been able to assist in the escape, even if most of them had been killed in the process.

Luke added, "It stings losing soldiers under your command, JD, but your soldiers died doing their job, a job they volunteered to do and a job they were proud of. You can't let their loss eat you up. Save that anger for the enemy."

"What do you suppose they'll do with me once they give me this medal? I've heard they don't let you go back into combat if you have 'the' medal," JD said. "All I've known is tanks and leading soldiers. I'm not sure I could stand being cooped up in an office."

Luke thought about that for a moment before responding, "I'm not one hundred percent sure what they'll do with you. I think they will probably want to integrate your experience into the armor school or maybe they will send you out on the road to do some public speaking events. If I were you, I'd try to get a position at the armor school and pass on as much of my knowledge to the new tankers as possible. This war isn't going to be over soon. It's going to drag on a while, and the President says the US is going to build a massive army to defeat the Russians and Chinese."

Luke hoped their conversation would give JD some optimism and guidance for his future. He hated seeing soldiers suffer like this from a combat loss. Luke had spent nearly his entire career in Special Forces and the infantry, and he had known more than his fair share of losses over the years. It had taken him a lot of time and hurt to work through his own issues, but he had put those demons to rest and did his best to help other soldiers around him who were going through the same thing.

JD thought about the instructor job, then smiled for perhaps the first time since he had arrived at the hospital. "I think I would like to work at the armor school. It would still keep me in the tank world I know and give me a chance to work with soldiers. Thank you for telling me about that—I'm going to put in a request for that assignment, and I'm sure they'll give it to me. You've given me a lot to think about. If you'll excuse me, I have an appointment with one of the docs. Maybe we can talk more later if you want?" JD said as he got up.

Luke smiled warmly. "I'd like that very much. Stay strong and I'll see you later."
****

Germany
Grafenwöhr Training Area

"Here they come!" came an excited voice over the radio. Seconds later, a dozen 155mm artillery rounds impacted along a mock convoy the engineers had set up in the impact zone.

"Excellent shot," replied Oberstleutnant Hermann Wulf. "Now let's see how well the battalion does at engaging the enemy," he said over the battalion net.

A minute later, dozens of Puma infantry fighting vehicles fired their 25mm chain guns at the enemy vehicles, scoring dozens of hits across their armored hulls. Some of the tracer rounds could be seen bouncing off the ground from nearby misses, while other rounds punched holes right through the vehicles, thudding into the ground behind them.

Hermann grinned with satisfaction. His troopers were finally becoming proficient with their vehicles' main guns and calling in supporting artillery. In the coming months, it was going to be imperative that they know how to function as a combined-arms unit. From everything the Americans and German units had been passing along to them, they would be having a tough go of it with the T-14 tanks and the T-15 infantry fighting vehicles. He had two more months to get his unit prepared to deploy. His battalion, the 35th Mechanized Infantry

Battalion, would be deploying to Belarus to help shore up the Polish and American forces facing down two Russian army groups.
******

Two Kilometers Away

Lieutenant Colonel Nikolay Tarnavskiy looked around the commander's side of the turret in the new German Leopard 2A6 main battle tanks his brigade was being given. He marveled at the fire control system, the internal safety features to protect the crew, and the raw power this tank projected.

"I'm glad I never had to face off against a tank like this. I'm not sure I would have survived," he thought as he pulled himself up and out of the turret.

He picked his still-lit cigarette off the top of the turret, placing it back in his mouth. Tarnavskiy took a long drag and filled his lungs before looking at his executive officer. "These tanks will do," he said with a grin on his face.

The XO laughed for a second. "These tanks are better than what the Americans were going to give us. You have to love German engineering—they really know how to make tanks," he replied.

Jumping down to join his XO, Tarnavskiy said, "When we receive the entire battalion's worth of tanks next week, I want the men to spend as much time as possible learning from our German instructors as possible. They need to become experts in these tanks if we are to take our country back. I want them trained hard—is that understood?"

His XO nodded. "It will be taken care of. We will not let you or our country down."

Prior to the war, the 17th Ukrainian Tank Brigade was going to be outfitted with surplus American M1A1 battle tanks. Once hostilities between NATO and Russia had started, the Americans had begun to activate its surplus equipment, and the job of outfitting the new Ukrainian Army had suddenly fallen into the Germans' lap. Germany saw this as a great opportunity to be the official military supplier of Ukraine. From an economic standpoint, this was a boon because once the Ukrainian army committed to using German military equipment, they would most likely stay with it for the next twenty or thirty years. Once the German manufacturing went into full military production, supplying

Ukraine along with their own forces wouldn't be too difficult of a challenge.

Chapter 16
Holding the Line

Moscow, Russia
Kremlin

The air outside the Kremlin had finally turned bitterly cold as winter arrived in full strength. While most people who lived in other countries detested the cold, the Russians had learned to live with it, and some even thrived in it. President Petrov swiveled in his chair and looked out the window, admiring the first major snowfall of the winter. The forecasters had said they would receive between 30 and 45 centimeters of snow that day. He watched as the guards near the entrance to the Kremlin began their traditional changing-of-the-guard routine. They were ever the professionals, the ceremonial guards of the Kremlin.

As he observed the ceremony and the snow steadily falling to carpet the ground below in its white wintery blanket, his mind drifted back to the meeting he was about to attend. While the war was not going poorly, it was not exactly going well either. His forces had managed to capture and hold more than sixty percent of Ukraine despite multiple attempts by NATO to remove them.

I had wanted to keep this conflict isolated to Ukraine, Petrov lamented. He had intentionally not invaded the Baltic or Nordic states in hopes that NATO would eventually accept the fact that Ukraine, for better or worse, belonged to Russia's sphere of influence. But obviously, once NATO invaded Belarus, it made that goal impossible. *I wish they would've left well enough alone. I couldn't very well sit by and let NATO build up its forces right on the borders of Russia and wait for them to attack again.*

A knock at the door broke Petrov from his thoughts. A second later, the door opened to reveal his Minister of Defense, Alexei Semenov.

"Good morning, Mr. President," Semenov began. "Would you like us to come in now, or should we meet in one of the other rooms?"

The man is clearly excited about something, Petrov mused. *He's normally not this chipper in the morning.*

He waved for Semenov to come in as he got up and walked towards the small table he had set up in the ante-room next to his office. The other generals filed in, along with Ivan Vasilek, his FSB director.

Ivan must have something important to discuss if he is joining this meeting, Petrov thought, no emotion or concern on his face.

"Gentlemen, please sit down. We have lots to discuss. Our great ally has finally arrived," President Petrov said as he began to pour a hot cup of tea for each of his trusted advisors.

"I hope you do not mean the tea you are pouring us," Admiral Anatoly Petrukhin joked, and everyone laughed.

Wagging his finger at his military advisors, Petrov said, "No, not the tea, though it does help on a cold day like this. I mean winter. It is the great equalizer of armies. With the arrival of the snow and cold weather, NATO and the Americans will now have to hold their lines and wait for spring."

The others in the room all nodded, except for Ivan. He knew something more was afoot but would hold his tongue until the proper time to speak.

Petrov placed the cups of tea on the table for everyone to grab one and then placed a fresh kettle of hot water in the center. "Generals, please begin. Bring me up to speed on what the latest developments are with NATO and where our forces stand."

Petrov sensed that Ivan had some private matters he would want to talk about with him afterwards, judging by the look on his face. The two men had known each other most of their lives, and Petrov trusted him, which was not something he could say of most people.

General Boris Egorkin, the head of the Army, started the briefing. "Mr. President, we've strengthened our lines across the various fronts. As of right now, NATO is not able to break through our defenses; however, that may change by summer. The NATO countries have announced a massive increase in military spending and the raising of a new army. While this is concerning, we are also increasing the size of our army and are focusing our industrial effort on producing the specific weapon systems that are giving our forces an edge," he explained.

Petrov jumped into the conversation. "What specific weapon systems are giving us the edge we need to hold our ground, or even advance?" he asked.

General Egorkin eagerly responded. "The T-14 Armata tanks and the entire Armata line of vehicles, for one. The second system is the S-400, or as NATO calls them, SA-21 surface-to-air missiles. The S-400s have proven incredibly effective at blunting NATO's airpower, and while complex, these systems are not terribly difficult for us to build in mass quantities, which we are currently doing. The Chinese are mass-producing these systems as well. Our goal is to continue to saturate the battlefield with S-400s to strip the Americans of the typical advantage they would have in the air," Egorkin said with a smug smile.

He continued, "Likewise, we have also moved forward with mass production of the Zhukov unmanned aerial vehicles or drones. The Zhukovs are cheap and easy to produce, and more importantly, unlike their American counterparts, they do not rely on satellite communications. We can control them via radio communication or by leveraging an existing cell tower infrastructure. To ensure the transmission signals are not tracked or jammed, we make use of an older technology the Americans pioneered in the 1990s—their single-channel ground and airborne radio system. It's incredibly hard to jam, as it jumps 111 frequencies a second. So, unless NATO wants to block *all* of their own radio communications, they are not going to be able to jam this drone," he explained, beaming with pride.

Petrov smiled at the enthusiasm. "Forgive me, General. I am not as versed in drone technology—are we currently able to jam *their* drones?"

Egorkin leaned forward. "Mr. President, the Americans rely heavily on satellite communications to control their targeting computers, their GPS, the transfer of large amounts of data and a large portion of their command, control and communications, or C3. While there has been an unspoken agreement that NATO and Russia will not overtly destroy one another's satellites, or attempt to cripple the other nations' power grid, it does not preclude us from jamming their ability to use this critical component of their C3. What our cyber warfare division has been doing is analyzing the cypher codes and frequencies their satellites use, and we believe we have a means of being able to remotely jam satellite usage within a specific quadrant."

Suddenly, the others in the room began to beam broadly as they realized the implications of what this meant.

"When did our cyber-warfare guys figure this out," Petrov asked, "and when can we start to implement it?"

"For that we have Director Vasilek to thank. It was his agents that infiltrated an American defense contracting company, providing us with the key piece of software code that enabled our people to create this new jamming system. It was only tested for the first time two days ago, and the trial run was determined to be a success. Now that we know it works, we are moving to build these jamming systems and place them around critical sites across the country. We are also working on incorporating them into a jamming pod that can be placed on some of our older Tupolev Tu-95 bombers, which can loiter freely inside our protected airspace as they project a 400-kilometer blackout zone."

Egorkin paused for a second before continuing, "I suspect the Americans will at some point figure out a way around this vulnerability, but until they do, it will provide us with a bit of a reprieve from their strategic bombers and cruise missile attacks. It will also aid in protecting our ground forces as we look to push NATO out of the Baltic states and expand our perimeter within the Nordic states."

Petrov grinned. "Ivan, you have outdone yourself yet again. Please pass along my compliments to your agents in America. I want this new technology implemented immediately. I also want it shared with the Chinese, so they can also implement it. If we both use this technology together, we can significantly dent the Americans' forces."

"Yes, of course, Mr. President," Egorkin responded happily.

Petrov's face darkened as he seemed to realize something. "Changing topics…what are we going to do about the Baltic and Nordic states who are allowing NATO to use their border with Russia as a springboard into our country?"

Alexei Semenov immediately jumped into the conversation. "This is exactly the problem we discussed last summer at the outset of this operation. While we avoided invading a NATO member directly, they have moved forces into the Baltic and Nordic states to both launch air campaigns against us, and to infiltrate Special Forces and other nefarious activities. We can no longer sit idly by and allow this to happen."

Alexei stopped to hand President Petrov a folder. "Before you now is our proposal for eliminating this threat. Now that winter has arrived, we propose launching a massive winter offensive into the Baltic

101

states to push NATO forces back into Poland. With regard to the Nordic states, we would only look to seize one hundred kilometers to act as a buffer zone. If the Nordic states continue to allow NATO to operate from their bases, then we may have to look at further plans for occupying them in the future."

Sensing that Petrov was about to object, Semenov quickly interjected, "With the new divisions we have brought in from central Russia and the reservists who have completed their familiarization training, we have the required forces to accomplish this limited offensive operation."

Petrov's left eyebrow lifted skeptically. "In the past, our reservists have not performed well. What are we doing to reverse that trend now?" asked Petrov.

Alexei nodded slightly. He had anticipated this question. "For the past two months, our reservist units have gone through intensive familiarization training on the equipment they will be using and our preferred combat tactics. While not all of these new divisions are using our top-of-the-line equipment, the gear they are using is functional for the tasks they are being given. With the activation of the reservists, we now have sixteen new divisions we can use, and as new equipment comes off the assembly line, the divisions will turn in their T-64s and T-72s for newer equipment."

Petrov grunted at the response but knew it was the best they could do. He was still very concerned about the military buildup the NATO members were now undertaking.

The meeting dragged on for a couple more hours, with the Air Force and Navy discussing their plans and operations. The Air Force was mostly going to focus on defending the air defense systems and letting the S-400s do the brunt of the work while the navy continued to marshal its remaining submarine force in the North Atlantic to snipe at and sink enemy freighters when possible. As the meeting concluded, Director Ivan Vasilek remained in his seat while the generals and the Minister of Defense exited the room.

Petrov stared at his long-time friend, knowing he had something important he wanted to discuss, or he would not have attended this meeting.

"Ivan, what is going on, my friend? What news do you bring?" asked Petrov, hoping for something they could easily deal with.

Ivan, ever the clandestine agent, showed little emotion as he pulled out his cigarette holder and lit a fresh cigarette. "I bring good news and bad news…but let's discuss the good news before we darken the mood with more troubling information," he said as he took a long pull from his cigarette, lightly tapping it on the ashtray.

Petrov eyed his friend with a bit of suspicion as he poured himself another cup of tea.

Vasilek continued, "Our misinformation operations on social media are having a profound impact in the Allied nations. We have successfully managed to splinter the NATO alliance and foment distrust in their governments. Turkey, Greece, Spain, Portugal, and Hungary have all left the alliance and pledged to remain neutral during the war. In the remaining countries, our operatives are organizing and spawning antiwar rallies and protests in the major Allied cities. I've actually detailed off a twenty percent increase in agents to help grow this movement." As he spoke, the corners of his lips curled up into the closest thing to a smile that Ivan's mouth ever approximated.

Petrov nodded in approval, taking a sip of tea.

"We have substantially increased our targeted ads on Facebook, Snapchat, Twitter and every other social media platform," Vasilek continued. "Our agents are live-streaming antiwar protests, speeches and rallies to gather more support and sow anxiety and hatred within the Allied countries. Two areas in which they have succeeded beyond our wildest imagination are on the college campuses and in the inner cities."

Ivan paused only long enough to take another drag from his cigarette. The man smoked like a chimney. "While we do have a vocal antiwar movement growing in the US, the North Koreans' nuking of California really turned the public against us. We may need to switch tactics in the US and start to focus more on economic sabotage. Maybe we should destroy a rail bridge, a tunnel, or some other critical piece of infrastructure near one of their key manufacturing hubs."

Petrov sat back in the chair, thinking about what Ivan had just said. Their last major sabotage operation against the American LNG facilities had not gone as well as he had hoped. *Sure, we destroyed the facilities, but it also hardened the American people's position against Russia,* he thought. *President Gates used that attack with great effect in rallying his nation against us.*

Petrov wondered what Ivan's thoughts were on the topic. "If you start more of these sabotage operations inside America, how will that negatively affect our situation with the population?" he asked.

Ivan snorted at the question as he blew smoke out through his nostrils. "Does it really matter at this point? The Americans are so enraged by the North Koreans obliterating Oakland and San Francisco, all they want now is revenge. They are drafting five million people into their military. Right now, I want to focus on figuring out how I can slow down the production of the military equipment that will be used against us. Come summer, the Americans are going to unleash an army on us not seen since the Great Patriotic War. I am not certain our generals fully appreciate that fact or understand how desperate a fight that is going to be."

Petrov grunted in acknowledgement.

"It's also not just the Americans," Ivan continued. "The remaining NATO members are also building up an army. While the winter is going to allow us to solidify our positions, it's also giving the Allies time to build an army to defeat us," Vasilek asserted angrily as he stubbed out the remains of his cigarette in the ashtray. He reached into his pocket, pulled out his jade-covered cigarette holder and retrieved another one to light up.

"Ivan, what about the Chinese and Koreans? Are they not sapping enough of the American military away from Europe? Are we truly in that dire of a situation right now?" Petrov asked, hoping in that moment that his military leaders' optimistic outlook was realistic.

"I think the Chinese have underestimated the ability of the Americans to strike at them. They believe they are such a large nation that little pinpricks here and there won't hurt them, but what they are finding out is that the Americans are focusing their pinpricks in just one area, concentrating all their bombing efforts and cruise missile attacks on dismantling the Chinese transportation sector. The Americans are bombing every rail and road tunnel they can find, hitting bridges and dams, causing all sorts of logistical problems. The Chinese are also finding out that the South Korean and Japanese armies are not as easy to defeat as they thought. Unlike in Europe, the South Koreans have a multimillion-man army," Ivan explained as he puffed away on his third cigarette since the start of their meeting.

"It sounds like you are not certain if the Chinese are actually going to win," Petrov said skeptically.

Ivan sold me based on the ability of the Chinese to defeat the Americans in the Pacific, the President thought a bit angrily. *That is going to be key to the success of our efforts in Europe.*

Vasilek looked at Petrov for a moment before responding, "I never said it would be easy or quick. I have spoken with Chairman Zhang. They are getting ready to launch a major offensive against the American Pacific Fleet and some of the Japanese islands. They anticipate having Taiwan fully secured by the end of the year." He seemed annoyed at being questioned like this.

Petrov leaned forward and looked Ivan in the eyes. "Ivan, continue to be straight with me. Do not lie or mislead me. I am counting on you to provide me with accurate intelligence and information to be the counterweight to the generals."

Petrov saw his message was understood. He then stood up. "I have other meetings I need to attend to. I will see you later in the week for our next update," the President said and then indicated that it was time for Ivan to leave. The two men shook hands, and the Russian spymaster left the Petrov's office and headed back to his own fiefdom, Lubyanka.

****

Vilnius, Lithuania
Fourth Infantry Division Headquarters

Major General Paul Austin was still fuming that his division had been forced to retreat from Minsk and fall back all the way to Lithuania. His division had fought fiercely in Belarus for nearly two full weeks before the order had come down from General Cotton, the NATO commander, to fall back to the country they had just invaded from.

If I had been provided the air support I was promised, things would have turned out differently and my division would still be in Minsk, he thought.

As he placed his coffee cup down, General Austin looked over to the right of his desk and saw the most recent newspaper sitting there. He briefly picked it up, reading the headlines. *Russian Troops Amass on the Borders of Baltic States...Russian Ground Offensive Underway in*

Nordic Countries...Korean Ground War Turning into Bloodbath...Taiwan's Beleaguered Military Continues to Hold Out. Austin placed the paper back on the desk.

These newspapers have no idea what's really going on, he said to himself, disgusted with how the media continued to portray the war. *They're just trying to scare people and drive up sales.*

A loud knock at the door brought General Austin back to the moment.

"Enter," he said loudly.

Colonel Wright, his G3 or operations chief, walked into the room along with Colonel Polski, his intelligence chief, or G2.

"What have you got for me, guys?" General Austin asked as they walked towards his desk and took a seat in the two chairs across from him.

"The Russians have moved several divisions towards Estonia and Latvia. It looks like they plan on invading them soon," Colonel Polski replied briskly. He was accustomed to General Austin's style at this point and never beat around the bush when talking to him anymore.

Austin nodded, then turned to his operations chief. "What orders do we have from headquarters on how they want us to handle this?" he asked.

Colonel Wright, a man who always had a determined and serious look on his face, responded gruffly, "Right now, the 82nd Airborne units are preparing defenses in Estonia and Latvia. The British are moving a tank division in that direction, but that's about as much support as those countries are going to get. With the 6th Tank Army still here in Belarus and three divisions sitting less than 100 kilometers from us, we've been ordered to stay in place." Wright seemed almost disgusted by the orders he had presented. He wanted to fight.

General Austin let out a soft sigh. *I hate playing defense*, he thought. He wanted the enemy reacting to them, not the other way around. *I guess no one wants to risk a couple of divisions getting trapped and cut off like what happened in Kiev again.*

Austin could see that his G2 was itching to tell him something, so he signaled for him to go ahead and speak.

Colonel Polski nodded and announced, "General, our intelligence drones and other assets in the area indicate that the divisions marshaling at the borders of Latvia and Estonia, along with the Nordic

106

states, will likely invade within the next month. The Russians are probably looking to establish a buffer zone to delay our forces when we launch our attack in the summer. It also looks like they're starting to prepare a network of defensive positions along the various approaches to Moscow and St. Petersburg." Like General Austin, Polski was a straight shooter, direct and to the point with information; he liked to present the facts directly and let the decision makers decide what to do with them.

Austin scratched his chin for a moment, contemplating the information he'd just received. *If the Russians do launch a winter offensive, then it won't be long before they hit our positions here. So, how do we best counter what we know is most likely going to happen?* he wondered. He picked up the wooden puzzle he kept on his desk, fiddling with it as he weighed the options. Suddenly, an idea came to him, like a lightbulb turning on.

"Here's what we're going to do," General Austin began. "I want our brigades to stay mobile. We're not going to get locked into a defensive position where we can't maneuver. Our best defense is our ability to shift and move our armor and mechanized assets to where they're going to be needed. Make sure our artillery is also staying mobile. I have no idea how much air support we'll be able to request or receive, so we're going to have to rely heavily on our own artillery support," he said, issuing his first orders for how he wanted the division to plan on defending Lithuania and their assigned area.

Once the two officers had the rest of their marching orders, they left his office to pass on the new orders and further develop the plans for what to do when the Russians launched their winter offensive.

Chapter 17
Battle of Taipei

Sergeant Lin pulled another cigarette out of his pack of Pall Malls; he frowned when he realized the pack was now empty. Sitting against the wall of the corner café his group of soldiers had taken up residence in, he lit up his last cigarette, taking a deep breath in and filling his lungs with the smoke and nicotine. He closed his eyes briefly, trying to clear his mind for a few minutes while he enjoyed his last Pall Mall. He knew there would be more heavy fighting shortly, and he was taking a few minutes to enjoy one of the last luxuries he had, not knowing if he would live another day or if this would be his last. There were only nine members of his company left alive since the initial invasion. His brigade was more like the size of a reinforced battalion than a brigade. His unit had fought bitterly from one defensive position to another, eventually being pushed back to Taipei.

With no Taiwanese air support to speak of, the PLA had been pouring tens of thousands of soldiers a day onto the island, with no way of being able to stop the incoming storm. It was only a matter of time until the island was fully occupied.

Sergeant Lin wondered, *What exactly are we fighting for now? If they had no hope of winning, then why did they continue this conflict? How many civilians are being killed on a daily basis because the government wants to keep fighting? We are destroying this city block by block...*

Just as his private thoughts were starting to run amok, a familiar voice called out. It was Major Wu, one of the few officers from their battalion left alive. "Sergeant Lin, one of the scouts has spotted a mechanized infantry unit moving in our direction. I need you to get the antitank missiles moved to the upper rooms of the building and get ready to engage them once they get within range," Wu ordered.

"Yes, sir. We'll set a nice trap for them," replied Lin as he got up, grabbing his rifle and heading to the other room, where a lot of the soldiers were currently resting.

When Lin entered the room, he saw roughly thirty soldiers lying in various positions on the floor, trying desperately to catch up on some much-needed rest. The fighting the last few weeks had been fierce and nearly nonstop, exhausting them all. Lin kicked one of the soldier's feet, causing him to stir.

"Everyone up!" he shouted. "We have enemy troops heading towards our position." Sergeant Lin spoke in a loud authoritative voice, making sure everyone heard him and started to get moving right away.

The men started to rustle, getting to their feet a bit slowly. As they pulled their minds out of the sleepy fog, they started to put their body armor back on and grabbed their weapons.

"I need the fire teams to take up your defensive positions. The antitank soldiers need to grab their rockets and come with me. We are going up to some of the higher floors to get a better angle on the armor units," he ordered.

Then Lin turned to his most senior sergeant left alive. "Sergeant Yang, you are in charge of the fire teams on this level. Understood?"

The sergeant nodded and started rounding up his group of soldiers, getting them moving to the various machine gun positions they had established. The group had strung together a series of machine gun positions that would provide them with interlocking fields of fire when the PLA ground forces made their advance.

Lately, the PLA had been using a lot of militia forces to bum-rush their positions, while the more experienced regular army units advanced behind them. This tactic had been working well for the PLA. While most of the militia units would get wiped out, they forced the Taiwanese soldiers to expend a lot of ammunition on them and give away their positions. This enabled the more experienced regular army soldiers to hit them hard with direct fire from tanks and indirect fire from artillery.

As Sergeant Lin trudged up to the emergency stairwell to the fourth-floor landing, he stopped for a minute while the soldiers below him caught up to him. He sent four soldiers into the fourth floor to set up their positions.

"Remember, don't bunch up, and make your shots count. We only have so many of those rockets left," he instructed. "Plus, once you fire from one position, make sure you move to a new spot because the enemy will likely send a tank round your direction, or at least some heavy machine gun fire."

The soldiers nodded in response and proceeded to fan out on the fourth floor.

Lin led the rest of the soldiers up to the top floor, the seventh floor, which would also act as their observation point. He had twelve soldiers with him. Four soldiers carried antitank rockets, three were snipers, and the rest made up two heavy machine gun teams.

"All right, I want you guys to fan out and find a good position," Sergeant Lin ordered the rocket-toting soldiers. "Make sure you have some cover and identify your next firing position and get those ready as well. I do not want you guys to sit in one position for too long."

He then turned to face his next set of soldiers. "Snipers, I want you guys to set up a little way back in the building, so you are not easily spotted. Your primary targets are the PLA officers. If you spot an officer or someone leading the soldiers forward, take them out."

The soldiers immediately went to work, identifying where the best positions would be and figuring out what they could use for cover. This was the third such building they had taken over and would fight from in the past week, so they were getting better at figuring out what would work and what wouldn't. If and when the fighting became too intense, they would be ordered to fall back to the next city block and take up another set of defensive positions.

The sounds of jet aircraft flying low and fast over the city echoed loudly through the shattered windows of the building. When they had moved into this building the day before, they had gone through and intentionally broken all of the windows, eliminating the glass as a potential source of shrapnel. It would also reduce the risk of giving away their firing positions when they started shooting.

Once the jets passed by overhead, they heard the thunderous booms of multiple explosions, not too far away. Then came the unmistakable sound of helicopters.

Lin looked to the soldier who was carrying their last two Stingers, signaling him to get the first one ready and move towards the blown-out window.

Thump, thump, thump. The helicopter blades grew louder as they echoed off the buildings of the city. Then they saw the first helicopter come into view. It was a CAIC Z-10 ground attack helicopter, similar to the American Apaches. As they watched the chopper move, it was clear that it was not headed directly for their position, but it was certainly advancing in their direction. They needed to neutralize that helicopter before it became a problem.

110

The young soldier prepped the Stinger and turned to Lin, signaling that he was ready. Then, he turned the surface-to-air missile towards the helicopter and activated the heat-seeking warhead. In seconds, the warbling tone from the launcher let the soldier know the warhead had acquired the target and was ready to be fired. As the soldier squeezed the trigger, the missile made a loud popping noise as it was ejected from the tube and the rocket motor ignited.

The missile streaked out of the building at lightning speed towards the Z-10. The helicopter immediately reacted to the threat and dispensed multiple flares in an attempt to throw the Stinger off. Unfortunately for the pilot of the Z-10, the Stingers the Americans had shipped to the Taiwanese days before the war had started were the newest, most advanced version of the missile. The seeker identified the flares and ignored them, directing the missile towards the helicopter as it desperately tried to seek cover by dipping down between buildings. In less than five seconds, the Stinger had closed the distance and detonated its warhead, spraying the chopper with its deadly shrapnel. The helicopter exploded a second later and crashed to the ground below.

Two more Z-10s appeared off in the horizon and headed towards their building now that they knew it was occupied. Sergeant Lin knew they had probably seen where the Stinger had come from and would likely try to lob a few rockets or missiles in their direction.

Lin immediately told the soldiers in his group, "Get down and be ready for impact!"

As he was about to hit the floor himself, out of the corner of his eye he spotted several Stingers racing towards the helicopters from a different building, several blocks away from them.

The helicopters immediately began to jink from side to side and dropped in altitude to get between the buildings and try to escape the Stingers heading towards them. One of the missiles slammed into a nearby building, missing the helicopters, but the second missile found its mark, obliterating another threat from the sky.

While the aerial attack was taking place, dozens upon dozens of enemy infantry fighting vehicles and tanks rumbled down the streets, heading towards them. The lead T-99 moved closer, until it was only two blocks away. Sergeant Lin's soldiers held their fire as they had been instructed, letting the tanks get closer. As the tankers moved forward, so did densely packed units of PLA militia.

Sergeant Lin lifted the small radio to his mouth and relayed a set of orders to the soldiers on the fourth floor, who had eight American-made AT-4 rockets with them. In seconds, he saw three rockets fly out in the direction of the enemy tanks. The T-99's self-defense systems immediately activated, destroying two of the rockets, while the third one plowed into the top of the turret's roof, causing a small explosion. In less than a second, that small blast turned into a much larger detonation, blowing the turret completely off as the ammunition on board caught fire and exploded.

Lin watched several more rockets fly toward the enemy tanks from the floors below him. Two rockets were destroyed by the tanks' defensive systems, but two more hit their marks, disabling the tanks they had hit.

Whistles blew, and suddenly the waves of militia units ran forward, right towards their positions. The machine gunners on Lin's floor immediately opened fire, pouring hundreds of rounds into the wall of militia soldiers charging their position. Enemy soldiers were dropping to the ground like ragdolls from the barrage of bullets being fired at them. The machine gun positions on the lower floors of Lin's building also added their fire to the melee, wiping out row after row of the militia soldiers.

How can they just run into our machine guns like that and not break? Lin asked himself as one of the machine guns near him began to reload. It was sickening how many enemy soldiers they were killing. It was like they were sheaves of wheat being cut down by a mighty scythe.

With nearly half a dozen tanks destroyed or disabled, several infantry fighting vehicles began to move around the wreckage and advance towards their positions. Suddenly, a loud ripping sound blasted Sergeant Lin's senses and he instinctually dropped to the floor, just in time to see chunks of the brick wall flying inward. The room he was in was ripped apart by dozens of heavy-caliber machine guns. The armored vehicles had turned their 25mm and 30mm auto cannons towards their little fortress, systematically trying to shred them and suppress their fire while the militia forces advanced.

In seconds, nearly half of the soldiers on the floor with Lin were torn to pieces by the heavy-caliber rounds. One of the soldiers' head simply exploded as a round tore right through one of the support beams the soldier had been hiding behind. Another soldier had both of his legs

112

ripped off when he tried to move to a position further within the building; his cries of agony could be heard over the roar of the enemy machine guns.

Despite this deadly chaos, Sergeant Lin's remaining machine gunners continued to pour their deadly fire down on the enemy soldiers advancing towards them. Just as Lin didn't think they would be able to hold out any longer, one of the few remaining M60 Patton tanks emerged from an alleyway nearby and fired an antipersonnel round into the militia forces that were about to overrun their position.

The tank's M1028 canister round was essentially a large shotgun round, spewing hundreds of steel ball bearings out the barrel at the charging enemy soldiers. As the tank's gunner continued firing antipersonnel rounds into the human wave, attempting to overwhelm them, the Patton's coax machine gun added its own fire, and so did the tank commander's M2 .50 turret-mounted machine gun.

In less than fifteen seconds, the tank had wiped out nearly 200 enemy soldiers as the militia attack faltered. Then, the PLA regular army soldiers began to advance, along with several infantry fighting vehicles. The M60 Patton switched from firing antipersonnel rounds to their high-explosive anti-tank or HEAT rounds, targeting the enemy armored vehicles. In short order, two of the armored vehicles were destroyed in a blaze of glory.

Out of nowhere, a T-99 suddenly appeared from around a nearby corner and fired a HEAT round at the M60. The Taiwanese tank exploded from the impact, killing the crew instantly, but not before they had helped to blunt the enemy attack.

Sergeant Lin was just about to report what was going on when Major Wu came over the radio. "Sergeant, have your soldiers fall back to the next defensive position!" he ordered.

"Fall back! Fall back now!" Lin yelled at his men over the sounds of the nearby conflict.

His soldiers immediately followed his orders, picking up their gear and moving out. However, as Lin's men took their gear and ran, the PLA soldiers noticed that the Taiwanese had stopped firing on them and tried to rush the positions that Sergeant Lin and his men were trying to vacate.

As Lin reached the ground floor, he pressed down on the detonator to the six Claymore mines they had daisy-chained together.

The sudden roar and boom of the explosion rocked the building Lin was exiting and wiped out a company's worth of enemy soldiers, who were just about to enter the building.

By the time Sergeant Lin's thirty-eight-man force made it to the next defensive line, they were down to just twenty-one soldiers. Lin looked around at the tired, scared and dirty faces and thought, *We can't keep fighting like this. There won't be anyone left. Someone needs to talk about a surrender so some of us can survive this hellish war.*
****

Explosions continued to rock the city of Taipei as the Chinese air force and ground attack helicopters continued to hunt for enemy strong points and armored vehicles. Colonel Wang's armored unit had been decimated during the past few weeks. While they'd had some initial success during the first day of the invasion, as the PLA had landed more tanks and their air cover and air defense systems had been systematically destroyed, his tanks were starting to get wiped out. When the order came down to fall back into the capital and prepare to fight block by block, he ordered his few remaining tanks to support the infantry as best they could.

Colonel Wang moved to one of the tanks in his unit to talk briefly with the tank commander. "How are you holding up, soldier?" he asked, genuine concern in his voice.

The tank commander, a young sergeant, looked down at Colonel Wang with tired yet determined eyes. "We are doing OK now that we've been given proper ammunition for this type of fighting." The soldier paused for a second, looking up at the sky as another jet raced somewhere high above them.

Then he looked back at his brigade commander and asked, "Sir, how much longer are we going to fight? We can't hold the city, and we are being systematically wiped out. If any of us are going to live through this, then we need to either withdraw from the city or surrender." The sergeant did not care if he sounded like a defeatist; he was tired of fighting and tired of seeing his friends killed.

Colonel Wang felt pained by the soldier's question. He had been pondering that same question for some time now. "I wish I had an answer for you, Sergeant. All I can say is we fight until we are told otherwise. Right now, division has not said anything about surrendering, and I am frankly not sure if we are going to surrender or fight until there is nothing left," he replied. He knew this was not the answer the young sergeant was hoping for, but it was the best answer he could give.

The soldier nodded in reply and then readied his helmet and went back to the task of getting his crew and tank ready for the next round.

Wang felt he needed to get some sort of answer from his own chain of command on this very subject, so he went back into his command center and tried to locate the division commander.

Thirty minutes went by as one of his operations officers worked to track down the general. Finally, they received word that the division headquarters had been destroyed during an airstrike. The general and two other division commanders in charge of the city had been killed. After some initial confusion, the military leadership in the Heng Shan Military Command Center wanted to speak with Colonel Wang.

"Colonel, this is General Wong. Right now, you are the most senior army officer in the city. I need an assessment of how things are going on the ground there and if you believe the units left can continue to hold the city," the general demanded.

Colonel Wang thought about this for a moment. There were three divisions fighting in Taipei; if he was the most senior guy left, then that meant a lot of the divisions had probably been wiped out or had suffered some serious casualties. "Before I can give you that assessment, sir, I need to know what the situation is outside the city. I've been focused on using my armor units to support the infantry in their various fortresses they've been establishing throughout the city, but I have no idea what enemy forces we are facing or what the situation is around us," he replied.

A short pause elapsed as the general was clearly talking with a few others nearby about something, perhaps gathering some of the information Wang had just requested.

"Colonel, I'm placing you on speaker so one of the other officers can provide you with that information."

A second later, another voice who had not introduced himself spoke. "Colonel, during the past two hours, the PLA have completed their encirclement of the capital. We are not certain about the number of enemy forces you are facing, other than to say we know a lot of units that are landing at the ports and beaches are being ferried directly to your position."

The voice paused for a second, perhaps trying to consider how much additional information they should provide him. "Right now, the island has been split in half. We estimate the PLA has probably landed around 200,000 militia forces and nearly 100,000 regular army forces, with more landing each day. We don't have any additional reinforcements we can send you. The few operational units we have left are retreating to the countryside right now to begin setting up an insurgency operation—"

"Colonel," General Wong interrupted at this point, "do you believe your forces can hold the city for a few more days?"

Wang grunted at that request. "With all due respect General, hold the city for a few more days to accomplish *what* exactly? We've been fighting across the city for more than a week. We are systematically destroying the entire city in the process, not to mention the hundreds of thousands of civilians that are still trapped in the city and are being killed. I'm being inundated with civilian casualties seeking medical help, and now the uninjured are desperately asking for food and water. These are supplies that I can barely scrounge up for my own men, let alone the people trapped in the city."

Angry, he passionately continued, "Can we hold the city for a few more days? Probably, but how many more civilians are going to die during this futile effort? I don't know—probably thousands or even tens of thousands. The PLA has not exactly been careful with their artillery barrages or air strikes. I never wanted to be caught in this position, but I believe our best course of action at this point is to either try and break out of the city to the countryside or surrender."

There, I said it, he thought. It was only what every soldier trapped in this city had been asking me for days. If the island was lost, then why continue to fight? *Why should we continue dying for a lost cause?*

For what seemed like a long minute, there was no response from the other end of the line. Wang thought the call might have been disconnected when he finally heard General Wong's voice. "I understand, Colonel. Your division has fought with great distinction. No one will ever say otherwise. You bring up a valid point about the civilian casualties. We never meant to turn Taipei into a street fight, but it just kind of happened, and unfortunately hundreds of thousands of people have been trapped in the city as a consequence."

An audible sigh could be heard on the other end. "I give you permission to surrender the city, Colonel. You may choose the timing of this, but if you truly feel there is no chance to break out of the city, then you are authorized to surrender the remaining forces and end the fighting in Taipei," General Wong said, finally acknowledging what everyone else already knew. The city just could not be held without completely destroying it and killing nearly everyone still trapped in it.

Colonel Wang responded, "Acknowledged, sir. I will assess our ability to break out and get back to you within the next couple of hours.

When Wang terminated the secured communication link, the others in the command center looked at him, their eyes almost pleading with him not to order them to fight to the death. Many of them had families that still lived in the city or the surrounding areas. They just wanted to live through the war and see their loved ones again.

Within a few hours, it was clear to Wang that they did not have enough fuel, vehicles, or ammunition to mount much of an offensive to try and punch a hole in the PLA lines. The mountain tunnels to their east had been captured and closed off by PLA paratroopers, and the tunnels to the south had also been captured, leaving him no real options to break out. At that point, Colonel Wang made the decision that he would surrender the remaining forces in the city and put an end to some of the bloodiest street fighting since World War II.

Chapter 18
Battle of the Mind

Sinanju, North Korea

The snow had been falling now for nearly three straight days, forcing a short pause in the ground war in Korea, although both sides' air forces were still bent on killing each other. The foul weather had limited the use of helicopters, drones, and artillery for the moment, so things were strikingly quiet.

Sergeant Ian Slater of the 2nd Infantry Division, 16th Mechanized Brigade, shivered as he found a nearby tree he could relieve himself against. He desperately wanted to avoid going out in the cold and snow, but his bladder demanded immediate attention. He wanted to do his business quickly and get back inside the Bradley fighting vehicle where the rest of his squad was staying nice and warm.

This sucks! he moaned to himself. *How in the world did I end up in the middle of a war? Join the Army, get the GI Bill—that's what the recruiter and my parents said I should do if I wanted to go to college. Forget the Army, and college—I just want out*! His anger was the only thing keeping him warm.

Ian's unit was supporting a Republic of Korea tank division that had driven the North Korean Army to the Taeryong River, the last major natural barrier before the Yalu River and China. The PLA, for their part, had rushed tens of thousands of soldiers across the border, slowing the ROK and American forces down, but not stopping them from pushing to this last barrier. Had the weather not slowed them up, they might have already crossed the river and finished capturing the rest of North Korea.

"Hey, Sergeant Slater, you almost done? The lieutenant wants to talk to you," one of his soldiers yelled from the opened hatch of their armored vehicle.

Ian finished his business, turned and yelled back, "Yeah, I'm on my way. Tell the LT to give me a second." He trudged back to the warmth of the vehicle.

As long as they had fuel, the vehicle commander, who hailed from Hawaii, was going to keep the track running, and the heater along with it. He kept the vehicle nice and toasty, which was fine by the soldiers packed in the back.

When Ian got into the vehicle, he grabbed the mic from one of the soldiers. "This is Baker Three, go ahead, Baker Six," he said, responding to the lieutenant. This was their second platoon leader since the start of the war. The first lieutenant had been hit by a sniper and killed, then their company commander had been killed in an enemy artillery strike. They had lost a lot of officers, so despite only being an E-5 sergeant, Slater found himself as one of the senior sergeants left in the company.

"Baker Three, this is Baker Six. I need you to come over to my vehicle. I need to pass some information to you. How copy?" asked his platoon leader.

Slater sighed at the thought of having to go back outside in the cold and snow and work his way through the several feet of it now on the ground to the lieutenant's vehicle.

"Good copy. I'm on my way," he answered, knowing that he didn't have an option.

"OK, you guys are on your own for a bit. I'm heading off to find the LT's vehicle," Sergeant Slater announced.

The other soldiers just grunted in response. Several of them were busy reading a book on their Kindles, or just writing a letter home.

It took Ian twenty minutes of trudging through the snow and cold before he found the lieutenant's vehicle. As he approached it, he saw the other sergeants were standing around a map that had been stuck to the outside of the vehicle. He also noticed they all had cups of hot coffee in their hands.

"Ah, there you are, Sergeant Slater. We have some coffee over there. Help yourself, and then I'll go over what the colonel just sent down," his platoon leader said jovially.

Eh, he's new and green, so he's still happy and excited. Give him a few weeks of this hellhole, and he'll be as disgruntled as the rest of us, Ian thought as he poured a cup of piping-hot coffee.

Walking back to join the other sergeants, he saw they were all wearing new ranks. Lieutenant Porter, the platoon command, also had captain's bars on.

What just happened? Did everyone just get a promotion besides me? he thought, angry and confused.

Seeing the puzzled look on Slater's face, Captain Porter pulled out a pair of sergeant first class chevrons and handed them to him. "The brigade has lost a lot of soldiers since the start of the war, and replacements are finally starting to show up. The colonel said to promote all the NCOs up two grades to start filling in for the losses. When you guys get back to your squads, I want you to pick two new people to promote to sergeant and one person to move up to staff sergeant. We have 62 new replacement soldiers that'll be arriving tonight. We'll be filtering them into the various platoons, and this should bring us up to one hundred percent strength. We're also getting several new Bradley vehicles and six Strykers," Captain Porter explained.

This brought a lot of happy nods from the group, as some were excited about the pay bumps. There were also a few concerned looks, as they all knew additional vehicles and replacements meant they were most likely going to see more combat soon.

One of the sergeants interjected, "No disrespect, Captain, but you just arrived with our unit not more than six days ago as a second lieutenant; now you're our new company commander, and all of us have been promoted up to sergeant first class or master sergeant. What the heck is going on?"

Captain Porter, for his part, did not look the least bit offended. "You know better than I do how many casualties we've been taking since the start of the war. The President has also announced a massive draft back home, so some of these new draftees and replacement soldiers are starting to arrive. They range from privates to specialists in rank, which means we need a lot more sergeants. On the officer side of things, it's even worse. Nearly fifty percent of the officers in the brigade have been either killed or wounded. The colonel is just trying to get the brigade back up to fighting strength. I know I'm new, and I'm going to rely on your experience to help me lead this company," he replied, which garnered a few nods and approvals.

At least this officer isn't naïve enough to believe he knows everything, Ian thought to himself. *He might yet turn into a decent officer.*

The captain continued, "Look, the weather is going to clear up in the next couple of days. The colonel said that when that happens, the ROK is going to try and make a final push to cross the Taeryong River and drive the Chinese and North Koreans to the Chinese border. While the ROK will continue to do the brunt of the fighting, our brigade is going to continue to support them. When the ROK armored units secure a hole in the enemy lines, our brigade is going to punch through that hole and try to drive the enemy to the Yalu River."

Captain Porter took a deep breath. "I don't know how much time we have to get our replacements ready, but I want you guys to focus on making sure they know what their responsibilities are and what to expect as best you can. I know this is a crappy situation we all find ourselves in, but we need to make the best of it and do our best to keep our soldiers alive. Everyone understand?"

They all nodded in agreement. The group talked a bit longer with the captain, making sure they knew what the next day's plans were before being dismissed to head back to their platoons and squads.

Promoted two ranks…so much for shooting myself in the foot and getting out of this mess, Ian thought as he struggled back through the snow to his squad's armored vehicle.

When he walked in, he was wearing his new rank, which caught everyone by surprise. While the soldiers in his squad respected him as their sergeant, they all knew he hated being in the Army and wanted out of Korea. They were surprised to see he had been promoted; they were even more surprised when he promoted three of them to sergeants and informed them of the new recruits that would be arriving in a few hours.

Slater suddenly realized that his little squad was going to be split up, and he was now in charge of an entire platoon. *How can I be a platoon sergeant?* he thought. *I've only been a squad leader for three months.*

That evening, the replacements arrived, along with the new armored vehicles. The next two days were spent getting everyone organized into their squads and making sure everyone had the right load-outs of ammunition, hand grenades and everything else they would need. Sergeant First Class Slater made sure they loaded the vehicles with enough food and water to last each squad three days. He also made sure they were packing three times their normal load of ammunition. Once the ROK secured a breakout, their unit would punch through the hole in the enemy lines and work to roll up the enemy position. It also meant they might be operating outside of their normal supply lines for a couple of days or more.

******

It was Christmas Eve, and the snowstorm had at long last cleared. High above the Allied lines, the soldiers below could see the contrails of dozens of B-52s as they moved north. Then, as if on cue, they heard the sound of falling bombs. The loud screaming noise they made as they fell from high altitude towards the targets below was terrifying. Off in the distance, the soldiers watched in wonder and terror as the enemy positions across the river were hit by hundreds of explosions across their lines. Trails of smoke and fire filled the horizon.

While they were observing the bombers turning back towards friendly lines, they saw several of the lumbering aircraft explode. Either enemy aircraft or surface-to-air missiles were finally catching up to them.

Once the explosions from the bombs fell silent, the unmistakable sound of artillery whistled through the air. ROK and American artillery started to fire hundreds of white phosphorous or WP rounds all along the enemy positions. While this was happening, dozens of engineering vehicles with portable bridging equipment rushed forward towards the river, establishing multiple pontoon bridges to ferry the Allies across.

Several of the engineering vehicles and crews were blown up by some unseen enemy. One of the pontoon bridges blasted into flying shards as the enemy artillery scored a direct hit.

In the midst of the Allied artillery barrage, the WP rounds were switched to smoke rounds, blanketing the river crossing area in smoke as the Allies tried to conceal their efforts to cross it.

Sergeant Slater winced when he heard the sound of incoming artillery flying high over their heads, heading towards where their own artillery was set up. The Chinese were starting their counterbattery fire in hopes of suppressing whatever the Allies were planning to do.

Under the cover of smoke, the engineers worked feverishly, connecting one section of bridging with another to get the pontoon bridges completed. As soon as bridges were assembled, they watched as one ROK unit after another crossed the river to engage the Chinese soldiers. Within an hour, they had observed probably at least three or four battalions' worth of tanks and other armored vehicles cross the pontoon bridges. Then, waves of light infantry soldiers ran across the bridges, trying to get to the opposite side.

While Slater's platoon seemed to be transfixed watching the river crossing, their radio crackled to life. "Bravo Company, we're moving out. Prepare to cross the river," Captain Porter announced. It was now their turn to work their way down the road that would lead them to the river crossing.

The soldiers in the vehicle with Sergeant Slater were mostly young replacements. Most of them had just finished basic and advanced infantry training less than a week ago, and now they found themselves on the front lines, advancing to contact with the Chinese People's Liberation Army. It was quite a shock to most of them. They reacted to the scream of each artillery round flying over their heads and flinched at the boom of any nearby explosion. Ian envied their naivety; he wished he still had that same innocence, but that had been stolen from him when the war had started without any warning.

After driving for a little while towards the river, their vehicle finally approached the pontoon bridge. Ian had actually never crossed a bridge like this in an armored vehicle, and he crossed his fingers that there wouldn't be any problems. He was terrified of being trapped inside if the vehicle fell into the water. He had heard from other soldiers in his unit about how some guys had drowned when a Humvee had been flipped over by an IED in Iraq and rolled into the river. Those soldiers had been unable to get their wounded comrades out of the vehicle before it had sunk, and the guys stuck inside had been too injured to push the heavily armored doors open against the water.

I could never be in the Navy, Ian realized.

"Sergeant Slater, when do you think we'll see some action?" asked one of the new soldiers, guilelessly believing in the romanticism of war.

Ian looked at the new guy for a second. He seemed eager to fight, while the others in the vehicle were a lot more reserved. They all looked like they would rather be anywhere than there, just like him. But not this guy. He wanted to be there. He wanted to kill.

"Once we get across this bridge, we'll be across our lines into enemy territory. After the ROK units force a break in the Chinese lines, our brigade is going to punch a hole right through it and push to the Yalu River. When that happens, we're going to see a lot of action. I want everyone to stay frosty, OK?" he replied, more to the rest of the group of soldiers than directly to the private who had asked him the question.

"Basically, another hour or three, then, right?" the private asked.

Is this kid serious? Slater thought.

"Private, I don't know when we'll be in combat, but trust me, you'll know when it happens," Ian replied, obviously annoyed. "Either our vehicle will be blown to bits and you'll all die in a fiery burning mess, or you'll start to hear bullets and shrapnel bounce off our armor. In either case, you'll *know* when we are in combat. Just listen to what I tell you guys, and hopefully we'll all live through the next couple of days."

I liked being a specialist or buck sergeant, Slater finally realized. *I was only responsible for a small group of soldiers. Now I have a whole platoon to worry about. If any of these guys get killed, I'm not writing any letters home to families. The officers can do that.*

As their vehicle moved forward, the vehicle commander yelled back to them, "We're holding up for a bit!"

Some fuel trucks were moving up, and they were going to top off while the ROK pressed their attack. A few minutes later, Ian's vehicle came to a halt.

Sergeant Slater told the guys, "Get out and stretch your legs while you can." They happily obliged. Some of the soldiers pulled out their cigarettes or chewing tobacco, while others did some stretches.

In the distance, they could hear the explosion of artillery rounds, the booms of tank guns, and the thumping of helicopters racing to the front. Ian looked up and saw two Blackhawks heading away from the front, back towards friendly lines. The helicopters had red crosses on them, designating them as medevacs. Surveying the scene around them, Ian realized they had essentially stopped in a Chinese armored graveyard. Dozens upon dozens of armored vehicles and tanks were strewn around the back side of the slope they were on. Some of the vehicles were still burning; others had dead or charred bodies near them or hanging from some of the hatches, a sign that they had tried to escape the burning vehicles but had failed in their effort.

While the vehicles were being fueled, Ian walked down the line to talk with a few of his squad leaders and make sure they were doing OK. He started talking with the corporal he had promoted to staff sergeant—the guy also happened to be his roommate prior to the war starting, so of course he was going to hook him up. In the middle of their chatter, they heard the whistling sound of incoming artillery rounds.

Everyone flattened on the ground or dove into a nearby armored vehicle. Four rounds landed around their vehicles and the fueling tankers. The ground shook violently as the overpressure from the explosions smacked the soldiers who had flattened themselves on the ground. Next came two large secondary explosions, which rocked their area further.

Then Ian heard the agonizing screams of the wounded. He looked up and saw the fuel tanker that had been refueling his Bradley exploding, throwing fuel everywhere, including his own vehicle. One of the soldiers that had hit the dirt near the vehicle screamed and rolled around on the ground, desperately trying to extinguish the fuel that had splashed all over him and ignited from the blast. Then, another soldier emerged from the back of the Bradley, also on fire and screaming. The soldier just ran in a straight line in the snow; he made it maybe ten feet, screaming and flailing his arms around, until he dropped to his knees and fell face-first, silent while the fire continued to consume his body.

Sergeant Slater and some of the other soldiers nearby grabbed fire extinguishers and ran towards the flaming Bradley. As they approached the vehicle, one of the two missiles that was stored in the launcher on top of the vehicle cooked off, blowing part of the turret off and throwing shrapnel everywhere. Ian felt something hot and sharp cut the side of his face as he fell to the ground.

When he pulled his mind out of the daze he found himself in, he realized that there was nothing he could do for the soldiers that might still be in the track. They were all gone, dead.

Medics ran towards the various wounded soldiers nearby. Grown men screamed for their mothers or wives or cried out in agonizing pain. Slater immediately waved to one of the soldiers with a radio that was nearby. "Call a medivac! Get us some help, and then radio the captain and let him know we took casualties from that artillery barrage."

Ten minutes later, a Blackhawk with a red cross descended towards them, just as Captain Porter arrived. The medics quickly carried the wounded to the waiting angels of mercy.

"Sergeant Slater! What the heck happened?" yelled Captain Porter over the roar of the helicopter.

Ian turned his back to the helicopter as the captain came running up to him. "We got hit by some random artillery fire. It nailed one of my Bradley vehicles, and then another Bradley was destroyed when a tanker exploded and doused the vehicle in fuel," he replied, disgusted by what had happened.

Captain Porter paused for a second, then looked Ian in the eyes. "You OK, Slater?" he asked out of genuine concern.

"I don't know, Captain. Half of my platoon is made up of replacement troops, and in less than 72 hours, I just lost them all. I was a sergeant three days ago; now I'm responsible for a platoon, and half of my guys are dead. And we haven't even attacked the Chinese yet," Ian stammered, clearly shaken by the events and starting to feel a bit of the shock of his own injury. While the cut on his face was not deep enough for him to be medevacked out, it still stung.

Captain Porter put his hand on Ian's shoulder, looking at him for a second. "I know this is tough. I know you don't feel like you're ready to be in charge of a platoon, but these guys are counting on you, and so am I. I need you to pull it together and lead your soldiers. Can you do that for me?"

Ian took a deep breath and closed his eyes for a moment before responding. "Yes, I can do that. I'll be OK, sir. You can count on me."

In that moment, Ian realized that no matter how badly he wanted out of Korea and the Army, he was stuck, and he needed to make the best of the situation. He had soldiers depending on him, and he didn't want to let them down. The cut on his face reminded him of his own mortality and how close he had come to being killed. While it was a minor flesh wound, had it been a few centimeters to the left, it would have torn right into his skull.

Chapter 19
Spies

Beijing, China

It was a cool November morning as Major Wong poured himself a cup of tea and sat down at his desk to review the week's flight plans for anything of interest. One item that caught his attention was a flight to New Delhi, India, at the end of the week. When he saw who would be on the trip, he became suspicious, and then a plan formed.

I need to contact my handlers about this immediately, he thought.
****

After completing a series of advanced training programs and extensive background checks, Wong had been assigned to a small cadre of PLA Air Force pilots who flew executive aircraft for high-ranking members of the Chinese Communist Politburo. Wong had been a member of this elite group for nearly four years, ferrying senior government officials around the country and the world, until one day he had impressed Chairman Zhang, the Head of Chinese State Security.

While making a routine flight from Beijing to Shanghai, Wong's aircraft had come into contact with a small group of birds. One of the birds had been sucked into an engine intake, causing the engine to fail. Had Wong not been as expertly trained as he was, the aircraft might have crashed. Ever since that day, Wong had become Chairman Zhang's personal pilot.

Unknown to Chairman Zhang, Major Wong had been secretly recruited by the American Defense Intelligence Agency nearly ten years ago, when he had attended a flight training program held by Bombardier Aerospace regarding various executive aircraft that the Chinese Air Force was purchasing. During his training, he had been approached by one of the flight instructors.

The instructor had told him casually, "If you're willing to provide information on the flight plans of certain individuals, you will be compensated handsomely."

At first, Major Wong had refused, but the more he'd thought about it, the more he'd begun to tell himself it really wasn't a "state secret" who was flying on his plane or where they were going—not with social media and the press always reporting on everything.

Then, during one of his training flights, when it was just him and his instructor on the aircraft, he asked what they would want to know, how much he would be compensated, and how he would communicate that information to them. Once these questions had been clarified, and he felt reasonably sure he could pull it off, he'd agreed to be a spy for the Defense Intelligence Agency.

After a couple of mundane years flying senior Politburo members around the country, he had been promoted to major and transferred to private service for Chairman Zhang. When he'd informed his handlers of this new posting, they increased his compensation considerably. At last check, he had accumulated over three and a half million US dollars in his account in the Cayman Islands. His plan was to retire to some white sandy beach in another few years, drinking Mei-Tais and chasing scantily clad women.

Then the war had started, and everything had changed. His handlers had tripled his pay for information to compensate for the increase in his risks. His handlers especially wanted him to identify when and where Chairman Zhang and President Xi would be traveling outside of China. While Chairman Zhang was not going to be traveling to India at the end of the week, his trusted aide Wu was. Major Wong was pretty sure his handlers would still be interested in this information. He was one step closer to a sunny, sandy shore.
****

Beijing, China
US Embassy

While the majority of the embassy personnel had been flown out of the country at the start of the war, a small skeleton crew still remained at the compound and carried out the daily functions of diplomacy, which, while minimal, were still important. Terry Bell, the head of the Defense Intelligence Agency in China, continued to man his post at the embassy, despite the risk of being detained as a spy in China during a time of war. This took an extraordinary amount of courage, considering that he could legitimately be shot if he were ever captured or his true identity discovered.

While he sat in his office, reviewing the latest military report from Korea, his smartphone chirped, indicating he had received a text message. Knowing this smartphone was only used by his sources to contact him if they had information he would value, he immediately opened the message. A grin spread across his face.

This could be the opening in the war we've been hoping for, he thought as his mind began to process what his source had just offered.

Terry grabbed a notepad and immediately wrote down a few details, then he developed a quick plan to capitalize on what his source had just offered them. He grabbed his secured phone and placed a quick call to the Deputy Director of the DIA to get the ball rolling.

The phone rang twice before a gruff, familiar voice picked up. "This is Marty."

Terry replied in an excited voice, "Marty, I think I found that break we've been looking for. My source that's been providing us with the travel details of Chairman Zhang and President Xi just told me that Chairman Zhang's righthand man, Wu, will be traveling to New Delhi in five days, and on top of that, he'll only have three security guards with him."

Terry went on to explain his plan for how they would abduct this high-value target, speaking quickly because of the adrenaline that was pumping through his veins.

There was a short pause on the other end before his boss replied, "This is a risky plan, Terry. You're talking about abducting a senior member of the Chinese government. Not to mention, this strategy would call for that individual to be kidnapped while visiting the soil of a neutral country."

Marty sighed. "We'd be breaking a lot of international protocols by targeting a government official while on official government business abroad. While I like the idea of grabbing Wu and interrogating him, there is no way we could move forward with nabbing him while he's on foreign soil. Is it possible for your source to take him to a location of our choosing on Chinese soil?"

This was not the kind of precedent Marty wanted the United States to set. It could make US officials prime targets while traveling abroad, which was not something they needed to add into the mix.

Thinking for a moment before responding, Terry replied, "I think I have just the plan that might work…"

****

Bhutan
Kangkar Pünzum National Park

The wind blew softly, ruffling the tent the four members of Operational Detachment Alpha 1110 were using to prepare for their mission. Outside, the rest of the base camp was set at the bottom of a picturesque scene of Mount Kangkar, covered in snow. Walking outside the tent in a nearby clearing, their helicopter pilot, a CIA agent and his source, who was dressed in khaki tour guide clothes, were busy performing a walkthrough and function check of the French Eurocopter AS365 Dauphin.

Despite the short notice of the mission, the CIA had somehow managed to acquire the helicopter from a wealthy businessman in Thailand. Through a herculean effort, they had flown the helicopter to Bhutan and repainted it to look identical to the Harbin Z-9, the Chinese military version of the same helicopter. The chopper would have a crew of two, the CIA pilot and his local guide, and would be carrying a Special Forces team of four men, but there was enough space to carry up to ten people inside the cabin. With a range of 540 nautical miles, this helicopter would be more than able to get them to Tibet and back for their mission.

Chief Warrant Officer Four Charles Lee, call sign "Chucky," was checking the duffel bag their CIA contact had provided for them a couple of hours ago to make sure everything they had requested was there: three Chinese-made QBZ-95 assault rifles, one AMR-2, essentially a Chinese version of the Barrett .50-caliber sniper rifle used by US Special Forces, and four QSW-06 pistols with silencers. It all checked out—everything they needed to carry out this snatch-and-grab mission was there. Because their mission was going to take them into China, they would be wearing Chinese uniforms and using Chinese weapons to blend in.

Everything about this mission had been rushed, from their rapid redeployment from South Korea to their marathon flight to India and then another flight to Thimphu, the capital of Bhutan, not to mention the drive to Kangkar Pünzum National Park. They had spent the better part of 60 hours in transit to get to this point. The cover story was that they were a group of Chinese and Russian mountain climbers who were going to attempt to reach the summit of Mount Kanghar, arguably the highest unclimbed mountain left in the world. However, their true mission was to infiltrate into Tibet and establish an ambush point where they would attack the vehicle carrying Deputy Minister Wu and abduct him for interrogation.

"You really think we're going to be able to pull this off, Chief?" asked Sergeant First Class Mark Wilson, call sign "Maverick." He had a bit of skepticism in his voice as he finished putting his Chinese uniform on.

CW4 Lee smiled at his friend's nervousness. "Come on, Maverick, I think you look every bit as Chinese as the rest of us do," he said, to the laughs of the other two members of their team, Spike and Bonefish. Maverick was six feet two inches tall with bright blue eyes and blond hair. Lee, Spike and Bonefish were actually of Asian descent and could pull off the appearance of being Chinese.

"You know what I mean, Chief. If anything goes wrong, we're screwed," he replied to their laughter.

Turning serious, Lee looked up at his team members. "This mission is no different than some of our past missions in Afghanistan, or even our last mission in North Korea. Yes, we're all alone, and no one will be coming for us if things do go south, but let's focus on making sure that doesn't happen. We have a solid plan. We need to execute and let the chips fall where they may," Chucky said as he went back to finishing the function checks on the weapons.

Two hours later, they were on board the helicopter, heading towards the Lhasa International Airport located in the small village of Jiazhulinzhen. Their mission required them to land their helicopter near a choke point on the 101-Provincial Road that would take Deputy Minister Wu from the airport to Lhasa, the regional government seat of power.

Chapter 20
Outsourcing

New Delhi, India
Rashtrapati Bhavan

As Deputy Minister Wu's vehicle arrived at the side entrance to the presidential residence, he couldn't help but marvel at the size and architectural design of the building. The residence used to be the Viceroy's house when India had still been under British rule, but now it was the seat of power for the President's and Prime Minister's offices. The building incorporated both Indian and British designs and was surrounded by hundreds of acres of beautifully kept gardens. It was an oasis of peace and tranquility in an otherwise overcrowded and busy city of twenty-one million people.

Once the vehicle Wu was riding in came to a halt at the covered entrance, a security guard dressed in a black suit opened his door and indicated he should follow him inside the building. Wu's two bodyguards followed him, along with several Indian security guards. As they moved towards the corridor that would lead them to the President and Prime Minister's offices, they were led to the guard station, where they were told they would be disarmed and searched.

Upon completing this formality, Wu was directed to an anteroom to wait to be called for his meeting. On entering the room, Wu spotted Ivan Vasilev, the Director of the FSB, sitting at a table near the window with his own bodyguards nearby. Wu signaled for his guards to wait by the door while he walked over to Ivan.

Ivan had seen Wu enter the room and was also sizing him up. While Ivan had met Deputy Minister Wu a couple of times, this would be his first time participating in a meeting with him without Chairman Zhang. He stood and extended his hand.

"Deputy Minister, it is good to see you," Ivan said warmly. "I take it Chairman Zhang was unable to attend this meeting?"

Wu read the surprise and disappointment on Ivan's face. "Hello, Ivan. It is good to see you as well. Unfortunately, Chairman Zhang has been sequestered in Beijing with the rest of the Central Military Commission for the time being," Wu explained.

"Yes, I understand. President Petrov very seldom leaves the command bunker after the Americans tried to kill him in the opening days of the war. These American dogs are relentless in trying to kill the leaders of the countries they go to war with. No decency or civility in war with these Yankees," Ivan replied with a bit of heat in his voice.

Just as they were about to discuss the purpose of their meeting, one of the aides to the Indian president walked in to inform them the President was ready to speak with them. Wu and Vasilek followed the aide, who led them to a very formal meeting room, where the Prime Minister of India, along with the President and two other senior aides, were waiting. As requested, only key people to the President and Prime Minister were present in the room for the occasion.

President Aryan Laghari stood as his two guests walked into the room. He immediately walked towards them and shook both of their hands, greeting each of them in their native languages. One of the key reasons President Laghari had won the presidency the year before was because of his critical role in brokering the normalization of relations between India and China. Of course, he had received a lot of help and prodding from FSB Director Vasilev and President Petrov, but the strategy had paid off, and he won the presidency by a large margin.

After the greetings and pleasantries were exchanged, Prime Minister Vihaan Khatri cleared his throat. "Gentlemen, please let us get this meeting going. We have a lot to discuss and not a lot of time to do it in," he said, indicating with his arm for everyone to take a seat at the couches in the nearby room. Some hot tea and cookies were waiting for them, neatly arrayed on the coffee table between the two couches.

While PM Khatri still didn't trust or like the Chinese, he did trust President Petrov, which was the only reason he had agreed to this meeting to hear the joint Chinese-Russian offer. As the group took their seats, Vasilev brought them up to speed on the war in Eastern Europe. Much to the surprise of India and the world, the Russians appeared to have accomplished the impossible. They had prevented the Americans from removing them from Ukraine, and had in fact inflicted a terrible loss on the Americans and NATO. The Indian leaders sat patiently, listening to Director Vasilev give them an unvarnished report of the war, which obviously differed from what the Western media tried to portray. Once Vasilev had finished his brief, they took a few minutes to refill their cups of tea and ask a few questions. All eyes then turned to Deputy Director Wu.

For the next half hour, Wu gave a similar brief on the status of the war in Korea and the annexation of Taiwan and parts of Southeast Asia. At some point, PM Khatri interrupted Wu to ask, "—Are you trying to lead us to believe that China is winning the ground war in Korea? We have all seen the media reports from the West, along with what the American Defense Department provides. The North Korean government has surrendered, and your army has been pushed back to the Yalu River."

Wu sat there stoically listening, not conveying any emotional response. He had expected these comments. Wu smiled softly and responded, "You must keep in mind, during the first day of the war, we succeeded in sinking one of the American supercarriers and severely crippled the 7th Fleet. Our armed forces have also secured Formosa, Mongolia, Myanmar, Laos and Vietnam. Our navy is about to begin an offensive to secure parts of the Philippines and the Japanese islands, which will extend our naval perimeter—"

PM Khatri interjected, "—You still have not answered our question about Korea and the fact that a large Allied army is now on the very doorsteps of your border."

Did this pompous idiot not hear any of the accomplishments China has achieved up to this point? he thought, anger starting to build a bit within him.

"PM Khatri, we have let the Americans and their allies deliberately push our forces to the Yalu River. We had to allow them to believe they were winning to lure them into the trap we have set for them. They are advancing faster than their logistical lines can keep up with. In addition, their rapid advance is burning through munitions and resources at a faster rate than the US's logistical capabilities can replace them. As December turns to January, the burn rate of their supplies is going to become a critical problem. At that point, we will launch our counteroffensive, which will push them back down the Korean Peninsula," Minister Wu explained, taking pains to remain calm and composed. "Furthermore, our navy continues to expand our maritime border by capturing additional islands and territory, which will make it increasingly difficult for the Allies to operate in the Pacific and keep their supply lines operational."

PM Khatri and President Laghari sat back on the couch, soaking in the totality what Wu had said. They had not previously ascertained the method behind the Chinese madness.

After a moment, Khatri leaned forward. "What is the end state of this war with the West? What do you want the world to look like after you have achieved your goal, and how does India fit into that world view?" asked the ever-astute Prime Minister.

Deputy Minister Wu eagerly responded, "The end goal of this confrontation with the West is to remove the old world order and replace it with a new world order. For nearly a hundred years, the West has led the world. In that timeframe, they have led the world into multiple wars, fueled religious and economic conflicts, and perverted the world with their immorality and lack of common decency. China is a nation of 1.6 billion people. Together with Russia, we control 11 million square kilometers of the entire landmass of the world. Our nations are no longer going to be subjected to the economic and political whims of the West. They have had their time to lead, and they failed. Now it's our time to lead," he said, concluding his passionate speech about the goals of Red Storm.

This statement appeared to have pleased the Indian leaders, who smiled and exchanged a few brief comments. When the two Indian leaders were finished with their side conversation, Laghari asked the obvious question: "What exactly is it that Russia and China want from India?"

Ivan leaned forward, wanting to answer this question before Wu stepped in. While Chairman Zhang was a natural businessmen and salesman, Wu was more of a bureaucrat—an effective bureaucrat, but still a bureaucrat nonetheless. "What Russia and China are requesting from India is access to your ports and manufacturing base. As you undoubtedly know, NATO is hitting parts of our industry and transportation system pretty hard. Russia, for our part, could certainly use your assistance in producing certain war products that are more difficult to produce. You would profit an economic gain, and we would have the supplies we need to end this conflict."

"Ivan, what specifically does Russia need our nation to produce?" PM Khatri asked casually as he sipped on his tea.

Vasilek answered in his typical matter-of-fact tone, "Armata tanks and infantry fighting vehicles, S-400 surface-to-air systems and missiles, and our Zhukov series of drones."

Once Ivan had said his piece, Wu moved forward with China's request. "There are several American and Australian submarines operating in the Indian Ocean that have proven to be quite effective in going after Chinese shipping of raw materials from Africa to our ports. We would like to request that we source our raw materials through Indian-flagged ships and have those ships deliver the goods to Indian ports, then transport those materials to our borders. Our industrial base is more than capable of meeting our war production needs, but we lack the raw materials to keep them fully operational."

President Laghari nodded at this request, knowing that the one weak spot to China's industrial might was their lack of natural resources. Their manufacturing base was enormous, but it was limited by their ability to find the resources to keep it humming.

The two Indian leaders leaned in closer to each other, whispering softly in their own language. Finally, President Laghari responded, "Gentlemen, we have heard your requests, and while we are sympathetic to your nations' plight, we have some concerns. First, our nation wants to remain neutral in this war. We do not want to appear to be taking sides or get drawn into direct conflict. With that said, we will agree to produce whatever equipment your nations are willing to license for production in India. We will also make available our maritime capabilities to move the raw materials China needs."

The President paused for a second before adding, "If the Americans question us or confront us over this, we will let them know that we are remaining impartial in this war, but we will not be bullied into not trading with one nation over another…"

The meeting continued for another hour before the representatives from Russia and China departed the presidential residence and began their separate journeys back home.

Chapter 21
Snatch n' Grab

30,000 Feet Above Tibet

Deputy Minister Wu had just concluded a successful business trip to New Delhi. As both China and Russia moved forward with the global objectives of Red Storm, it was now time to start bringing the Indians into the loop. India's agreement to supply China with the resources they desperately needed and the manufacturing of war materials for Russia should be enough help to turn the tide against the Allies.

I was wrong to doubt Chairman Zhang when he said this plan could work, thought Wu. It was like what that General Yang told us during the briefing of the Formosa invasion: 'A poor plan executed violently is better than a great plan executed poorly.' *Two years from now, China will be the lone superpower in the world, with Russia at our side.*

Wu let a smile slowly spread across his face.

A couple of hours into their flight back to Beijing, a flight attendant approached one of Wu's bodyguards, whispered something into his ear and then walked away. The guard approached Wu. "Sir, the pilot says we are going to make an unscheduled stop at Lhasa."

Wu looked up at the guard, a bit uncertain as to why they would make a stop in Tibet. Lhasa was way off the beaten path. "Go find out why we need to make a stop. We need to make best speed to Beijing," he ordered.

"Yes, sir," the guard replied dutifully, rushing off to do as he was told.

After a few minutes, the guard returned. "The pilot says one of the engines is reporting an oil pressure problem. He wants to stop at Lhasa and have it checked rather than risk the engine cutting out."

The guard looked a bit nervous. While it was significantly safer to fly than drive, when a problem with an aircraft happened, it tended to be fatal at 30,000 feet.

Wu just nodded and went back to preparing his notes for his eventual meeting with Zhang. He wanted to make sure he brought up the possibility of approaching the Russians about letting China mine inside

Siberia for certain materials that would help keep their manufacturing base running at full capacity. If they could get the Russians to cede control of certain mines, the Chinese could increase production of war materials, and in turn help the Russians by manufacturing certain pieces of equipment, just as India would be doing for them.
****

An hour later, their aircraft landed to little fanfare at the small airport outside of Lhasa. The pilot came into the cabin and spoke to Wu directly. "Sir, it will take the mechanic approximately four hours to check the engine and various sensors to make sure there is not a problem."

Wu was annoyed at being temporarily stranded in Tibet but recognized that it was better to be cautious with a mechanical problem than try to press their luck and end up crashing.

Seeing that it was nearly lunchtime, Wu decided he would head into Lhasa and get something to eat. *I've never actually been to Lhasa. Perhaps there's a nice restaurant to eat at here. Look on the bright side—I'll get a chance to see another side of China I wouldn't have otherwise seen*, he thought as his stomach grumbled.

He caught the attention of one of his bodyguards. "Find a vehicle we can use to head into town for some lunch," he ordered.

In short order, the group of four men were in the vehicle and on their way to Lhasa while the pilot stayed behind with the aircraft and the mechanics.

Twenty minutes into their drive, they spotted a small checkpoint manned by several PLA soldiers. There were a couple of cars being stopped and then waved through, nothing out of the ordinary. Wu's vehicle slowed down, and the bodyguard driving it lowered his window and produced his Politburo security credentials, letting the guards know that they were escorting an important person and to let them pass.

Deputy Director Wu was busy reading a message on his smartphone, completely oblivious to the fact that two of the three soldiers at the roadblock were moving towards each side of the vehicle. The bodyguards, however, caught this deviation from what they had observed with the vehicles that had been stopped prior to them and tensed up. The guard sitting next to Wu said something to his partners in the front seat, and they immediately reached inside their jackets for their sidearms.

In one swift and fluid motion, the three army soldiers moved their rifles to the ready position and opened fire on the car. The windshield and the side windows of the car shattered, spraying the individuals in the vehicle with small glass shards. The guard sitting next to Wu tried to raise his pistol to fire at the attackers but was suddenly pumped full of lead as half a dozen bullets hit him in the chest and one round met its mark in the center of his forehead.

The driver, who had already been hit by multiple bullets, immediately smashed his foot down on the accelerator in an attempt to get his charge and comrades out of the ambush taking place. The vehicle lurched forward maybe ten feet, nearly running down one of the attackers before a large-caliber round hit the engine compartment, causing the vehicle to stop almost instantaneously. The attackers shot the driver several more times, and he slumped forward onto the steering wheel. The horn blared under his weight.

The guard in the front passenger seat managed to get his pistol up and fired two quick shots off, hitting one of the attackers before his head exploded in a red mist, spewing blood, brain matter, and bone fragments across the entire car, splashing Wu in the face and dirtying his fancy designer suit.

Before Wu knew what was happening, one of the soldiers had reached his side of the vehicle, opened the door, and grabbed him firmly by his suit jacket, yanking him out of the car. Wu felt himself being spun around and thrown to the ground face-first, as if he were some little girl's ragdoll. He hit the ground with a loud thud as the wind was knocked out him.

What on earth is happening? he wondered, still dazed by the speed of the events unfolding around him.

Suddenly, he felt the pinch of what felt like a needle in his right thigh. In seconds, he felt a slight burning sensation, and then his world began to turn black as all the pain he had just been experiencing faded into the darkness of his mind.
****

Once CW4 Lee had slammed the autoinjector syringe into the right thigh of Deputy Director Wu, he felt the man stop struggling as he began to drift off to sleep. Prior to their mission, the CIA operative had given them the syringe, telling them to just slam it into their subject's leg and the drug would do the rest. Director Wu would wake up 24-hours later, a little groggy but otherwise unharmed.

As the body below him went limp, Chucky radioed Maverick, speaking in Chinese to keep up their cover. "Take out the blue truck before he gets away. Spike, Bonefish—grab the civilians from the other vehicles and get them lined up on the road facing the ditch now! We have to move quick and get this done. We don't have long before this gunfire is reported!" he yelled to his other teammates.

Spike and Bonefish immediately ran to the two other vehicles that had been in line behind Wu's car. They grabbed the two old men and a young couple out of the two vehicles, dragged them to Wu's now-bullet-riddled vehicle, and had them drop to their knees, facing the ditch.

While this was happening, Maverick fired a single shot from his Chinese-made .50-caliber rifle directly into the engine block of a blue truck that had turned around and begun to race to the closest village to seek help. Once his vehicle came to a halt, the man jumped out of the truck and made a run for it on foot. Maverick sighted him in and gently squeezed the trigger, sending a single round 800 meters away, where it slammed into the man's back. He tumbled over then ceased moving; the round had pierced his heart.

As the sound of Maverick's shots echoed off the surrounding ridges, it only heightened the team's awareness that they didn't have a lot of time to execute their plan and get out of there. One of the ODA members unfurled a black Islamic State flag and draped it across Wu's shot-up vehicle with the four civilians kneeing in front of it.

One of the soldiers pulled out a smartphone, and CW4 Lee got himself ready as he stood behind the civilians. He pulled out a postcard with a brief statement that had been prepared for him by the CIA's ISIS group. The language, phrases, and demands on that card were all in line with rhetoric ISIS had used inside China in the past. While Chucky read off the statement, Spike filmed it and Bonefish continued to guard the hostages.

While Lee and the ODA members were filming their video, Maverick took one last look down both sides of the highway to make sure there was no unwanted attention heading their way before he grabbed his remaining gear and started running down the hill towards his

ODA team members. He needed to move quickly as their ride would be landing soon.

I can't believe we're pulling this off, Maverick thought as he began to pick up speed.

As he ran, he heard the four single shots and knew Lee had just completed his part of the deception. Just then, he heard the *thump, thump, thump* of the helicopter blades as their Eurocopter rose above the ridge where he had just been set up, racing towards the Special Forces soldiers and their high-value individual or HVI.

Less than a minute later, the chopper landed, and the ODA members loaded up their HVI and any evidence that could be linked to them. They made sure to leave behind a copy of the video they had just made, along with a written list of demands, ordering the freeing of Islamic militants who had recently been captured or were being held by the Chinese government, along with a few other requests they knew the government would never accede to.

Within minutes of landing, the helicopter was already fully loaded and lifted off, heading back towards Bhutan as quickly as possible. It would not be long before local police or an army unit was dispatched to the ambush site and discovered what had happened. They needed to place as much distance as possible between themselves and the Lhasa Airport. There were still some PLA Air Force fighters at the base that could hunt down their helicopter, if they knew where to look.

Maverick looked at Chucky with a wicked grin on his face. "Did you ever think you'd make a terrorist execution video, Chief?"

The other two operators both laughed at the reference. For his part, Lee just smiled and shook his head.

Two hours later, their helicopter landed at the base camp they had left more than five hours before. The CIA agent ran up to the helicopter, eager to see if they had succeeded in capturing their HVI. Once he saw Wu was indeed on the chopper, he took possession of the four others they had brought with them.

Another man drove a small fuel truck towards the helicopter to get them refueled. Once he got close enough to use the hose, he ran it out to the chopper, filling up the tank with the engine still running.

The Americans had no idea if the Chinese had been able to track them back to the base camp just across the border in Bhutan, so they planned on getting their HVI as far away from the scene of the crime as possible. Once they arrived at the capital, they would transfer everyone to a waiting executive jet that would whisk them away to a safe house in Singapore, where they would finally debrief Wu.

Chapter 22
Dr. Roberts

Singapore
CIA Safe House

Placing the manila folder marked TOP SECRET on the table in front of him, Sebastian Roberts closed his eyes and brought his right hand up to rub his eyes and the bridge of his nose. The marathon flight from Langley across Europe to the Middle East, and then eventually across the Indian Ocean to bring him to Singapore, had been no small feat. Had he not been flying in a luxurious Learjet that had a couch he could lie down and sleep on, he might have been even more exhausted than he already was.

Looking briefly out the window, and then at the flight map on the wall, he saw he had less than an hour before they landed. Sebastian closed his eyes and began to go over the case file the Agency had built on Wu, calculating how he would exploit that information to get the answers they were after.

Sebastian was both a psychologist and a psychiatrist, and he had studied at some of the finest institutions the world had to offer. He was a master of understanding the mind, and more importantly, what made people tick. He was also adept at employing the chemical mixtures that regulated and controlled both the mind and emotions. Between his pharmaceutical concoctions and his clever choice of words, Dr. Roberts could have the most hardened person babbling like a baby in minutes, spilling their guts out during an interrogation.

While serving a number of deployments with the US government in Iraq, Afghanistan, and a myriad of other countries, Sebastian had developed an extremely effective method of obtaining critical information quickly from even the most uncooperative prisoners. Much to the horror of those in his chosen profession of psychiatry, he had pioneered the term "medical interrogations" and had become the most sought-after subject matter expert in the field by both governments and academia. After the war with Russia had started, Sebastian had once again been contacted by the government and asked to perform his services.

For a price and anonymity, anything is possible, he had learned at the outset of the War on Terror.

His current subject, Wu Bangguo, was a bit of an enigma. Having read everything that had been provided to him by the CIA and Defense Intelligence Agency on the flight here, he had come to his own conclusions. Wu had left little in the way of an electronic footprint, and what trail he did leave had been carefully constructed by the Chinese State Security Service, making it difficult to know what was true versus planted information.

It won't matter how much information we have or don't have on Mr. Wu, Dr. Roberts thought. *In a few hours, he will tell us everything we want to know.* A wry smile spread across his lips; he had yet to find a person who did not give up the goods once they had been injected with his drug cocktail of choice.

After what felt like an eternity in the air, the plane ferrying Sebastian finally landed at the Changi International Airport in Singapore. Once the lone flight attendant opened the outer door, the hot, humid air began to waft into the aircraft, assaulting his nostrils and lungs with the thick moisture and the exotic smells of the city. Exiting the aircraft, he placed his white fedora on his head and draped his sports jacket over his shoulder. A black unmarked car was waiting near the bottom of the stairs, along with a man in his mid-fifties wearing khaki pants, a Hawaiian shirt, and sunglasses.

"Sebastian, it's good to see you again," Jonah Chang said with a warm smile as he walked forward to greet his friend. Jonah was the station chief for Singapore and was the lead CIA agent for Southeast Asia. If there was a secret mission or operation going on in Asia, chances were, Jonah either was involved or knew about it. His group had done a superb job in snatching Wu from Tibet. Staging the snatch-and-grab to look like a terrorist abduction was simply brilliant. The Chinese government was in an absolute tizzy right now over what they called the most brazen terrorist attack on their soil in decades. The fact that a junior Politburo member had been kidnapped and was being held for ransom incensed them to no end.

"Jonah, it's been too long since we last met. How are the wife and kids doing these days?" replied Dr. Roberts warmly.

"Oh, they are doing good," Jonah answered. "My oldest is in his second year of college, and my youngest is a junior in high school.

Linda is also doing great. She loves being here in Singapore. You know, we're just an hour flight from Phuket, Thailand. She makes us take nearly all our vacation days in Thailand; it's simply beautiful."

The two men made their way into the car. Almost as soon as they were seated, the driver took off towards the CIA safe house.

After the vehicle started moving, Sebastian leaned over towards Jonah. In a low voice, he asked, "How long has Mr. Wu been exposed to the sensory deprivation goggle therapy?"

SDGs were a relatively new tool that had been incorporated into the interrogation process. They were essentially a virtual reality headset that flooded a person's eyes with various types of lights—strobes, pulses, bright and then fading lights in a multitude of colors. While the visual effects were happening, the noise-cancelling headsets began their own assault on the individual's auditory sense in conjunction with this. The person would hear a series of noises: crying babies, nails being scratched across a chalkboard, etc. The subject's brain was bombarded with more stimulation at one time than a person could hope to deal with, leading to sensory overload. Ten minutes of this treatment would feel like hours to the average person—an hour with this headset on and anyone would feel like they had been dealing with it for a day or more. It completely and utterly wore the mind out.

Jonah smiled at the question. "Mr. Wu has been undergoing the SDG therapy now for the past 48 hours. Not all at once, of course. We don't want the poor man to become insane before you arrive. We've given him the therapy for roughly ten minutes every hour. At this point, he now believes several days or even a week has passed since he was abducted."

To anyone listening in on their conversation, it almost sounded like this was a conversation between two doctors as they discussed a patient, and in a way, it was almost like that—only Sebastian was the doctor, and Wu was the patient.

"Have the soldiers remained in character the whole time?" Sebastian asked.

Because they had staged the entire abduction to appear as if it had been Islamic militants who had abducted him, they wanted to keep that storyline going for as long as possible. It was imperative that they keep Wu believing he was being held by the terrorists for a while longer.

Once he realized he was being held by the Americans, his resolve might strengthen, and that was not something they wanted to allow.

"Yes," Jonah confirmed. "They have done an exceptional job pretending to be terrorists, by the way. The mock execution of the civilians with the Islamic State flag in the background and the bullet-riddled vehicle was superb. You would not believe the hornets' nest they've stirred up with the Chinese in Tibet and other western regions. Our source, the pilot who arranged for the plane to land in Tibet, said his superiors are going crazy trying to find Wu." Jonah said, almost giddy at the chaos their little operation had sown.

Any distraction or drain of resources from the fight against US forces is a welcome distraction as far as I'm concerned, thought Jonah. *I just hope the PLA won't look to invade Thailand next.*

Thirty minutes later, their vehicle arrived at the safe house and Jonah led Sebastian up the stairs to the second-story office where they were holding Wu. As they entered the hallway, a secretary seated below a corporate sign that read *Southeast Shipping* smiled and hit a buzzer under her desk, which unlocked a door to her right. The two of them walked through the opening towards the two rooms they had set up for the interrogation. Jonah led Sebastian into the first room, the observation area, where a multitude of computer monitors and other equipment was carefully arranged. From here, they could watch everything happening inside the interrogation room.

Mr. Wu's hands and feet were taped to a chair that was suspended in the air by a chain anchored to the ceiling. This technique caused Mr. Wu to be tilted forward at a 45-degree angle, causing a sense of weightlessness and further adding to the confusion that their subject would be experiencing. Inside the SDG, it would feel as if he were floating or falling, depending on how his mind was reacting to the images and sounds being thrown at it.

"I want Mr. Wu lowered back to the ground and his restraints removed," Sebastian ordered. "Take the SDG off him as well and have someone prepare some tea. Now it's time for me to earn my keep and have a discussion with Mr. Wu."

While several agents began to get Wu set up, a pot of tea was heated up in the observation room. Dr. Roberts prepared his concoction of drugs. He had two methods of introducing the drug into a person: through a shot, or in a drink of some sort. Knowing that Wu would most likely be thirsty and that he would be eager to eat and drink something, Sebastian opted to introduce the drug via the tea he was having prepared.

Dr. Roberts knew that Wu was fluent in Russian as well as English, so he chose to use Russian to try to keep the Islamic militants ruse alive. Sebastian's cover story was that he was a hostage negotiator, sent by a Russian company to help secure his release. This would be the genesis of their meeting and how he would start the questioning.

Twenty minutes later, Wu was seated at the table and ready to begin. Opening the door, Dr. Roberts walked in carrying a cup of hot tea and a small tray with some food indigenous to the western regions of China, where the Chinese Islamic militants were known to operate.

The CIA really went to great lengths this time to ensure this deception is as real as possible, Sebastian thought with admiration.

A man who appeared to be of Chinese descent stood in the corner, acting as a guard. Dr. Roberts sat down at the chair across from Wu. His subject lifted his head slightly. His eyes looked bloodshot and exhausted.
****

Lifting his head slightly, Wu looked around the dimly lit room to see if he could possibly identify where he was. His captors' accent sounded like they were from southern China, not from the western portion of the country, where most of China's Muslim population resided. Yet everywhere he looked, he saw items that suggested he was being held by an Islamic militant group. The guard in his room would stop to pray at the appropriate times of the day. When the guard wasn't glaring at him, Wu observed him reading the Qur'an, and his captors either spoke Arabic or Mandarin and Uyghur dialects.

As his gaze drifted back down to the floor, his thoughts began to race.

I don't know if I can take much more of this. Who the heck are these guys and what do they want with me? Wu thought as a new person walked into the room.

As he surveyed the figure before him, he tried to figure out if that man was of European or Russian descent. Wu was suddenly distracted when he smelled the food being brought in, and his stomach grumbled. *This must be a trap*, he thought. *I'm being interrogated...but by whom?*

147

The European-looking man placed the meal on a small table next to Wu. He smiled warmly and had a look of genuine concern on his face.

"Mr. Wu, I am sincerely sorry for the way these animals have been treating you," Dr. Roberts said in perfect Russian. "My name is Ivanov. I work for a hostage rescue company that has been contracted to try and obtain your freedom from the Islamic State," he said, which elicited a surprised look from Wu. He clearly had no idea who had kidnapped him.

Pushing the tray of food and tea towards him, he said, "Please, eat and drink. I am sorry you have been dealt with so horribly. I will do my best to ensure that you are given proper food, water, and more humane treatment. Do you know how long you have been held here?" he asked, wanting to see how's Wu's sense of time had developed.

"I don't know, maybe a week or two. Can you tell me what happened?" he asked, almost pleading as he quickly ate the meager amount of mutton kebab and naan that Ivanov had brought him. He then downed the entire cup of tea, despite it still being rather hot. The life in his eyes started to return a bit; he began to feel better with some food in his belly. Just as he was about to start asking more questions of the hostage negotiator, he suddenly felt a little bit lightheaded. Then, for some reason, he felt a lot happier, euphoric even.

The negotiator responded, "You've been in captivity for nearly five weeks."

Wu burst into tears.

"Why are you crying, Mr. Wu?" asked Dr. Roberts in a comforting tone. "You have done nothing wrong. Your capture was not your fault. It took many weeks, but eventually Chairman Zhang Deijang was able to track you down and contacted my firm to work on getting you released. I've been authorized to provide your captors with a large sum of money if they release you. I am confident we will be able to get you back to China within the week."

Wu seemed to perk up at this comment, though the drugs were clearly working their magic now. He suddenly felt incredibly chatty and started asking all manner of questions to find out more information about the status of the war.

Knowing that this was the time to start asking his questions, Sebastian began his initial approach. "Mr. Wu, can you tell me what is supposed to happen next in Korea?"

Wu looked at him for a second and then smiled drunkenly as he answered, "If things went according to plan, the Americans will push our forces past the Yalu River, and then we will spring our counterattack. We have allowed the Americans to naively believe they are winning in Korea, driving our forces out of the country while we lure them further into our territory. A special trap is waiting for them...."

The two of them continued to talk for three more hours about what China had prepared for the Allies in Korea. Finally, Sebastian changed the topic. "How is China going to deal with the US Pacific Fleet? Won't they prevent your plan from working?" he asked.

Wu just grinned at this simple, yet benign question. "We have thought about that for years," he said. "During the war with Vietnam, we tested a series of new anti-ship missiles that we will unleash on the Pacific Fleet. What the Americans do not know is that we have built an armada of drones that we will use to attack the Americans—"

"What exactly do you mean by a drone armada?" Sebastian interrupted. "How are you going to be able to get past the American anti-aircraft systems? Their Aegis system is nearly impregnable."

Wu just laughed at that suggestion. The drugs were clearly still having their effect on him. He was almost giddy with excitement of the trap they had laid for the Americans. "We are simply going to overwhelm their system. They may be able to shoot down 500 anti-ship missiles, but can they shoot down 1,000, or 2,000 missiles? No system is impregnable, and the Americans are about to discover that firsthand."

Mr. Wu laughed some more before continuing, "The Americans believed our attack on their two supercarriers was the best we could throw at them, but we only sent them a small portion of what we have available. We wanted to make them think we were unable to pull off a complex attack to sink their fleet, but the next attack will have a significantly different result."

As he concluded, his eyes drooped. The side effects of the drug were now in full swing, lulling Wu to sleep before Sebastian had been able to extract everything he was after. As Wu's head dropped down to his chest and he fell asleep, Sebastian signaled for the guard to take him to a small cell where they would allow him to sleep for a few hours.

When he woke up, he would be given some more of Dr. Roberts' truth serum, and they would continue their discussion. In the meantime, Sebastian needed to write up what he had learned so far and get this information disseminated up the chain of command, so they could warn the Allies in Korea of what was going to happen next.

Chapter 23
Ambush

Liaoyang, China

"Could it possibly get any colder in this miserable place?" Sergeant Ian Slater said, more to himself than anyone else.

The 16th Mechanized Brigade had crossed the Yalu River a couple of days after Christmas. They'd had to fight like hell at the river as it was a natural barrier to their advance, but once the ROK forces had broken through, Sergeant Slater's brigade had punched right through the hole they had created and gotten right into the PLA rear guard units. Within a day, they had rolled up twenty-two kilometers of the enemy line, trapping nearly 19,000 PLA soldiers and then forcing them to surrender. Once the PLA had realized they had multiple American brigades in their rear area, the entire front had collapsed, and they had withdrawn to just outside of Liaoyang, where they had finally stopped the American and ROK forces.

"Sergeant Slater, the captain is on the radio," announced his radio operator. "He's trying to reach you, says it's important." As soon as he finished speaking, he ducked his head back inside the new vehicle he had been riding in.

Taking one last pull on his cigarette, Ian filled his lungs, letting his body soak up as much nicotine as possible before exhaling it through his nose. He flicked his cigarette butt on the snow-covered ground and began to walk back to his tracked vehicle. After eight straight days of combat and racing all over the Chinese countryside and small villages and towns, his unit had been enjoying a down day a couple of miles behind the newly established frontlines. They all needed to catch some rest, rearm, and get some new replacement soldiers for the ones who had been either injured or killed.

Slater ducked his head as he stepped back into the track, and his radio man handed him the mic.

"Baker Six, this is Baker Three. How copy? Over," he said.

As he waited, they heard several low-flying aircraft head over their position towards some unseen target. Moments later, there was a series of thunderous explosions.

Those must have been off in the distance, thought Sergeant Slater. *I didn't feel any rumbling. The impacts must have been at least a mile away.*

"Baker Three, this is Baker Six. Get your platoon ready to move. We've been ordered to reinforce Echo Troop. I need your platoon to advance to their position. Make contact with them and then report back to me. How copy?" asked Captain Porter, a bit of urgency in his voice.

I have to give the captain credit, thought Slater. For having been thrown into command of the troop three weeks ago, he'd done a halfway decent job of keeping the unit together and ensuring they didn't get wiped out doing something stupid. *Our troop losses have gone down significantly.*

Slater depressed the talk button on the mic. "That's a good copy, Baker Six. We'll be on the road in five mikes. Out."

With that, he turned to the platoon frequency, ordering, "Everyone, be ready to pull out of your positions and follow my tracks in five mikes."

Five minutes went by with little activity. Once Sergeant Slater was ready to roll out, he suddenly heard the screams of artillery flying over their heads towards the PLA positions.

Friendly fire. Hope they smash the crap out of them before we get up there, Slater thought.

They had just started moving their lead vehicle forward when the area around them suddenly erupted in thunderous explosions. The Chinese army was launching their own counterbattery fire, seeking out the guns that had just been firing on their troops.

"All Baker elements, move out!" Sergeant Slater yelled over the platoon net.

In seconds, their vehicle lurched forward and picked up speed, heading down the dirt path that would lead them to Echo Troop's position. Fortunately, none of Slater's vehicles took a direct hit as they made their way out of the artillery barrage and towards the front lines.

As they neared Echo Troop's positions, the overwhelming percussion of heavy machine gun fire, explosions, and other sounds of war grew in intensity.

"Echo Six, this is Baker Three. We're approaching your position. Where do you want us to deploy? Over." Slater hoped the Echo

Troop commander would respond quickly. It sounded like the front line might be getting overrun, given the volume of enemy fire.

"Baker Three, this is Echo Six. Move your vehicles to grid CH 7634 6538 and plug the hole in our lines. We have additional air support and artillery fire inbound," the Echo Troop commander yelled back. In the background, Slater heard the 25mm main gun of the Bradley firing away at some unseen enemy.

Geez, what the heck have we walked into? Ian wondered.

He directed the four Bradleys in his platoon to the coordinates given to them and looked at the video display next to the vehicle commander. He saw an M1A2 Abrams battle tank burning, with the tank commander's body half hanging out of the turret, burned and charred from the fire. Next to the tank were two Bradley vehicles, both torn apart by whatever weapon had hit them. At the berm in front of the destroyed American vehicles were a dozen infantry soldiers, doing their best to lay down suppressive fire against the Chinese infantry soldiers trying to advance towards them.

"Guide our vehicles between those burned-out tanks and tear into those enemy soldiers," Slater directed. "Also, start looking for enemy tanks and other armored vehicles. If you spot them, take them out first. They're the priority."

Ian turned to look at the soldiers behind him. "When we stop, I want everyone to dismount and get yourselves positioned against the berm. Support the soldiers already there and hold the line. Is that understood?" he yelled to them.

"Yes, sir!" they all yelled back, and they steeled their nerves as they prepared themselves to follow orders.

Slater grabbed the mic and relayed the same orders to the other three Bradleys in his platoon. Within seconds of arriving at the little hill, the enemy fire shifted from the soldiers who had been manning the berm to his four armored vehicles. Dozens and then probably hundreds of rounds started to bounce off the armor turret and body of their vehicle. The gunner in the turret swiveled the gun slightly to the right and fired off a short burst from his 25mm chain gun. He whooped and hollered, letting them know he had just wiped out half a dozen PLA soldiers who had tried to charge the hill.

"Enemy tank identified!" the track commander yelled.

153

"Switching to TOW!" the gunner shouted. In less than a second, they had acquired the enemy T-99 and had fired their TOW antitank missile, which leapt from the carrying tube and made its way quickly towards the enemy tank.

"Oh my God, he's turning towards us. He's going to shoot!" yelled the gunner.

"Hold steady. Our missile is almost there," replied the tank commander in a much calmer voice.

Should I even try to get out of the vehicle? I think it may be a bit too late, Slater thought as he realized he might be about to die in a few seconds if that tank fired first.

Then, miraculously, the track commander yelled to his gunner, "Hit! We got him. Start looking for any additional tanks."

Seeing that there was nothing Slater could do to help the guys manning the tracks, he grabbed the radio mic and tried to raise Captain Porter again. "Baker Six, this is Baker Three. How copy? Over."

It took a minute to get a response, but Porter finally replied. "This is Baker Six, I copy. What's your status, over?"

"Baker Six, we've reached the berm that is essentially the front line. We're encountering massive numbers of enemy soldiers advancing on our position. We've destroyed one T-99 and believe there to be many more armored vehicles operating in this area. We've identified multiple friendly M1A2s destroyed. Requesting additional armor and infantry support if we're to hold this position. How copy?" relayed Sergeant Slater.

Roughly thirty seconds went by before he heard a response. He was starting to get nervous as he waited, wondering what was going on at the other end of his call.

"Baker Three, I just received orders that the entire battalion is moving to your position. Stand by for assistance. Air support should also be inbound, so please be prepared. Out." With that, Captain Porter signed off, and they were officially on their own until the rest of the battalion showed up. They just needed to hold the line until additional help arrived.

Since there was nothing left for Slater to do in the track, he reached over and grabbed his M4 to head out of the back. Fortunately, the snowfall had lifted; however, the temperature had dropped significantly. At last check, it was hovering around 10°F during the day, and roughly -20°F or even -30°F at night. Slater trudged to the berm, where a couple of his soldiers were, and plopped himself down next to them. They were taking turns popping up to fire off three to five rounds at enemy soldiers before dropping below the crest of the hill and moving slightly to the right or left, alternating their firing positions.

Sergeant Slater stood up slightly, placing his head and rifle above the hill line and scanning the horizon for a target. What he saw scared him half to death. No more than 500 meters away from them was a wall of enemy soldiers moving towards them. A line two or three soldiers deep would run forward maybe ten meters and then drop to the ground, while another line of two or three soldiers deep would run past them for ten or twenty meters and then drop. Each line was leapfrogging each other as they advanced towards the American positions.

Holy crap, that's a lot of enemy soldiers, he thought. *How in the world are we supposed to stop that?*

He aimed his rifle at the incoming horde, firing off a series of ten shots before dropping behind the ridge. Dozens of enemy rounds slammed into the earth, right where he had just been standing.

Soldiers from his platoon lined the berm, pouring as much rifle fire into the advancing enemy as possible. One of his heavy machine gunners swept his weapon back and forth, cutting many of Chinese soldiers down.

"Keep firing! Don't stop!" Slater yelled to be heard over the roar of gunfire.

Ian popped up one more time, firing into the wave of humanity that kept charging their positions. He saw multiple enemy soldiers go down from the impact of his rounds, but they just kept coming. Slater looked back to the Bradley behind him (which was still firing its main gun into the enemy soldiers) and saw two of the vehicle crew members doing their best to get the TOW launcher reloaded. Just as it looked like they had completed that task, Slater heard a swooshing sound right over his head.

In shocked horror, Slater watched as the Bradley exploded. The two crew members who had been reloading the TOW missiles were simply blown apart, their bodies ripped into multiple pieces as they were thrown into the air.

"Tanks! Dozens of them!" shouted one of the soldiers about ten feet away from Ian.

Sergeant Slater pulled himself over the edge of the ridge and poked his head over to observe for himself. He saw a dozen T-99s heading towards them and a myriad of other infantry fighting vehicles, along with even more waves of soldiers behind them. They were still roughly 1,500 meters off, but it was enough to make his stomach churn.

Slater felt like he was going to throw up. They were already facing thousands of enemy soldiers, who were now less than 200 meters away and advancing quickly.

Captain Porter and the rest of the company will be arriving shortly, and that will help with the enemy near us, but that won't help us survive that second onslaught, Ian realized.

Sergeant Slater yelled to his radio operator, "Raise the battalion! I need to let them know what we are facing!"

As he started to relay to battalion what they were seeing, two of the remaining Bradleys both fired off their TOW missiles at the incoming tanks.

"Sergeant! We have air support inbound," said the forward air controller. "I need you to guide them in. Switch to channel six. Their call sign is Raven One."

Slater could hear a lot of yelling in the background of the radio. *Sounds they have a lot going on there too*, Ian thought as he switched the radio preset.

"Raven One, this is Baker Three. We have troops in contact. Requesting emergency air support. How copy?" Ian yelled into the receiver to be heard over the cacophony of war happening all around him.

A second later, the pilot replied, "This is Raven One. We copy, Baker Three. Please proceed with coordinates and let us know what we're looking for."

Ian grabbed his notepad, which had their exact grid location written down, and relayed it to the pilots. "We have multiple human wave assaults danger close, 200 meters from our position. We also have nearly a dozen T-99s and close to two dozen assorted infantry fighting vehicles roughly 1,200 meters to our front. What type of ordnance do you have?" Slater asked.

"Baker Three, we're a flight of four A-10s, and we have full combat load. Our first pass will be against the infantry assaulting your current position. Then we'll move to focus on the enemy armor. Please pop yellow smoke so we can make sure we have your lines identified," directed the pilot.

Slater looked up and yelled to several of the soldiers around him, "Start throwing your yellow smoke grenades behind us. Pass this order down the line!"

After a momentary flutter of activity, a yellow pillar of smoke appeared behind Slater and his men.

"We see the smoke. We're coming in hot from the north," the pilot said as their aircraft appeared out of the clouds from the north.

I don't think I've ever been so happy to see an A-10 as I am right now, Ian thought as he fought the fear that was still growing inside of him.

As the aircraft descended, the four of them leveled out in a line, slightly behind each other. Their 30mm chain guns made their unmistakable *buurrrppp* sound as thousands of rounds began to tear into the waves of PLA soldiers that were nearly on top of them. In seconds, hundreds, maybe even thousands of PLA soldiers were obliterated into chunks of flesh and mists of blood.

While the Warthogs were going in for their attack run, a heavy volume of tracer fire erupted from the Chinese lines, in an attempt to blot the four-attack aircraft from the sky. A couple of missiles leapt into the air, leaving ominous trails of smoke in their wake.

The A-10's defensive systems went into effect, launching out multiple flares to distract the missiles. Two of the missiles went right for the flares and detonated harmlessly. The other missiles missed entirely, and the sweet angels of death circled around for a second pass at the enemy armor.

As the Warthogs lined up for their next attack, nearly a dozen anti-aircraft missiles were shot at them from the Chinese lines. One of the flying tanks took a direct hit to one of its engines, but the pilot still continued his attack run, relentless in his effort to provide Ian and his men as much help as possible. Fortunately for Ian, none of the other incoming missiles did anything to stop the A-10s from completing their mission.

When the Warthogs flew across the enemy lines, they released a series of hellfire missiles and cluster bombs across the entire enemy position. Explosions rocked the area. Parts of armored vehicles, tanks, and even enemy soldiers were launched into the air, and the horizon filled with smoke and flames.

Ian heard a lot of his soldiers whooping and hollering at the destruction the A-10s had just wrought. The victory would be short-lived. Seconds later, Ian saw one of the Warthogs explode into a million tiny little pieces.

As he surveyed the scene, another missile streaked in from the clouds above and landed a direct hit on one of the A-10s, blowing the right engine apart. The three remaining aircraft immediately broke formation and began spitting out additional flares and chaff canisters. Seconds later, two additional missiles flew in from high above and hit the flares.

"Baker Three, this is Raven One. We have enemy fighters engaging us now. We're breaking off and heading for home. We'll see what we can do to rustle up some additional help for you guys," the pilot said, speaking loud enough to be heard over the warning sirens blaring in his cockpit.

That's it for these guys, realized Slater. *They're bugging out, and rightly so.*

"Thank you, Raven One. You just saved our lives. Stay safe and we'll see you next time. Good luck. Out," Ian said. They were going to need it as much as his platoon was.

As the aircraft left the area, the Chinese attack resumed, albeit with a lot fewer armor and infantry soldiers. The human wave that was about to crash against them had largely been wiped out. What remained of the infantry was content to stay where they were, firing at his men from a distance while they waited for the next wave of soldiers to join them.

"Sergeant Slater, look behind us!" yelled one of his soldiers. Ian turned around and smiled at the sight of the rest of his company, along with eight M1A2 Abrams battle tanks, heading towards them.

The cavalry has arrived, he thought.

Chapter 24
Supplies and Reinforcements

Seoul, South Korea
Yongsan Garrison

It was dark outside. Snow once again drifted down on the Korean Peninsula. The temperature had continued to hover around 2°F as General John Bennet poured himself a cup of coffee, his fifth of the day.

He snickered as he looked at his coffee mug, which his brother had bought for him as a gag gift. Designed by some veteran-owned company, it bore the inscription, "Filled with Blood, Tears, and Whiskey."

As Bennet sat down at his desk, his eyes wandered to a family photo, a picture of him, his wife and their four kids, two boys and two girls. His eldest son, John Junior, who went by JR, had just joined the Marines four days ago.

Why the heck did he join the Marines? I could have helped him out so much more if he had just gone into the Army like I told him to, he thought. Then again, JR was a strong-willed young man bent on doing things his way. Bennet decided he'd have to speak with General Cutter about his son once he finished officer basic course. *At least he went officer—I really wish he'd stayed in and finished law school, though.*

John snapped himself out of his thoughts and looked down at his desk. He had been reviewing the latest casualty reports and the burn rates of their current war stocks. The Chinese had just launched a massive offensive the day before. The new attack was turning into something fierce as the PLA brought a lot more forces to bear than he had thought they had in the region. He had chewed out his intelligence directorate for not knowing about the increase in PLA soldiers moving towards them. It was their responsibility to identify these units before they became a big problem.

As he was scanning through the casualty reports, two of his colonels popped their heads into his office. "Sir, we have a situation developing up north," one of them said. "You should come to the operations center."

General Bennet sighed. He knew this was probably not good if they were asking him to come back to the ops center so soon. He'd only left there forty minutes ago.

"All right, I'm on my way," he said, reaching down and grabbing his coffee cup to take with him.

I might need more of this, he thought as he followed his officers down the hall.

"General Bennet, we have a break in our lines—here at Dashiqiao," said Brigadier General Phillips, his operations officer or J3 as he pointed to a spot on the digital map.

The map displayed the various US, ROK, and Japanese units all along the front lines, along with a red line showing the enemy's front line and a blue line marking the edge of the Allied forces. As the general examined the image, he saw that the break in the line was serious.

If the PLA is able to exploit this break, they could potentially roll up the entire front line, forcing us to give up the past ten days of hard-fought gains, Bennet realized.

"OK, everyone, let's keep our cool. What's happening? Let's start from the beginning," John said, trying to calm everyone down. It had been a trying few weeks, and nerves were becoming frayed as exhaustion and stress continued to mount.

General Phillips, who was standing nearby, sighed. "The Chinese appear to have moved an entire army group to the area. Right now, most of the troops we've been encountering are militia, but following the militia units are the regular army groups. I talked with the brigade commander from the 16th Mechanized Brigade. His brigade is just south of the main enemy assault, and he told me the PLA's been hitting his entire side of the line with multiple human wave attacks throughout the day."

General Bennet frowned.

Phillips continued, "His brigade isn't the only one experiencing this problem, either. All up and down the line, they're reporting massive human wave attacks. The only thing that's stopped them from being overrun up to this point has been close air support. However, even the Air Force is starting to buckle under the pressure from the PLA Air Force."

Phillips went on for another twenty minutes, bringing everyone up to speed on the status of the front line and the Allied positions.

After a while, Colonel Vince Sutherbee, the Air Force liaison officer or LNO assigned to General Bennet's command, jumped into the conversation. "Sir, now that most of the Taiwanese military has officially surrendered, the Chinese are winding down their primary combat operations in Taiwan. What we're seeing now is a transfer of those air assets from the southern theater of command to northern China. We are starting to see a massive increase in the number of Shenyang J-11s and Chengdu J-10s. These aircraft are starting to mix it up with our fighters in significantly greater numbers than we'd seen in the past."

Before anyone could ask him about the Air Force providing additional ground support, Colonel Sutherbee added, "Our aircraft are doing their best to maintain air superiority over the battlefield. Our A-10 Warthogs, which have been instrumental in blunting the PLA attacks, have been taking a terrible beating with the increase in PLA fighters. In some cases, we've had pilots flying their aircraft back into combat despite one of their engines being completely inoperable or blown out. The demand for air support is so great, we just don't have enough aircraft to support the ground forces and keep the enemy fighters off the battlefield."

General Bennet looked distressed. Turning to his Navy LNO, Captain Amber Michaels, he asked, "What about the Navy? When are those additional carriers going to get in range to use their aircraft over the battlefield?"

Captain Michaels was a new addition to Bennet's staff, having transferred to his headquarters shortly after the sinking of the USS *Ronald Reagan*, one of the lucky crewman to survive that tragic day. Bennet was glad to have her at his command and knew he would have to rely on the Navy a lot more going forward for their air support, especially with the Air Force still recovering from the loss of Kunsan Air Base at the outset of the war.

Amber responded, "Sir, I spoke with Admiral Kinkaid an hour ago. His strike group is now entering range of our most forward front lines."

She motioned towards her Air Force counterpart. "Working with Colonel Sutherbee, we're going to break up the air war into two sections. The Navy, with the support of our EA-18 Growlers, will begin to assume control of air superiority from the Air Force. After viewing the latest satellite imagery, it appears the Chinese are preparing for not only a much larger ground offensive, but an air offensive as well—"

Colonel Sutherbee interrupted, "You're talking about their H-6 strategic bombers?"

She nodded, adding, "That, and their Xian JH-7 ground attack aircraft. We thought those aircraft might be used against our facilities in Guam, but the latest updates show those squadrons have been moved to just east of Beijing, which tells us they're most likely going to be used to support their ground forces."

Everyone in the room sat there for a few minutes, thinking about a possible course of action.

General Phillips chimed in, "What about our B-1s or B-2s? Perhaps we can have them go after the airstrips housing those strategic and tactical bombers."

Up to that point, the B-1s had been focusing on troop concentrations and heavy industrial centers. The limited number of B-2s they possessed had been focusing on going after the Chinese infrastructure: taking out train tunnels, bridges, and key railyards deep inside of China. While the strategic attacks did not always yield immediate fruit, their long-term impact—disrupting the Chinese economy and ability to move men and material around the country— would be realized soon enough.

Bennet held up his hand before anyone could respond. "The B-2s are under presidential order to keep hitting their specified targets. We aren't authorized to redirect them unless we get permission directly from Gates. The B-1s, however, I can redirect under my own power."

He turned to face Sutherbee. "Send a message over to the B-1 squadrons to begin going after the PLA airfields that house the H-6 strategic bombers. I want the Lancers to start hitting the Chinese airfields as often as possible," he ordered.

Then Bennet turned to his logistics officer. "What's the status on our supplies and replacement soldiers?"

Brigadier General Amy Tibbits had known this question would eventually be asked, and unfortunately, she did not have any good answers for the general. The US logistics system was stretched beyond its breaking point. It had gotten so bad that the Department of Defense had been contracting UPS and FedEx to use their aircraft to assist in moving critical war material to Asia.

It's a sad day when you have to rely on FedEx to keep you supplied with tank rounds and bullets, but that's where we are, she thought. She swallowed nervously as the general and the others at the table all turned their eyes towards her.

"Our burn rates are starting to become a major concern. With the renewed Chinese offensive, we're churning through a lot more ammunition. The other challenge we're running into is that as we move the supply depots forward, we run the risk of them being overrun if the lines continue to collapse. I will say, FedEx and UPS have really stepped up. They've begun to deliver an enormous amount of supplies from the States to Seoul. This has allowed us to use the C-130s to do the more dangerous work of moving the supplies from Seoul to our forward depots."

Tibbits quickly changed topics and moved to replacement soldiers, which was just as important as supplies. "US First Army is finally starting to graduate the first set of draftees. While most of these draftees are being slated for units in Europe, I have managed to get some of our open requirements filled. We're going to start seeing an influx of 7,000 Army soldiers to Seoul, along with 15,000 Marines a week. These recruits will be arriving in country starting next Monday, and every Monday thereafter."

This was the first piece of really good news the group had had in more than a week. While the Allied offensive had been going well and they had been capturing a lot of territory, the casualties had been mounting, and replacement soldiers had been arriving at a trickle, which was not sustainable given their losses.

General Bennet sat back in his chair and looked up at the ceiling. He had been left with one bad choice after another. The Secretary of Defense had directed them to attack the PLA hard and push them back out of North Korea.

The US needs some wins, he could hear the SecDef saying, almost as if he were still in the room.

Well, I gave them the wins, but I've nearly run my army into the ground in the process, General Bennet thought. *Now we have a major enemy offensive brewing up, and I have no way of realistically stopping it.* John tried to crunch through the scenarios, hoping he could somehow pull a win out of what would be certain defeat if he kept his forces where they currently were.

Looking at his senior leaders, Bennet's eyes narrowed as he determined what they would do. "It's clear the PLA is launching a major offensive. Looking at the map, we don't have nearly enough forces to stop them. We have roughly 101,000 US forces, and that's if we include the two Marine Expeditionary Forces. The Koreans have suffered some heavy losses, and so have the Japanese. We have no real Air Force replacements coming for many months, and no additional naval ships for at least the same amount of time."

He sighed, pausing for a moment, but he knew he needed to make the tough decision. "I want our forces to begin a fighting retreat to the Yalu River, establish a defensive line there and hold. We will not retreat beyond the river. That river will be our last stand. This will allow us to shrink our front lines to a more manageable front. The Yalu is also the best natural barrier we could ask for. If we start our withdrawal now, we can control the retreat and allow our forces time to get entrenched and prevent a larger breakout."

The others at the table nodded in agreement. No one wanted to retreat, but to stay and try to hold their current lines wasn't tenable given the size of their current force and the lack of air assets being allocated to them. Seeing a consensus between his officers, the general closed the meeting. "I'll tell the SecDef our plan. Let's get the ball rolling right now and make sure we can hold at the Yalu." With that said, the group broke up and began to get their parts of the plan set into motion.

Chapter 25
Revelations

Washington, D.C.
White House, Situation Room

Tom McMillan had just spent the last fifteen minutes bringing everyone in the Situation Room up to speed on the interrogation of Wu Bangguo, the Deputy Minister for Chinese State Security and Chairman Zhang Deijang's righthand man. His capture had been an absolute coup and had provided a treasure trove of information. The CIA had spent the better part of five days debriefing Mr. Wu and then going over every piece of information with a fine-tooth comb, authenticating as much of it as possible before passing the information up to Tom and the President.

Gates looked at his NSA with a bit of a bewildered look. "So, what you're saying, Tom, is that this whole war, this 'Operation Red Storm,' has been methodically planned out for years? Basically, no matter what we had tried to do at the outset of this war with Russia or Korea, it was still going to happen?" Gates asked.

Tom nodded. "Yes, Mr. President. This entire war comes down to China and Russia seeing this as their time to replace American hegemony. With our forces bogged down in the Middle East, Afghanistan, and parts of Africa dealing with Islamic terrorists, they felt Europe and the rest of Asia were ripe for the taking—"

The Secretary of Defense jumped in at this point. "—Tell me more about the social media plan, and this techno-communism argument they're launching."

The Secretary of State held up a hand before anyone could say anything further. "Listen, I know everyone wants to get wrapped up in this social media business, but we have a real problem in Europe and Asia right now. Don't you think we should focus on the military situation there first Jim?" asked Travis Johnson.

Waving the question off, SecDef Castle insisted, "The social media angle is huge, Travis. If we don't find a way to counter this message they're planning to blanket the internet and social media platforms with, then we're going to lose the war of public opinion and confidence in the government. While I'm not one to lead by opinion polls, we can't turn a blind eye to the propaganda they're about to unleash. We can't let the Russians and Chinese turn the perception of the war in their favor. I mean, they're calling for rioting in the streets, work stoppages and all kinds of other civil unrest. This is a tactic right out of the old communist playbook, and I, for one, do not want us to fall prey to it."

The others at the table thought about that for a moment.

"Jim's right," the President asserted. "We need to get ahead of this. We know what they're planning, but we also know we don't have much time."

He turned to one of his trusted security advisors, John Winters. "John, I want your team to put together a social media campaign to counter this techno-communism message they're about to flood the internet with. Do your best to preempt them and get our message out before theirs hits. Maybe we can blunt it and discredit it before it starts."

The others in the room nodded at this suggestion. They just hoped they would be able to counter it soon enough to make a difference. Dr. John Winters had been a premier expert in counterterrorism at the Department of Defense under the previous administration and a special advisor to the President during his campaign and now into his presidency. There wasn't a single person in the room who didn't respect him. If anyone could pull a rabbit out of a hat, it was Dr. Winters.

"We'll get on this right away, Mr. President," John replied confidently. "Now that we know what they're planning, we'll be a step ahead of them."

With a game plan in place to deal with the social media firestorm that was about to kick off, they moved back to the kinetic part of the briefing.

Admiral Meyers signaled to his briefer, who immediately brought up the slides for their presentation. "After reviewing the information Mr. Wu provided, we now have a firm understanding of what the Chinese army is planning to do in Korea. Two days ago, the Chinese launched a massive counterattack against our forces. While we anticipated them doing this at some point, we were caught a bit off guard by the volume of troops they were able to bring to bear against us so quickly. Per Mr. Wu, this had all been part of an elaborate plan and trap. The PLA's intent was to allow us relatively tough, but winnable engagements to overinflate our confidence in our ability to take and hold ground in China proper. These initial successes led us to rush forward faster than we probably should have. Unfortunately, this is exactly what the PLA had wanted us to do."

A few of the men in the room grunted; no one liked walking into a trap.

Admiral Meyers continued, "General Bennet, the Allied commander in Korea, has ordered his forces to fall back to the Yalu River and use this as a last line of defense. It's a natural barrier that will be hard for the Chinese to cross under fire. The real challenge is going to be controlling the northern part of the Korean border between China and Russia. That area is a lot more rugged, and the Yalu is not nearly as wide or deep there. The Tumen River is the next natural barrier. For the moment, we are leaving that portion of the country largely to the ROK and Japanese to defend while we focus our forces to face the main Chinese army—"

McMillen interrupted to ask, "—What about troops and equipment? How are we faring in that department?"

The SecDef signaled he'd answer this question for the admiral. "We've moved the *Roosevelt* Strike Group into position to take over the air superiority mission from the Air Force; we need the Air Force to focus on providing air support for the ground troops. We just made this change a couple of days ago, and so far, we are seeing good results. For each Allied aircraft we are losing, we are shooting down eight PLA Air Force fighters. As for troops and equipment, our forces in Korea are hurting in both areas. I've had to divert some of our new recruits from our buildup in Europe to Korea to keep up with the casualties our forces have been sustaining. I highly recommend that we divert more resources to Korea until we can stabilize the lines a bit more."

Jim sighed as he explained the situation and then sat forward in his chair, looking the others in the eyes before turning to the President. "We have to slow the pace of the war in Korea, along with Europe, so we can catch our breath. The draft has started, and we're finally starting to fill out the ranks of the new units we've reactivated. We need time to get those units the equipment they need. While I recognize that time is not on our side, this is also not something we can rush any further than we already have."

The President rubbed his temples. None of this was what he wanted to hear.

Jim cleared his throat. "Another issue we're running into with the new draftees is the high percentage of them that are medically unfit for service. Never in my life did I think we would have so many young people unable to serve in the military because they were so fat or out of shape that they're more of a liability than a help. Shoot, half of the new recruits showing up for training can't go more than a few hours without access to their smartphones or they freak out. We're having a host of new discipline, morale, and medical problems we never thought we'd have. It's truly concerning, especially if we have to increase the size of the military again."

Jim's cheeks were red. It was tough enough trying to get the military the equipment they needed without having to deal with new personnel issues.

The others in the room also seemed concerned by what the SecDef had just brought up. While several media stories about this very subject had been making waves, the issue itself had not made it into a presidential meeting until now. It was clear that Gates was also not happy with the new information.

Lack of parts, ammunition, fuel and money had plagued the military prior to the war. Now, with a major war going on between Russia, Korea and China, the military found itself stretched beyond its ability when the country needed it most.

Disgusted at the situation, the President thought, *It always comes back to time. How has our country been so thoroughly unprepared to handle a war like this? Have we truly been a paper tiger?*

After weighing his options for a moment, Gates asserted, "OK, then we have to slow the war down. How do we do that and not lose the conflict in the process?"

All eyes turned to Jim. Placing his reading glasses on the table, the SecDef looked at the President and bluntly stated, "We change tactics with the Air Force. For the last month, we've had them focused on strategic bombing missions, going after Russian and Chinese infrastructure, blunting their ability to move personnel, equipment, and material from one part of the country to another. We've been able to hurt their ability to produce war stocks and other materials, but while that effort will help us win, it isn't helping our situation on the ground right now."

"My recommendation is that we change their target set and have them start near round-the-clock bombardments of enemy positions. In the case of Korea, we have our B-2s and B-1s work in tandem with our B-52s to carry out massive bombing runs of enemy troop positions. Let's keep them from massing their forces. We can insert more Special Forces behind enemy lines to specifically call in air strikes against enemy troop concentrations wherever we find them."

The President nodded. *Makes perfect sense to me*, he thought.

Jim continued, "In Europe, we should do the same thing—have the bombers specifically work over the Russian troop positions. We should also rely a lot more on our NATO allies in Europe to do more of the air strikes. The challenge we face in Europe is a bit different than in Asia. The Russians new SA-21s are really hurting us; until our electronic warfare guys can figure out how to defeat their new targeting systems, we're only able to use our F-15s, F-16s, and B-52s in a limited fashion. It's the same with our European allies."

Jim paused for a second as he reached for his bottle of water, opening it to take a quick drink while the others in the room thought about the situation.

"I will say this," Castle insisted, "the Germans and French have really come around since the start of the war. I spoke with my German counterpart this morning, and he assures me they will have two full German army groups ready by the start of summer. That's 125,000 combat soldiers. Both army groups will have two full armored divisions with 2,500 Leopard 2A6 main battle tanks. Their automotive groups are producing tanks and other armored vehicles on near round-the-clock production cycles right now. Likewise, the French are also looking to field two army groups by the start of summer. I'm very pleased with how fast both nations are moving towards being ready for our summer offensive."

Castle managed a smile, the first one he had cracked since the start of the meeting.

Admiral Meyers added, "With the French and German army groups, and the reactivation of Fifth Corps and the added units to Third Corps, that will place the US and NATO Forces at roughly 560,000 combat troops by the first of June, with another 310,000 support troops. At that point, we will no longer need to stay on defense, and we can push the Russians out of Ukraine once and for all and threaten Moscow."

Meyers then turned to the Secretary of State and the Director of the CIA. "If Operation Strawman is ready, we may not need to invade Russia proper, but we'll be ready if we have to."

The new Director of the CIA, Jedediah "JP" Perth, cleared his throat at the mention of his pet project. "After consultation with my counterparts in British MI6, and BND, the German Federal Intelligence Service, we are moving forward with Operation Strawman. This is an incredibly closely held operation, with very few people having been read into it. In two weeks, we will begin to insert the clandestine team that will make contact with Strawman, Alexei Kasyanov. Once the offer has been made and he has agreed to it, we will set into motion a plan to break him out of house arrest and arrange for a series of safe houses for him to begin the resistance movement."

"Because of the summer offensive, we obviously don't have a lot of time to get the ball rolling, but with the help of my social media gurus from Google and Facebook, we're going to spread his message far and wide within Russia and will hopefully be ready for our part when the time comes. It is my firm belief that the Russian people will rally around Alexei, and he will successfully become the new Russian president," JP explained.

Some of the men in the room smiled, while a few of the military members looked at him with obvious skepticism.

Gates grinned at his new CIA Director. *I knew JP was the right guy for the job. If he can pull this off, this may be the single biggest coup of the entire war*, he thought.

Jedediah Perth had taken over as the Director of the CIA roughly two months prior. As a senator, JP had been an ardent advocate for the intelligence community, though he'd often butted heads with many of the leaders within the various organizations. Prior to becoming the junior senator from Arkansas, JP had been an intelligence officer in the US Air Force and had continued to serve as a reservist until he'd accepted the director role at the CIA.

As an intel officer, and a man who had served in both Afghanistan and Iraq, he brought with him real-world firsthand experience that the leadership of many of these organizations either lacked entirely or had experienced in a completely different time. JP understood that the wars of the future would be fought not just on the battlefield, but in social media and cyberspace, areas JP felt the dinosaurs who been running the various agencies did not fully understand. While JP had only been at the Agency for two months, he had been hard at work gutting it of the political appointee holdovers and bureaucrats who were more interested in proving a point or advancing their careers than they were in defeating America's enemies and moving the Agency into the twenty-first century.

Prior to the war with Russia, JP had been analyzing the political opposition groups within Russia. In short order, his two-man research team had identified the People's Freedom Party, or PARNAS, as a real possible alternative to the Petrov regime. Their party motto, "For Russia, with free will and without corruption," along with their strong anticommunist stances and alliances with other liberal European organizations, meant they would probably have strong support from other countries in Europe. That would be critical in any post-Petrov period. The problem was that the current leader, Alexei Kasyanov, was currently under house arrest. An article in the *Wall Street Journal* had claimed this was the one man Petrov feared most. A self-described nationalist democrat, he might be the one man that could replace Petrov and still hold the country together.

The President closed the meeting. "Whatever resources or assistance you need, JP, just let us know and we'll make sure you get it. If your plan works, it may save us from a costly invasion and occupation."
****

Three hours after the national security meeting ended, Dr. John Winters walked into his office and called his small cadre of team members to his office to discuss their new task. It was important that they develop a plan to counter the upcoming Chinese and Russian propaganda campaign. Thanks to the information provided by Mr. Wu, they had a heads-up on the overall strategy and details of the message. Now they needed to create a counter-message.

Clearing his throat to get everyone's attention, Dr. Winters began. "As you all know, I was just at a meeting with the President and the national security team, discussing the war. What you are about to hear is highly classified and extremely sensitive information. Clare is going to hand out a special nondisclosure agreement that you all will need to sign to work on this next project. I'm giving you the option to

171

opt out if you want to, but if you opt out, you are not going to be able to join this special project later. Also, if you do sign the NDA, you will *only* be working on this project for the next couple of weeks."

They all seriously considered their options. Of his team of twelve team members, only four opted not to be a part of the project—not because they didn't want to participate, but because they felt they were already over-tasked and didn't want their other projects to suffer. The four of them were excused from the room and went back to work.

"Those of you who are still here are about to work on one of the most sensitive and perhaps important projects of the war," Dr. Winters began. This introduction caused everyone to perk up. "A little while ago, the CIA carried out a snatch-and-grab mission of Chinese Deputy Director of State Security Wu Bangguo, the righthand man of Chairman Zhang Deijang. During his interrogation, Mr. Wu revealed to us a propaganda campaign that has the real possibility of not just turning the public opinion of the war in their favor but resulting in open revolt within our countries. We don't know the exact time when it will start, other than it will begin soon, perhaps in the next few days or within a couple of weeks. In any case, the President has directed our office to put together a counter-message."

The members of John's team were excited now. An opportunity to go head-to-head with their adversary in the ultimate battle: the conflict of the mind.

One of the women in the group asked, "Why would this new propaganda message be more powerful or effective than what they've already been flooding the internet with? No disrespect, but the millennials of the country are already practically siding with them as it is, and college campuses are practically socialist embassies for all intents and purposes." She spoke with contempt in her voice.

Several members of the team chuckled at her comment, and one of the women couldn't help but roll her eyes at Cindy, who had come to be known as the group's extremist. "I don't know if it's *that* bad," she insisted.

John watched his team go back and forth for a few minutes as the group discussed the flood of propaganda that had been hammering the Allies. The Russians had expertly used raw combat footage of the war, the death of Allied soldiers, and the proliferation of fake news stories; it had all been taking a terrible toll on the populations of the

Allies. Already, this campaign had succeeded in getting Turkey to leave NATO, and massive protests across Hungary, Spain, Portugal and Italy had forced those governments not to back NATO. The protests had gotten so out of control in many parts of the UK that the Labour Party members of parliament had almost garnered support from the Tories to hold a no-confidence vote in the government and had only been narrowly defeated. The Russians were using information technology to wage war in a way the Allies had not anticipated, and frankly had discounted. Now the Allies were paying dearly for that mistake, and it was not one they could make again, with China now entering the fray.

One of the men, who had stayed out of the conversation up to this point, put down his folder and looked up at the team. He had just finished reading the summary of "techno-communism."

"You guys, I think that this new approach could be incredibly effective against the younger generations in the Allied countries. You should really give this a read."

They all took a break from their conversation and dug into the files before them. Finally, Cindy asserted, "Frank, you're right. This 'techno-communism' is going to be very alluring to the restless youth of society, since it basically guarantees them a job as a right. The Chinese are selling this as a way to use technology to enforce a 'social justice' model, punishing those who have views that are considered hateful, racist, or otherwise harmful to the population or government as a whole."

Dr. Winters cut in at this point. "If we're going to counter this appeal, then we need to pick it apart piece by piece. Do you all have any suggestions?"

One of the younger women on the team, Stephanie, spoke up. "We need to sell that this version of communism is not only a disaster for the future, but also means a complete and utter censorship of free speech. We could have a commercial where someone is being kicked out of college because they disagreed with their professor, and another person is fired from their job for working too many hours because that would deprive another individual from obtaining a job."

Frank added, "I can just picture a Google Home or Amazon Alexa device being used under this system to rat out an individual's non-sanctioned beliefs. What if an Xbox recorded someone praying and their religious convictions were not considered legal under the State's demands?"

Cindy chimed in, "You know, a lot of people don't realize that the microphones on their phone are never really turned off. Picture a commercial where all these devices are listening in on conversations and reporting actions, and the jails are filled with political dissidents."

Dr. Winters nodded emphatically. "Exactly, Cindy. Those are the exact points we need to make to counter what the Russians and Chinese are proposing. The enemy is going to use our open society, our freedom of the press, and the internet to flood the minds of our young people and those disenfranchised voters to turn the people against not just the war, but against our form of government. Their arguments will sound appealing, but in the end, techno-communism would be the death of the very freedom our people now enjoy."

Winters' teammates nodded.

"We have a lot of work to do and not a lot of time to get it done in," Winters asserted. "I need everyone to work together on this and crank out some ideas quickly. I would like to start getting some of our messaging points ready over the next couple of days."

As John finished giving his team their marching orders, the group went to work tackling the challenge.

Chapter 26
Operation Strawman

Moscow, Russia

The snow was beginning to fall more heavily in the Bibirevo district of Moscow, where Alexei Kasyanov remained under house arrest.

Why in the world would a reporter want to meet with me on a day like this? thought Alexei as he prepared a fresh kettle of water on the stove. His guest would be arriving within the next ten minutes, and he wanted to make sure he had something warm to offer him to drink. The cold of the Russian winter had finally settled in across the country.

A couple of months ago, a reporter from *Der Spiegel* in Germany had reached out to him, asking if he could write a biographical piece on him and his political opposition party. Of course, Alexei had jumped at the chance, but he had to be incredibly careful about how he communicated with Gunther. He was still technically under house arrest; however, with the war with NATO consuming so much of the Petrov government's focus and resources, Kasyanov felt this was the right time to connect with an outside journalist, especially in light of President Petrov's suspension of the next election, which had been scheduled to take place in March, until the end of the war.

So far, Gunther Brinkbaumer had written two exceptional pieces about Alexei's efforts to lead the People's Freedom Party or PARNAS against Petrov's United Russia party. Gunther had done a superb job thus far in conveying the struggle faced by any political party other than the ruling party and how the opposition parties often found themselves the target of any number of government charges and allegations just prior to each election cycle. Satisfied with Brinkbaumer's reporting up to this point, Kasyanov had agreed to his first sit-down with the reporter. Since Alexei's wife and two children were temporarily living with friends in Sweden, he was not as worried as he normally would have been to have Gunther meet him at his home.

Alexei thought wistfully, *This year is supposed to be the year reformers like myself bring an end to the Petrov regime. We need to reassert Russia as a country ruled by law and the constitution and not by the politically connected oligarch class.*

Looking out his apartment window, Alexei saw a taxi pull up to a building down the road from him. A single figure got out of the vehicle and slowly walked away from the cab. As Kasyanov watched the cab turn down another street and disappear out of sight, the passenger crossed the street and headed towards his building.

Good, just as I instructed, thought Alexei. *Always have the taxi drop you at one point, wait for him to leave, and then walk down to your true destination.*

He buzzed the reporter into the building. After a soft knock at the door, Alexei walked over and opened the door.

"Alexei?" the reporter verified.

"Yes," Kasyanov confirmed.

"I'm Gunther Brinkbaumer from *Der Spiegel*. It is good to finally meet you," he said, extending his hand.

"Please come in. It's cold out there. I have a fresh kettle on the stove. Would you care for some tea?" Alexei offered.

Gunther smiled and nodded as he took his jacket off, hanging it on the hook on the wall next to the door. The two of them sat down at his kitchen table.

Gunther began the interview by asking Alexei a lot of questions about his political beliefs, how he felt Russia could prosper under a different leader, and how he would govern Russia if he were elected president of the country. About an hour into the interview, the conversation started to turn more serious, almost as if it were a job interview. Alexei could sense the difference in the tone of the questions and grew suspicious.

"Alexei," Gunther said as he leaned forward in his chair, placing a small device on the table between them, switching it on.

"What is this? What are you up to?" Alexei demanded as he sat back in his chair, ready to defend himself should he need to.

Gunther held up his hands and explained, "I have activated an electronic scrambler in case anyone is listening to our conversation. I need to ask you some serious questions, and I need a sincere response." He searched Alexei's eyes and facial features to make sure he understood what he had just been told.

When Alexei simply nodded, he proceeded. "My name is Gunther Brinkbaumer, and I do work for *Der Spiegel*. But I also work for the BND, which I am sure you already know is the German intelligence branch. We have a plan. We would like to replace President Petrov with a new leader, and the Allied nations believe that you, Alexei Kasyanov, leader of the People's Freedom Party, may just be our best hope."

A smile spread across Alexei's face. *It's about time the Allies looked for someone to replace Petrov*, he thought.

Inside, Alexei was giddy with joy. This offer was beyond his wildest dreams.

The two of them talked for many more hours and went over how the BND, CIA, and MI6 were going to break him out of his house arrest and establish a series of safe houses and underground networks in Russia for him to operate within. Their goal was to provide him with a secure means of communicating with his supporters to organize peaceful rallies across Russia and begin garnering public support. As that support grew, they would look to find ways to erode Petrov's backing and eventually replace him as the leader of Russia.

Chapter 27
Expansion & Government in Exile

Zhanjiang, China
South Sea Fleet

President Xi looked proudly at the sailors and Marines before him. They had fought gallantly in Vietnam and now they had been a part of the successful reacquisition of Formosa. Today, however, was a special day. After this ceremony, these men would return to their ships and head out on the next adventure to expand China's control of Asia.

As the sailors took their seats, Xi began to speak, "My fellow countrymen, I applaud the success you have achieved thus far in helping our nation to achieve its rightful place as the new leader of the world. Our grandfathers were part of the great revolution that saw the rise and unification of China. Today, you are taking their place as you help to unify Asia under Chinese control and assert our dominance as the new leader of the world—a title of which the Americans are no longer worthy."

He paused for a moment as people stood and applauded at his opening statement. Slowly, the fanfare died down, and he resumed his fiery speech. "During the first hours of the war, the Navy showed it could defeat the American Seventh Fleet. You even killed their commander in the opening hours of the war," he said, openly giving praise to the men before him. They stood and clapped once more.

Xi raised his hands to get the men to resume their seats. "What we ask of you now is to demonstrate to the world once again that it is China, not the US, that controls Asia. You will lead a campaign to expand Chinese control to the Philippines, Malaysia and Indonesia. We need you to do your best in hunting down the remaining American submarines that can threaten us and ensure our armies stay supplied and able to hold our new territories. With the acquisition of these three countries, China will not only have secured our future petroleum needs, we will also have protected passage for our African mining operations. The work you sailors are going to partake in will help shape and define the future of the twenty-first century. China, our great nation, is depending on you men to accomplish your mission. We wish you the best of luck and a safe return," he concluded, then stepped back from the mic.

The sailors jumped to their feet, clapping excitedly once again. They loved hearing their leader not only praise them but give them a reason for why they were fighting and dying. While the victories against America had been great, they had come at a heavy price to the navy, and the American Pacific Fleet had not yet been destroyed. A final battle would still have to be fought, and in the meantime, they had to take down those American submarines who were tearing apart the entire Northern Fleet.

Xi turned and walked off the stage. While he enjoyed the applause, he had a meeting to get to.
****

A few minutes later, President Xi and Admiral Shen were alone in a small private room without any maps, computers or other electronic devices. Xi signaled they should sit in the two chairs waiting for them. The Chinese president was feeling a bit paranoid and had taken great pains to make sure that what was said in this room would not be discovered by anyone, including Chairman Zhang, the architect of Operation Red Storm.

"I wanted to meet privately with you so you could give me your honest opinion without fearing losing face if you admit failure," Xi began. "I have ensured that no one is listening to our conversation. I need a frank assessment of how the naval war is going against the Americans, and I need to know if Chairman Zhang is accurate in his assessments."

Nodding, Admiral Shen sat back in the chair. "We are in a precarious position right now. The Northern Fleet is shattered. The American submarine and cruise missile attacks are devastating our forces and our ability to continue to operate in the northern parts of the country. Nearly every aircraft we had assigned there was destroyed, along with some of our best submarines and destroyers. It is fortunate that we kept our carrier group south of Taiwan; we could have lost it if the Americans had attacked it." Admiral Shen felt relief from the confession but immediately started to sweat, worried that he should not have been so open in his response.

Xi nodded solemnly and leaned in. "Can we still win?"

Shen took a deep breath, relieved that Xi was genuine in seeking a real assessment. He paused for a second as he calculated his answer. "It depends. If we can produce more of our anti-ship cruise missiles and anti-ship ballistic missiles, I believe we can win the surface warfare part of the fight. What we are not going to win, at least not right now, is the underwater fight. While we won a great battle in the East China Sea, it cost us dearly; we lost over half of our naval aircraft and a large number of our submarine force. The American submarines are incredibly effective weapons. We are working with the Russians to try and help solve this problem, but right now we do not have a good answer as to how we are going to defeat them. If we cannot defeat the American submarine force, then it will be nearly impossible for us to keep our carriers safe and not lose our southern fleet," Shen answered.

For a moment, the President's countenance appeared sad and defeated. Then, he lifted his head, and a fire burned in his eyes.

"Are you in need of more destroyers to defeat the American submarines?" asked Xi.

"We have five new *Luyang III*-class destroyers and nine additional *Jiangkai II* frigates. These ships are going to be a part of a new antisubmarine warfare task force I have assembled. This specific group of ships and aircraft will focus solely on hunting and then sinking the American submarines operating in the South China Sea. Until I can fully secure the South China Sea, I need to have them stay local to this area," Admiral Shen explained.

The President nodded, then leaned in and looked Shen directly in the eye for a brief moment. "We need to win this fight, Admiral. What more do you need to win it?"

Chapter 27
Exile

Kyoto, Japan
Four Seasons Hotel

Following the collapse of the Taiwanese military, the democratically elected leaders of the Republic of China had been forced to flee the country and establish a government in exile. Since this outcome had always been a possibility, several possible locations had been identified in advance. Japan had not been one of those preselected locations, but ultimately, there was no other choice. The Phillipines, Indonesia, Malaysia, and Thailand had all rejected them; in desperation, they'd turned to Japan and had been told they could set up their mobile government in Kyoto. They had opted to rent out all 123 guest rooms at the Four Seasons Hotel, which would provide the security services with a safe and controlled location for the government officials to sleep and work.

While the government fled the country, the military continued to fight on for several more weeks before they had to surrender or face certain death. A small cadre of soldiers, mostly Special Forces units, would continue to operate in secret. They would collect information and carry out an insurgency. Minister of Defense Lu, who had been a soldier in his youth, had opted to stay with the military and continue the fight. While their military had been largely destroyed, their ability to collect intelligence and keep tabs on what was happening on the island was very much intact.

Walking along the corridors of the second floor, President Hung Hui-ju couldn't help but marvel at how her staff had turned the entire hotel property into a functioning government building for them to live and work in. It had taken a week, but they had transformed the entire first and second floors into functioning offices. The third floor had been designated as sleeping quarters for the senior government members; the rest of the staff that had been able to evacuate stayed in a separate hotel nearby.

Foreign Minister Chang was hard at work in one of the suites that had been converted to a work space. When he saw the president enter the room, he smiled warmly. "Madam President, it is good to see you," he said as he stood and walked around his desk to greet her.

"Please, let's sit over here." Chang gestured at a pair of chairs with a small coffee table next to them.

President Hung got right down to business. "Have you spoken with the Americans yet about helping us retake Taiwan?" she inquired. She knew the Americans could not help right away, but Taiwan had now been under the control of the communists for nearly five weeks. Each week, each month, meant it would be that much harder to liberate her country.

Chang had a sparkle in his eyes. "They are developing a plan now to neutralize the Chinese navy. Once the Americans can control the sea, the PLA will not be able to stay in control of the island for long. As you know, the American Secretary of Defense was in Tokyo two days ago. I was able to meet with him for roughly an hour before he left for Seoul. He assured me that when the US Pacific Army is fully formed up, Taiwan will be among the top priorities to retake. Right now, we have to bide our time and wait." His voice rang with hopeful optimism.

Hui-ju thought about that for a second while trying not to betray any emotion on her face. *While it's reassuring that the Secretary of Defense has prioritized the liberation of Taiwan, I'm under no illusions about how long that would take*, she thought. The Americans and Japanese might control the waters around Japan, but they hadn't ventured further south to confront the Chinese carrier strike group, and now that the mainlanders controlled Taiwan, they could turn it into a fortress to defeat any American-led efforts.

"I am glad you were able to speak with Jim Castle," she responded. "However, I suspect it will be at least six months until the Americans attempt anything to help us."

Seeing her sad expression, Chang hoped the President would be pleased with this next concession he was able to get from the Americans. "He did say it will probably be more like seven or eight months until they will have the ground forces necessary to start an operation. However, he said they will direct additional submarines to start operating in the straits. They will also continue to carry out strategic strikes against high-priority targets that our forces identify in Taiwan. He said his hope is to provide some Special Forces troops within the next couple of months to help keep our insurgency operation going for as long as possible."

This news managed to elicit a glimmer of a smile from President Hung.

"There was something else we discussed during the meeting," Chang said, the corners of his mouth curling up in such a ridiculously devilish grin that Hung chuckled.

"Oh, and what was that, Chen? Do not keep your president guessing," she said lightheartedly.

He leaned in closer and said softly, "The prospect of a future united China…" He sat back as the President's smile began to grow.

Chapter 28
Bigwigs

Seoul, South Korea
US Forces Korea Headquarters
Yongsan Garrison

Secretary of Defense Jim Castle was in a foul mood as he surveyed his senior military leaders. He scowled at the US Pacific Commander, his new Marine Corps Commander for Asia, and the US Forces Korea Commander, who were present for this secret meeting along with several other generals. While it was a risk for so many of the senior military leaders to meet in Seoul, it needed to be done if Jim was to meet with everyone at the same time. None of these men could afford to fly back to Washington to meet, or even to travel to Hawaii; they were all needed at the front, so Jim had made the decision to travel to them.

He furrowed his brow. "What the hell is going on along the Yalu River and why have we not captured Vladivostok and the rest of the peninsula?!" shouted Castle using his former Marine General voice. His eyes darted between General Bennet, the US Forces Korea Commander and his new Marine Asia General, Roy Cutter.

General John Bennet saw Cutter look at him with uncertainty, so he spoke up to try and help his friend out. "I instructed General Cutter to keep his Marines focused on the ground war in northeast Korea until we could stabilize our lines along the Yalu. When the Chinese lines fell apart, I pressed forward, trying to keep them on the defensive. We now know that was a deliberate trap and I fell for it. I should have been more cautious and not charged into China until we had our entire position in North Korea stabilized," Bennet explained.

Jim wasn't buying it. Cutter hadn't captured Vladivostok because he was waiting until he had more troops and fighter support. "That may be partially true, General, but Cutter has known since the outset of this war that his forces are to stay mobile—hit an objective, secure it, and transfer it over to the Army, so you can keep your forces on the go. Instead, Cutter, you charged ahead when you saw a fleeing enemy army, as if you didn't want to be left out. While I'm not going to admonish you for being aggressive, you failed to listen to your orders," he barked, clearly incensed. "Now the brunt of your force is bogged down at the northern border and unable to break contact until General Bennet here can send you reinforcements. By the way, he can't send you reinforcements because he charged forward into China seeking a quick and easy victory."

Jim paused for a second, needing to calm down for a second before he kept talking. "Look, things happen in the fog of war," he conceded, "but I need you guys not to get carried away like that. We need to close off the Russian Pacific bases and begin to encircle China. We can't do that unless both of you are working towards that goal. What I need to know now is how soon can your forces secure Vladivostok and the rest of the Russian Far East strategic objectives?"

General Bennet leaned forward in his chair. "Secretary Castle, until I can get more reinforcements to Korea, there's no way I can detail off enough forces to relieve General Cutter's Marines. Our hold on the Yalu has been tenuous at best. It's only been through the massive bombing and air support we've received that the Second Korean War hasn't played out like the first. The irony of how things are turning out right now isn't lost on me either. I will win, but I cannot do it if I'm not given the support I need."

Jim snapped back, "General Bennet, it is now February tenth. This is going to be the first full month the military starts to graduate some 90,000 infantry soldiers a week. I have to prioritize where to send them, and right now, that has been Europe. We are gearing up for a major offensive at the start of the summer, and we need to get those troops in place and prepared. The best I can do right now is to send you roughly 15,000 army soldiers a week, and of course, you'll start to see 30,000 Marines arriving each week. That's the best we can do until we reach the troop levels we need for Europe."

General Cutter broke in at this point. "These new soldiers and Marines were supposed to start arriving a month ago—what's caused this delay?"

That had been the million-dollar question a lot of the senior military leaders in Europe and Korea had been asking. Jim had been getting hounded about that issue by nearly everyone from the President on down. Castle sighed, knowing he owed these guys an explanation, especially since he was there in person.

"We have had a heck of a time getting qualified recruits through the draft. Nearly a third of the young people being drafted fail to meet either the physical or the medical standards to join. Between being too obese and having a host of chronic illnesses like diabetes, the failure rate has been horrific. When you lose a little over a third of your draftees each week because they can't pass the physical fitness standard, it slows up our ability to fill the ranks. After this happened for four straight weeks, we increased the draft size each week by thirty-five percent, and we seem to have finally solved that problem. Starting next week, we should be back on track with expanding the armed forces," he said, almost feeling guilty that this problem had ever developed. Despite knowing there was a war going on and a desperate need for soldiers, he was unwilling to lower the military physical standards just so they could fill the ranks.

Laughing at first, General Cutter retorted, "You have to be joking, sir—you're saying that nearly thirty-five percent of the people between the ages of eighteen and twenty-six are unfit for military service?"

Jim stared daggers back at Cutter, whose smile disappeared. "That's exactly what I'm saying, Cutter."

Castle allowed a moment for the reality of that to sink in before he changed topics. "Now, General Cutter, I want a definitive timeline for when you are going to secure your objectives and extricate yourself from the cluster mess you've entangled yourself in." He spoke in a stern voice, not letting his newly appointed Marine Commander off the hook just yet.

His demeanor once again serious, Cutter responded, "You said I should start to see 30,000 new Marines each week starting next week. If that's the case, then I should be able to start moving on the Russian objectives by the end of February. That should give me enough time to gather my reinforcements and get them in place with the Navy to start hitting them."

He continued, "As to my forces already engaging the Chinese, I will work with General Bennet on how best to extract them from the border region before the end of the month. Will that suffice, sir?" he asked.

I sure hope that will be enough, because I don't know what other options I have, Cutter moaned to himself. He hadn't anticipated his forces getting bogged down at the Chinese, Korean and Russian border, but that's exactly what happened. *Now I have 63,000 Marines I can't disengage from the enemy and no Army reinforcements to fill in the positions I've already secured.* His forces had sustained such heavy casualties, far heavier than he'd thought he would have in such a short time.

Castle thought about Cutter's timeline for a minute, finally nodding. "One month, General. Unscrew yourself and get those objectives captured, or I'll find someone who will. I need you to start preparations for our invasion of China next fall, and that can't happen until you finish securing your assigned objectives."

Jim then turned to face the Pacific Commander, Navy Admiral Harry Fenton. "Now let's talk about the naval situation. What are your forces doing to counter the PLA Navy's anti-ship missile swarm attacks, and how soon will your forces be able to defeat the Chinese fleet down in the South China Sea?"

All eyes turned to look at Admiral Fenton, who had so far survived the President's leadership purges. Everyone knew that if he didn't get things sorted out in the Pacific soon, that would change.

Fenton was almost always calm and organized, even to a fault. "Let me address your question in parts, Mr. Secretary. With regard to the South China fleet, we have surged seventeen submarines to the Philippines to interdict Chinese naval forces from attacking the Philippines. We've also redirected twelve submarines to the Taiwan area, and soon they'll begin to attack any and all surface ships ferrying troops and equipment to or from the island. Until we can achieve some semblance of air superiority over Korea, northern China and the Russian Far East, I can't afford to move my carriers down south. Right now, their air power and the Aegis systems are in continuous need. If we can move the Atlantic Fleet carrier strike groups to the Pacific, I believe we can finish the Chinese navy off within the next sixty days. Then, it'll just be a matter of time until they have to surrender Taiwan and we can continue to harass their entire coastal line and industrial centers."

Castle sighed. To him, this was probably the most frustrating part of the war thus far. They had already lost *two* supercarriers, and a third had taken heavy damage. These weren't ships the US could just crank out in a few months like a tank; they took years to build, even with round-the-clock operations.

"Admiral, here's what I would like to see happen," the SecDef began. "Keep the pressure on the Chinese with your submarine force. Keep your carriers focused up north here for the time being. Until General Cutter finishes securing his Russian objectives, I'm going to need you to hold that fleet in the area to support him. As to the Atlantic Fleet carriers, I will speak with the President about having them moved to your theater of operation. They will most likely be needed in the summer, but for the time being, we can put them to better use out here in the Pacific."

Jim paused for a second, surveying the faces before him. "Look, I know it's been a tough war, and we've taken a lot of losses," he acknowledged. "It hurts, and we've all lost a lot of friends and people we've known and served with for years. All I can tell you is that the President and I are both incredibly proud of you and your service. We are doing everything we can to get you the men, ships and aircraft you need to win. I can't guarantee you'll have everything you want in the next couple of months, but make no mistake, gentlemen—the President has turned the economy loose on producing the materials and equipment we need. In the very near future, we're going to be producing more aircraft, missiles, tanks, and ships than we'll know what to do with."

Jim turned to each leader. "John, you've got to do what you can to slow the pace of the war down in Korea. Hold the line at the Yalu, but don't go looking for a fight. I need you to stabilize the front until the Navy and Air Force are in a better position to help you. Admiral, until I can get you those additional carriers, do what you can, but don't lose what remains of our fleet. I can't do anything to help replace your losses until probably the end of the year or early next year. Roy, you've got to secure the Russia Far East. We have a major operation going on in the summer, and your piece of the puzzle has to be in place before that operation starts."

The meeting went on for a few more hours as they ironed out the various details of how the war with China was going to be fought. One thing was clear—nothing substantial was going to happen for at least six to nine months.

Chapter 29
Battle in the Atlantic

North Atlantic

The weather was terrible this time of year in the North Atlantic. The waves were larger, and the winds were stronger. The winter storms made flying nearly impossible. The constant rolling and pitching of the decks of the destroyers and icing made it difficult to run continuous anti-submarine warfare operations like they needed to. While the Allies had sunk fourteen Russian submarines in the Atlantic since the start of the war, there were three *Oscar II*-class submarines that were wreaking havoc on the supply convoys. The introduction of the SSN-26/P-800 "Strobile" anti-ship missiles had come as a rude shock to the US Navy.

While they had known of the missiles' existence, they had assumed the Russian Navy would have stuck with their older P-700/SS-N-19 "Shipwreck" missiles. The older missiles carried a significantly larger warhead, but their guidance and targeting system was also easier to spoof, which was why they had been phased out. While the SSN-26s carried a smaller warhead, their hit rate hovered around forty percent, and the fact that they could engage a convoy from as far away as 600 kilometers made them incredibly hard to counter.

Following the opening salvos of the war, the three *Oscar IIs* had strung themselves across the most likely sea lanes the convoys would travel and then waited for their prey to arrive. When the targeting satellites identified a convoy, the *Oscars* would maneuver themselves to the flanks of the convoy and then engage them once they had entered the kill box. Because each *Oscar* could carry seventy-two missiles, they could likely score between eighty and ninety hits against the convoy. Until the Allies could increase the number of ships protecting the convoys and intercept the barrage of cruise missiles, the losses would continue. The only saving grace was the fact that once the *Oscars* had launched their attack, it would take them close to three weeks to rearm and get back on station to repeat the process.
****

As the *Churchill* slid down the trough of yet another large wave, Captain Gilbert expertly shifted his hand to ensure that not a single drop of his Calle San Juan Costa coffee would go to waste. Lifting his mug to his mouth as they rode the next wave up, he savored the sweet-toned Costa Rican java.

I'm going to miss riding the waves in a destroyer when the Navy does finally retire me, Patrick thought.

The others on the deck appeared more like they were holding on for dear life as they crested yet another large wave. At least the weather report said things should be clearing out of the area shortly; they just had to ride out a few more hours of rough weather.

After the first two NATO convoys had been savagely attacked, the Navy had seen fit to give Captain Gilbert command of twelve escort ships: seven American, one French, two Canadian and two British frigates and destroyers. Now that he had a proper security detail, he had also been given a World War II-sized convoy to protect. His twelve escorts were now protecting 107 tankers, freighters, transports and other heavy roll-on, roll-off ships, which were transporting the tanks and other heavy armored vehicles needed for the war effort. The US and NATO were gearing up for a big action in Europe, and that meant the NATO supply convoys were going to be busy.

Lieutenant Commander Tiffany Brewster, Gilbert's second-in-command, was really looking forward to their next port of call. The end destination for this particular convoy was Antwerp, Belgium. She was bent on trying one of these famous Belgian beer tours.

There may be a war going on, but that doesn't mean we can't find something to entertain ourselves with, she thought as she entered the bridge.

She needed to speak with the captain about the approach to the English Channel. When she entered the bridge and saw the captain showing off his skills by drinking coffee on choppy seas without losing a drop, she chuckled.

He's such a ridiculous coffee snob, she thought with a smile, *but at least he shares his good coffee.*

When they finished cresting the wave, she got his attention. "Captain Gilbert, we just received a message from one of the P-8s flying out of England. They said they have a possible contact at bearing 133, fifty-two miles. They are requesting that we send a ship to check it out."

"You could have just called the bridge to let us know that; no need to make a special trip up from the combat information center," he replied.

"If I did that, sir, I wouldn't have been able to witness how a true coffee connoisseur balances his java between the troughs," she replied with a wry grin. "Plus, I needed to stretch for a minute—"

As she was about to say something further, a message came in from their lone French ship, the *D654 Auvergne*. "Bridge, CIC. We just received flash traffic from the *Auvergne* of a possible underwater contact at bearing 257, ten miles from our current position," the voice from the combat information center announced.

Lieutenant commander Brewster immediately turned around and ran back to the CIC. Captain Gilbert turned to the watch officer and ordered, "Set Condition One! Man battle stations for possible underwater contact."

A couple of the destroyers and frigates nearby converged on the possible enemy contact.

A few seconds later, Captain Gilbert heard LCDR Brewster's voice over the intercom. "Bridge, CIC. We have multiple torpedoes in the water. *Auvergne* has reported they are engaging the underwater contact."

****

On the *K-560 Severodvinsk*, Captain Rubin Malahit's hand involuntarily shook a bit from nerves as the NATO convoy continued to approach their ambush. Two days ago, the joint Russian-Chinese RORSAT had tracked the projected path of the convoy, giving a high probability of crossing their current positions. Russian naval command had immediately looked at the current locations of their submarine force and begun to move the various subs into place to maximize their chances of really hurting NATO. The *Severodvinsk* had immediately been ordered to trek 243 kilometers to the position they currently found themselves in.

Looking at the map of the current NATO positions, Rubin could see the hour of attack was nearly upon them. He looked up briefly and saw his executive officer approach him.

"Sir, the other submarines should be in position to launch their attacks shortly," he said, confirming what the captain already knew.

Several *Akula* submarines would attack the convoy escorts to distract and move the escort ships towards them, while Captain Malahit and the captain of the other *Yasen*-class submarine were ordered to slip inside the convoy and begin to deal the real damage. Of course, the attack was also supposed to be coordinated with the *Oscar* ships that were also operating nearby.

Everything sounds good on paper, until you actually have to coordinate things, Malahit thought.

Just as he was about to issue a set of orders, one of the sonar operators yelled, "Torpedoes in the water!" In that instant, everyone turned to look at him to determine if the torpedo was heading towards them or another target.

"It's from one of the *Akulas*. They're engaging a destroyer," he explained.

A string of obscenities jumbled in Malahit's head. *I knew this was going to be impossible to coordinate*, he cursed inwardly. The Akula had engaged the escorts far too early. *The other submarines aren't in position yet, and my boat is still too far out to penetrate the convoy's protective perimeter.*

The captain turned to face the bow of the ship. "Helm, move us ahead two-thirds. Make our depth two hundred meters."

Then, he turned to face his weapons officer. "Find me targets. We're only going to get one shot at the enemy, and I want to make it count."

A flurry of activity both above and below the waves played out as numerous Allied warships started to head in the direction of the *Akula,* which was now acting as bait. Twenty minutes went by…more torpedoes were launched by both sides.

An American submarine joined the fray and appeared to have a torpedo with a solid track on the Russian sub. Then, a second *Akula* launched a pair of torpedoes at the American sub, which forced them to shift their focus from hunting to evading the new threats heading towards them. While the waters churned with activity, the *Severodvinsk* moved in for the kill.

"How far away are we?" the captain inquired.

"Sir, we're now less than 3,000 meters from the first group of transports, with the nearest potential threats over 15,000 meters from our current position," one of the sonar operators responded.

It's now or never, Captain Malahit thought. He turned to his weapons officer and issued the final order. "Fire torpedoes one through six!"

As soon as the sub had rocked with the launching of the torpedoes, the captain turned and yelled, "Increase speed to 20 knots and drop us down another 100 meters! Let's put some more distance between us and the launch point of the torpedoes!"

Silently, they tracked the torpedoes as they moved towards their targets. The captain had only held two of their torpedoes in reserve, in case they encountered a threat that would require them to engage. The remaining six torpedoes sped towards their unsuspecting targets. After a breathless wait that felt like forever, the torpedoes homed in on their prey. One by one, they exploded against the hulls of the freighters and tankers that had been delivering the much-needed supplies to NATO.
****

The CIC of the *Churchill* was abuzz with activity as Captain Gilbert looked at the map of the battlespace and had that sickening feeling that, once again, he would be the commander of yet another ambushed convoy. As his lone French destroyer took off after an *Akula* submarine, one of his own American destroyers chased down a second one. Then, the radar screen began to populate with over 200 anti-ship missiles flying in towards them from three different angles. While his destroyers and frigates were attempting to prosecute and hunt down three underwater contacts, they now had to deal with a massive missile raid.

The *Churchill* shuddered several times as the vertical launch systems spat out the ship's 60 RIM-66 SM-2 standard missiles at the incoming threats. Five other destroyers in the convoy fired off their own SM-2 missiles in an attempt to swat as many of the threats from the sky as possible.

"How many torpedoes are heading towards the convoy?" Captain Gilbert barked at one of his battle managers.

Not taking her eyes off the screen she was monitoring, the young officer replied, "Ten torpedoes heading towards the convoy. They're going to start hitting ships in the next couple of minutes."

"We have to thin out of those incoming missiles or they're going to finish off the convoy," Gilbert realized.

He looked to one of the weapons officers. "How soon until our interceptors start hitting the enemy missiles?"

"They should start reaching the incoming missiles in the next minute or so—"

As the officer was relaying the information, the ship rocked hard to port, almost throwing the ship completely onto its side before it righted itself in the water. The power briefly flickered out before coming back on again, and everyone looked around trying to figure out what had just happened. They obviously hadn't been hit.

"What the hell just happened?" the captain yelled.

"CIC, this is Bridge. One of the LNG tankers just took a torpedo hit and was vaporized. We got hit by the blast wave of the explosion— I'm also seeing nearly a dozen other freighters and transports heavily damaged and on fire. A couple of them look like they're going down," Lieutenant Commander Brewster reported. She and the captain had switched positions once it had become apparent that the Russians had laid an ambush for the convoy and it was not just a lone Russian submarine they were dealing with.

"Get me a status report on those incoming missiles now!" the captain demanded of his lead weapons officer.

"The missiles are engaging the targets. The number of incoming threats has dropped from 216 to 61. They are now coming into range of our 5-inch guns and the CIWS systems," the officer replied.

That's still too many missiles for them to handle, Gilbert realized as he ran the calculations in his mind.

As the remaining missiles streaked in at Mach speed, the convoys close-in and point defense systems began to take over and started to thin out the incoming threats, but a large number of the missiles still got through, causing considerable damage among Gilbert's convoy.

When the attack finally ended, Patrick headed back to the bridge so he could see the state of his convoy for himself. Grabbing a pair of binoculars, he saw that the damage was obviously extensive. Pillars of black smoke billowed into sky from several ships that had been hit; one of the ships was clearly actively in the process of sinking.

Thankfully, the storm that had been regaling his ships prior to the attack had given way, which would make recovery of the sailors floating in the dozens of life rafts a lot easier.

"Order the helicopters to get airborne and start recovery operations," the captain ordered. "We need to get the survivors pulled from the water before they freeze to death."

After many hours of recovery operations, the captains of the remaining escort ships compiled their battle reports and a full assessment of what happened began. Reviewing the initial battle accounts, Captain Gilbert found some consolation in the fact that this attack had not been an entirely one-sided event. His escorts had managed to sink three *Akulas* and one of the newer *Yasen* submarines.

However, what angered Gilbert most was that no one, including the *P-8 Poseidons,* had spotted or sunk any of those three troublesome *Oscar*-class submarines until it was too late to counter their attack—all three had escaped the conflict unharmed.

During the attack, the lone French destroyer assigned to his fleet had been sunk, along with two more American destroyers. Both British destroyers had sustained damage but were still operational. The one bright spot was that the Canadian destroyer had not only survived the attack unscathed, they had scored two of the enemy submarine kills. It was a tough loss, but the convoy would continue, and most of the much-needed supplies would make it to the front.

Sighing as he looked over the results, he moaned to himself, *This was not how I wanted to end my naval career—as the NATO convoy commander who had two of his convoys mauled by the Russians.*

Chapter 30
Valentine's Day Massacre

Lviv, Ukraine

Ambassador Duncan Rice understood why the Ukrainian government did not want to set up a government in exile in a neighboring country, but as his driver turned down another detoured road, he wished they would. Despite a lot of the ground fighting in Ukraine having subsided for the winter, the Russians had still made a concerted effort to hit the city with random cruise missiles and the occasional mortar attack. They especially liked to target the major road and rail networks, which made moving around the city rather challenging.

I think Prime Minister Groysman feels like he is being a true leader by keeping his government in one of the last major strongholds left under his control, thought Duncan as they neared the hotel that was acting as the PM's primary government center. Looking out the window at the damage the city had sustained over the last five months of war, Duncan felt angry that his warnings had not been heeded regarding Russia.

As they approached the overhang entrance of the hotel, a guard stepped forward and opened Ambassador Rice's door. Duncan unfastened his seat belt and then got out of the vehicle; he was already running late for his meeting, and he hated to be late.

Too many road detours, he grumbled to himself.

Duncan had flown in from Washington the night before and would be flying back to Washington tomorrow, once he had a chance to speak with the various parties he had arranged meet with. For the past four months, Duncan had been working with a small group of diplomats and security experts at the State Department and the National Security Council to try and bring an end to the war. Once it had become clear the Russians were not going to surrender and the President had made the decision that regime change was the only acceptable outcome, his task had changed dramatically. Now Ambassador Rice's primary task was working with pro-democratic and anti-Petrov groups within Russia and Ukraine.

After a quick check by security, Ambassador Duncan was led into a room where Prime Minister Groysman waited for him. The PM stood and extended a hand and a warm smile. "It is good to see you, Duncan. I miss the frequent talks we used to have before all this craziness started. Can I get you a cup of coffee?" he inquired.

Smiling at the thought of some hot java, Rice nodded. Once they both had their drinks, they sat down in a pair of comfortable chairs with a coffee table between them.

"I wanted to ask you how things are going here in Ukraine—how are the people holding up?" Duncan inquired. He had been the ambassador to Ukraine, so he still felt something for the country and its people.

"Honestly, it has been hard," Groysman admitted. "Many people have friends and loved ones trapped on the wrong side of the battle lines. Many more have lost loved ones from the fighting as well, especially in the major cities. While the entire country has not been turned into trench warfare, it is still too dangerous for people to try and drive between the two warring parties. Life has been difficult but thanks to the generosity of the American people, at least we have natural gas and food to get us through the winter."

The two men talked for another hour before Duncan brought up the name Alexei Kasyanov. "What do you know about Alexei, if anything?"

Groysman smiled ever so slightly at the mention. "I know he is probably the one person that Petrov would fear most if he could run for political office. Since Petrov has postponed the election until the war has ended, I would suspect Alexei will try to run. I also suspect that Petrov will do what he can to have him disqualified through the courts," the PM replied before taking another sip of his coffee. He noticed he had run out and signaled for one of his guards to have some more brought in, along with some sandwiches.

"So, in other words, you like him," Duncan said coyly.

"You guys are going to go for regime change in Russia, aren't you? That's why you haven't tried to attack yet?" Groysman probed.

Holding up his hands in mock surrender, Rice responded, "I can neither confirm nor deny that Washington will seek regime change after we win this war. What I am at liberty to say is that our forces will resume offensive operations once they are ready."

There was a knock at the door. One of the security guards opened it slightly, checking to see that it was in fact the food and coffee they had ordered. As the guard brought the rolling table with the food on it to them, they continued their conversation.

"I still cannot believe Petrov invaded the Nordic countries," Groysman commented. "Attacking the Baltic states was no surprise, but invading Norway and Finland…can you tell me if you guys are going to stop them from taking Lithuania or wait until they reach the Polish border?"

The guard who brought the rolling table placed it between them and then left the room. Prime Minister Groysman smiled at the aroma of fresh coffee wafting around them. He reached over and grabbed the coffeepot to pour them each a fresh cup.

As the PM lifted his hand, Duncan noticed a small wire had been attached to the bottom of the ornate coffeepot. Duncan immediately shouted, "*Stop!*" but it was too late.

A loud thunderous *boom* sounded, and a fireball expanded outward, killing everyone in the hotel room before they even knew what had happened.
****

Across the street, a man wearing a hotel uniform stripped his jacket off and changed out of his pants and into a neatly pressed suit. He proceeded to put his new pants, shirt, and jacket on when he heard the loud rumble of the explosion. He paused for a second, smiling at his handiwork.

He had spent the better part of four months infiltrating the security of the hotel to get to this moment. The fact that the PM was meeting with a US ambassador only made the moment of their death that much more satisfying. After changing into his new outfit, the man who had designed the bomb inside the rolling table cart hailed a cab that would take him to the train station. He was on his way to his next target— London.
****

Washington, D.C.
White House

The weather report said that the D.C. area was supposed to get close to twelve inches of snow today, prompting all nonessential government operations to close for the day. The President was lost in a moment of tranquility as he watched the snow outside his window blanket the city; it was so calm and serene.

This peace was rudely interrupted when the phone on his desk rang. Turning his chair around to look at the phone, he saw that the call was coming from the Secretary of State. Then, his Chief of Staff walked into the room and immediately turned on the TV.

With the phone still ringing, Retired General Liam Greeson asserted, "Mr. President, there's been an explosion in Ukraine. It's bad."

The image of a hotel with multiple fires bursting through blown-out windows filled the entire screen.

Picking up the phone, Gates answered in a matter-of-fact tone, "This is the President."

"Mr. President, I just received word that Ambassador Duncan Rice was meeting with Prime Minister Groysman when a bomb was detonated, killing them both. We still don't have any word on what type of bomb was used, or how it got into the room they were meeting in, but we do know it was not a result of Russian artillery, rockets, or air strikes. It was an inside job," Johnson said.

Suddenly saddened by realization that Ambassador Rice had perished, the President softly replied, "Thank you for letting me know. If you can, I would like to call Ambassador Rice's wife later today. He was a voice of reason in these troubled times, and I am going to greatly miss his expertise and friendship," Gates said.

They spoke for a few more moments before the President concluded his call.

As he watched the TV images of the hotel, it was clear it was a fairly large bomb that had gone off—more than enough to kill everyone in the room and those next to it.

A reporter narrated, "Reports are that twelve people were killed and another 37 injured during the blast. Still no information yet on the cause of the blast that killed the Prime Minister and an American diplomat, but it is suspected that Russian intelligence may have been involved."

"Turn it off, please," Gates instructed. "We've seen enough. Keep an eye on the situation and let me know if anything major is discovered. Otherwise, I'm heading up to the residence. I want some time alone to think."

199

The President stood up. It was clear the death of Ambassador Rice had shaken him. The two had become close, even good friends, over the last four months. Duncan had met with the Director of the CIA, JP, on multiple occasions and had been a real help in determining who could potentially replace President Petrov. It had been Duncan's idea for how to reshape not just Russia, but China as well.

I can't believe he's dead, Gates thought in despair. He was going to make Rice the provisional administrator for Russia to work with the new government once the war was over. *This is a terrible loss.*

He climbed the stairs to the residence. He needed some time alone and to be with his family.

Chapter 31
The Errors of the Past and a New Future

Provo, Utah

As Air Force One began its final approach to Provo, Utah, the President looked over the notes for tonight's discussion one final time.

If we cannot learn from our past, we are doomed to repeat it again. We cannot allow the twenty-first century to become a duplication of the last century, he thought. If they couldn't make the world see reason when it came to how to deal with these autocratic tyrants, then this current war would just be the beginning of yet another bloody chapter in the annals of human history, and all this bloodshed would have been for naught.

Tonight's meeting and tomorrow's conference would hopefully set a new course for humanity, hopefully one filled with optimism. The site for the meeting had been chosen carefully many weeks in advance. They'd found a wonderful ski lodge that had a phenomenal panoramic view of the mountains surrounding Provo and Utah Lake. While the rooms were not five-star like these world leaders might be used to staying in, they were secluded and quiet, away from prying eyes and potential threats. There were also a few thousand US soldiers roaming the surrounding woods, along with enough Secret Service agents to ensure there were no unwanted surprises.
****

Three hours after Air Force One landed, President Patrick Gates surveyed the group of world leaders who had traveled to meet him and smiled warmly at his guests. Looking down, he finished pouring the glasses of Merica Bourbon for each of his visitors and began to serve each of them individually. As the idle chitchat died down, he opened the informal meeting.

"My fellow leaders—first, I want to thank each of you for your willingness to meet with me during these trying times our world now faces. As leaders of our respective countries, our first and foremost charge is the protection and well-being of our people. I know many of you see me as a novice to the political scene, or someone who is in over my head. Perhaps you are right; I am a novice to politics. However, what

I am *not* a novice to is understanding human nature and knowing how to solve problems. I also know that if we cannot correct the mistakes of the past, we are doomed to repeat them."

He paused for a moment as the men and women at the table sipped their bourbons. "When World War I ended, the Treaty of Versailles was implemented, and it set into motion the course that would lead to the Second World War not more than thirty years later. That war then led to the Cold War, and the endless conflicts that have embroiled humanity ever since. We have to learn from those mistakes and commit ourselves to not making those same errors."

Several leaders nodded in agreement. "Right now, we find ourselves in yet another major world war. Two days ago, I ordered the Central Intelligence Agency to share with each of you and three other individuals of your choosing in each of your governments what we had obtained from Deputy Director for State Security Wu Bangguo. What we now know is that the Russian Federation and the People's Republic of China had planned this war out for many years. They colluded to cause a series of events that would ultimately lead to war. They built intricate social media plans and campaigns to stir up trouble in our home countries and did their best to sow as much chaos and discord as possible. For all intents and purposes, they have succeeded beyond their wildest dreams," Gates said, observing their reactions to his words.

The leaders continued to sip their bourbon and listen intently.

"While none of our nations sought this war out, we now have to deal with it—"

Before the President could say another word, the Prime Minster of England chimed in. "With all due respect, Mr. President, what more would you have us do? I have already committed my nation's military to this fight, and I have reluctantly agreed to the drafting of 600,000 young men and women to our armed forces. We have accepted £450 billion in loan guarantees from your treasury to give us the capital we need to rebuild our military. What more can we offer?" she asked in her clipped English accent.

The president of Brazil, Castelo Branco, added, "This war with both Russia and China does not concern my country. Brazil is a long way away from the fighting, and neither of these nations have expressed a desire to attack us or even threatened us. Why should I even consider getting Brazil involved in this fight?" he asked.

Gates smiled at the question; this was exactly what he had wanted someone to ask. Patrick stood from his chair but signaled for the others to remain seated. He walked over to a map on the wall that had been set up prior to everyone's arrival. On the map were the current battle lines and the national flag of each nation that had provided troops to the war effort. "Ladies and gentlemen, I spoke of the Treaty of Versailles and how we should not repeat the mistakes of the past. You see"—he paused as he waved his hand over the map—"we are going to win this war."

"We are going to defeat the Russians and the Chinese. What I want to discuss with you today is the creation of a new military and economic alliance that will shape the postwar future and the rest of the century. When we defeat Russia and China, we are not going to impose terms that leave them filled with nothing but hate and a desire to resume hostilities when the occasion presents itself. Rather, we are going to work with them and inspire them to be a part of our grand alliance once their new governments have stabilized."

Continuing, he added, "We have to inspire not just our people, but also our defeated enemy, that there is something more to look forward to other than revenge, that there is a real future for our nations and the world if we can learn to work together, rather than against each other. I want to propose that at the end of the war, we collectively work towards a global project. For example, I believe that if all our scientists put their minds together and truly share their data, we could collaborate to find a cure for cancer within our lifetimes."

A few of the leaders smiled, while others looked perplexed.

"In addition, I feel strongly that a clean energy solution is just around the corner. With a little engineering, we're not that far from harvesting the energy of the Earth's waves or space-based solar panels," President Gates asserted.

Some of the other national leaders seemed to catch his point, nodding.

"As national leaders, we need to inspire our people to think beyond just themselves. We need to instill in them that there is more to life than just having a fancy car…and I believe that if we form a true partnership, the boundaries of the problems we can solve will dissolve," Gates said passionately.

"I see a vision for a New World Alliance based on common interests, one that isn't geographically specific. There are fundamental principles we all believe in: protecting those we love, creating a better future, and preserving our most precious resources. Let's work together and ensure that those values continue."

The conversation went on for hours. President Gates truly listened to the other world leaders' goals, and at the end of the meeting, he had them all agreeing to be a part of this New World Alliance. Even the president of Brazil agreed to commit forces to fight in Europe and Asia. They had a lot of work ahead of them, but the foundation had been laid.

Chapter 32
Shields Up

Seoul, Korea
Yongsan Garrison

"General Bennet, the PLA just broke through our defenses near Gulouzixiang and this entire stretch of the Yalu line!" a colonel from the operations center warned as soon as the general entered the room.

They had been monitoring the PLA assault for fifteen hours as both sides relentlessly launched attacks and counterattacks against each other. The Chinese had been hitting the Allied lines at eight different points now that the river had finally frozen over enough for them to move large numbers of soldiers across it. To make matters worse, a major snowstorm was blanketing most of northern Korea, dropping visibility down to practically nothing. With swirling snow and little visibility, they couldn't make use of their helicopter gunships or close air support, which meant that they had to rely on artillery.

Bennet immediately walked towards the wall map. He saw multiple areas on the line that were blinking red, indicating they were under attack, and three spots that were now fully red, showing where the enemy had broken through.

This blasted weather—if I could get my fighters airborne, we could stop this attack immediately, he thought angrily.

"What units do we have that we can send to plug those holes immediately?" he barked at his operations officer.

Major General Tim York, the J3, responded, "We have the ROK 702nd Special Assault Regiment and the US 15th Infantry Division moving to plug the hole in the line here"—he pointed to one of the breaches—"and the ROK 27th Infantry Division, along with the entire 1st Stryker Brigade Combat Team, is heading to plug the line here, and then and the 81st Stryker Brigade Combat Team is moving to stop the PLA advance through the line here, across from Gulouzixiang, China."

Pointing to another area, he frowned. "That area there I think is of great concern. Prior to the heavy snowfall, satellite imagery showed a massive concentration of enemy artillery, troops, and armor units that was forming up there when the storm hit."

Turning to his Air Force LNO, Colonel Sutherbee, Bennet pleaded, "I know we have a major snowstorm going on right now, but is there *any* possible air support we can get?"

Colonel Sutherbee shook his head. "Not right now, General. I'm working to see if we can get support from our bases in Japan. They may be able to fly above the storm and drop some precision-guided bombs on a series of predetermined targets. I've also spoken with the group commander at the 2nd Bomb Wing out at Guam, and they're going to get airborne and provide us with a series of arc light flights." Sutherbee walked over to the map. "They'll deliver one bombing run along this position here and then hit this hole in our lines here. They're going to be flying high to get above the snowstorm and will be dropping 500 lbs. dumb bombs, so it's going to be a straight carpet bombing run."

General Bennet almost sighed in relief. If he couldn't get tactical ground support for his forces on the ground, then getting the Air Force to bomb several miles of their lines that were captured was the next best thing.

Turning to one of his other officers, he asked, "Does anyone know how long this snowstorm is supposed to last?"

A naval weather officer assigned to the command spoke up. "At least two days. It's a really heavy blizzard coming down from northern China. To make matters worse, sir, it's supposed to eventually envelop most of the peninsula as it moves towards northern Japan. It's going to have a major impact not just on our air operations, but also on our naval operations in the Sea of Japan."

The others in the room thought about that for a minute. If neither the Air Force nor the Navy could provide direct ground support to the Allies for a few days, they could be in serious trouble.

John realized the dire straits they were in. "We need to rush more troops to the front immediately," he asserted. "If the PLA is able to break through our lines here, then we're toast. It'll roll up our entire defense."

As General Bennet further reviewed the situation, another officer nearly jumped out of his seat. "Sir, you have to hear this!" he shouted. "I just received a radio message from Major General Pike, the 7th Infantry Division Commander. He said the PLA broke through the ROK forces and the 2nd Infantry Division all across the Yalu. He's encountering the lead elements of the PLA advance party all the way south in Taechon, some forty kilometers south of the Yalu River," he said to the disbelief of everyone present.

"Get me General Cutter on the phone immediately," Bennet barked to one of his operations officers.

Man, I hope his Marines can help bail us out of this, or we're finished, John thought as he waited for the Marine general to be tracked down.

A few minutes later, one of the officers signaled for him to come over to his desk and held out the phone for him. "Roy, this is John. Where are your Marines right now?" he said, urgency in his voice.

Cutter was taken aback. He had finally been able to extract most of his Marine force from the front lines and moved them down to Busan before loading them back up into the transports to start the next offensive. "My boys are in the south at Busan, resting up. What's going on, John? Are you guys in some sort of trouble?" he asked. He knew John had stripped away a lot of his reserve forces to free up his Marines.

"It's this blizzard, Roy. The Chinese used it masterfully. As you know, they've been hitting most of our lines for the past fifteen hours. While they've broken through in a few areas, we've largely been able to keep them contained—but Roy, I just received an urgent message. The 7th Infantry Division just reported running into some lead elements as far south as Taechon. I'm working to verify that, but if it's true, we are in real trouble. They'll be able to cut off nearly 40,000 of my soldiers and be within spitting distance of Pyongyang."

He paused for a second to catch his breath and to let some of what he just said sink in for a moment. "I hate to do this to you, Roy, but do you think you can pull off a George Patton move and get your Marines on the road to Taechon? If the PLA has truly broken through and is driving that far south under the cover of this blizzard, we're toast. I don't have any more forces I can throw at them without sacrificing the rest of the Yalu line, stretching all the way to the Russian border."

A pause in the conversation gave General Cutter a moment to soak it all in. He had been under orders to get his forces ready to secure Vladivostok, but if he didn't come to the aid of the ROK and US forces now, they could end up losing control of most of North Korea. Taking a deep breath, he suddenly knew what he had to do.

A smile spread across his face as he responded, "Well, General, I guess it's incumbent upon the United States Marine Corps to save the

Army's butt once again. I'll get my Marines on the road immediately and keep you apprised of their progress. I've got to go—lots to get ready." He concluded the call and then turned to face his officers, who were now eagerly looking at him, wondering what he had just signed them up for.

"Fear not, gentlemen," he said jovially. "The Marines have been called up to save the Army…and save the Army we will."

A few of his officers managed a chuckle before they turned serious again.

Cutter spent a few minutes bringing them up to speed before turning them loose to get the various units roused and on the road. Now it was a race to see if they could get north fast enough to prevent the Chinese from recapturing what they had fought so hard and long for these past few months.
****

Yalu River
Opposite Gulouzixiang, China

As the Allied forces fought a drawn-out retreat to the Yalu River, US and ROK engineers worked tirelessly to turn the Korean side of the river into a veritable fortress. They built a series of reinforced trenches, machine gun bunkers and other hardened facilities for the soldiers who would be manning the defenses to both ride out enemy bombardments and seek warmth from the cold. With temperatures routinely dropping below zero, frostbite was becoming a major concern.
****

Sergeant Slater was in an even more foul mood than usual as he walked among the trenches. *This cold is reaching all the way into my bones! Forget this—I'm going back in the bunker!* Sergeant Slater grumbled to himself.

He rushed past a few other guards on the trench line and made his way into the heated bunker. As he entered, the heat from inside welcomed him with its warm embrace. A couple of the other soldiers yelled at him for letting the heat escape, and Slater quickly closed the door. He snarled at them and they quieted right up. Ian wasn't the most-liked sergeant in the company, but he was respected, which he supposed was just as good.

"Sergeant Slater," one of the young privates called to him, "do you know if our unit is getting pulled from the line anytime soon?"

Snorting, Ian responded back, "You just got here three days ago, Private. Now you want to know when we're getting pulled from the line? We'll get pulled from the line when the higher-ups are good and ready. Until then, we'll man our positions in the shift rotations we've been doing for the past three days."

The soldiers went back to reading or doing whatever they had been doing prior to his return to the bunker. Most of them would be returning to the cold in the next hour, so they were enjoying the short respite from the freezing temperatures for the time being.

After the long retreat, Sergeant Slater's battalion had been ordered to help hold this line of trenches with two other Stryker brigades that had just arrived from the US. The two new units were mostly green troops, draftees fresh from training. The only thing keeping those units alive right now was that most of their officers and sergeants were battle-hardened warriors who had been injured either in Europe or at the outset of the Korean War and now made up the nucleus of the new leadership.

While the soldiers of his platoon were kvetching and whining about the cold, more snow began to fall. It was under this cover of snow that the first barrages of the new Chinese offensive began. In an instant, the entire world these soldiers were living in was suddenly under attack. Hundreds upon hundreds of Chinese rocket artillery began to pound their positions and rock their bunker.

This lasted for nearly an hour before the field phone in the bunker rang. Somehow, despite all the noise of the explosions going on, Slater heard it and immediately answered.

"Sergeant Slater, this is Captain Porter," came the voice on the other end. "I need you to get your platoon on the line and ready to repel the enemy. This is it! We can see thousands of them moving towards the edge of the river bank. I've already requested the quick-reaction force to be sent forward to our positions, but I need your platoon to hold your two bunkers and that trench line. Do you understand?" he yelled to be heard over the thunderous booms of the rockets and artillery.

"Understood, sir. We'll hold the line. Out!" Slater shouted back.

He screamed at his men, "Get moving to the trench line! Man your fighting positions!"

The noise level assaulting their ears was horrendous. The continuous thudding of dozens of rockets against the ground above them was terrifying, and now he was ordering everyone out into it. When they opened the bunker door leading them into the trench network, not only were they slapped with subzero temperatures, they were smacked with the overwhelming rumble of explosions and the percussion of hundreds of rifles and machine guns firing at each other. Some of them froze up from the shock of it all.

Undeterred, Sergeant Slater screamed at his men, "Move! Get to your fighting positions quickly!"

The soldiers began to shove and push their way out of the bunker.

Ian immediately turned left when he came to the T-intersection of the trench and headed towards his heavy machine gun bunker, while his other soldiers filtered into the firing positions on the trench. When the engineers had built the trenches, they'd placed heavy 4x4 planks of wood over the top of each trench, both to keep out the snow and to provide overhead protection against flying shrapnel. Every meter, there was a short break to allow the soldiers to pop above the trench line and fire down into the enemy below. As Slater ran into the machine gun bunker, he saw his two M2 .50 machine gunners firing away at the enemy soldiers across the river. His other two M240 machine gunners had their weapons angled a little lower and were firing into the enemy soldiers that were currently racing across the frozen river to get at the concertina wire below.

In the distance, he could see friendly artillery fire reaching out to hit the Chinese artillery positions that had been pounding them mercilessly for the past hour.

Lord, I hope that counterbattery fire can silence some of those guns, or they're going to pound us into the dirt, he thought before returning his focus back to the enemy in front of him.

Looking down at the maze of concertina wire and other obstacles the engineers had built, he saw waves of enemy soldiers rushing towards it. When the engineers reached the impediments, they began to attach the Bangalore torpedoes together into long tubes and slid them through the lines of concertina wire, landmines and other obstacles, blowing them up and creating holes large enough for the infantry soldiers to follow through.

210

"Take out those Bangalore troops!" yelled Slater to his machine gunners. "We can't let them breach our defenses."

One of the M2 gunners shifted his fire away from several infantry fighting vehicles that had just arrived at the edge of the river to the enemy engineers attempting to breach their defenses. The soldier fired off a series of three-to-five round bursts, decimating an entire squad of enemy soldiers as they were attaching and then sliding the ever longer torpedo through the concertina wire. Seconds later, a loud explosion rocked the bunker, throwing Ian to the ground as some debris from above fell on top of him.

Slater slowly regained consciousness, pushing the blackness from his mind as he fought to reclaim control of his body. He looked to his left and saw one of the original guys from his platoon from before the war, lying on the ground not more than a few feet away with blood coming out of his nose and mouth. He coughed, which only caused more blood to flow out of his mouth. As he struggled to breathe, little foamy blood bubbles escaped from his lips and he looked at Ian, terrified and pleading for help.

Slater shoved aside the debris that was on top of him and crawled over to his friend. "Hang in there, Joe! You'll be OK. Let me roll you over onto your side," he said as tears started to stream down his face.

He rolled his comrade onto his side, so the blood wouldn't just collect in his lungs and drown him. To his horror, the lower part of his body didn't turn, but just separated from the rest of him. Ian saw some of his intestines fall out of his friend's stomach and he convulsed for a second before looking at him, a single tear running down from his face. The light in his eyes showed briefly for the last time. Ian knew his friend had just died, and it made him furious and immensely sad that there was nothing he could do for him except try to kill more of the enemy that had just robbed him of a great friend.

In that instant, Slater got up and surveyed the damage to the bunker. They must have taken a tank round or some other projectile, because nearly everyone in his line of sight was either dead or injured. One of the wounded soldiers, his right arm nearly severed, had resumed his post at the M240 machine gun and was pouring fire down into the enemy soldiers that were now rushing through a breach in their concertina wire.

Ian grabbed the field phone and got out an urgent request for medics and more soldiers to help him in the bunker. Then he ran over to one of the M2 heavy machine guns and took aim at a wave of enemy soldiers that was rushing across the ice.

Sergeant Slater squeezed the trigger, firing a ten-round burst into the cluster of enemy soldiers. He was glad to see most of them get shredded by the .50-caliber slugs as they ripped through the gaggle. There were just so many enemy soldiers charging across the river, it was nearly impossible to miss them. All he had to do was point his weapon in their direction and he was all but assured of hitting one of them. Because of the high velocity of the M2, a single round could often hit two or three enemy soldiers, making it an ideal weapon to use at a charging human wave.

A minute after Ian had started firing into the Chinese soldiers, eight soldiers from his company's QRF arrived and immediately went to work on getting the other machine guns back up and running. While Slater's machine gun bunker had only been out of commission for maybe two or three minutes, the enemy had made it count. Hundreds, maybe even a thousand enemy soldiers had made it across the frozen river and were now at the base of the ridge. As more and more of the obstacles were breached, an increasing number of enemy soldiers were now racing up the ridge towards the troops in the trench.

Across the river, not more than 2,000 meters away from the American positions, dozens upon dozens of Chinese T-99 main battle tanks appeared through the swirling snow, their shapes barely discernable, but there. At 58 tons, they were too heavy to cross the frozen river right now, but they could provide excellent direct fire support to their infantry counterparts. Once Slater spotted the tanks, he knew that must have been what had hit them the last time.

I can't let us get nailed like that again, he thought.

Just then, Ian saw two of the tanks fire in his direction. The rounds looked like they were coming right for him, but they impacted on his trench line, sending part of the wooden roof, sandbags and body parts flying into the air. Slater ducked from the explosion, nearly losing his footing as his feet slipped on the brass casings that carpeted the floor around him. As soon as the shrapnel stopped flying, a wave of Chinese soldiers jumped to their feet and charged into the hole the tanks had just created.

212

Not manning a machine gun anymore now that another soldier had taken over for him, Ian jumped up, raised his M4 to his shoulder and took aim at the enemy, hitting one soldier after another as they charged towards the opening in the defenses. While he was firing away, he heard the whistling sound of more artillery fire overhead—only these rounds were bound for the enemy tanks. Dozens of explosions lit up the entire area around the tanks, a few even scored direct hits. One tank exploded in spectacular fashion, contrasting starkly with the near blizzard-like conditions; Slater lifted his arm involuntarily to shield his eyes.

Seconds later, Ian turned his gaze back to the enemy soldiers charging up the ridge. To his horror, he saw even more enemy soldiers than before. As all seemed lost, Slater saw additional American reinforcements starting to show up all along the trench line, and then five more soldiers filtered into his bunker as well.

A lieutenant walked into the bunker and yelled out, "Who's in charge in here?" as he tried to be heard over the roar of the machine guns.

Sergeant Slater walked over to the lieutenant and leaned in closer to his face. "I'm in charge. What can I do for you?" he barked angrily, annoyed that he had to stop shooting at the enemy so that he could deal with this officer.

The lieutenant looked at Slater and smiled. "I've got an A-10 on the radio. He wants to know if we want a gun run on the enemy troops at the base of our ridge or if we want him to focus on taking out those tanks," he said, pointing to the opposite side of the river, where the remaining tanks were continuing to fire rounds into the Allied positions.

"LT, have him focus on taking out those tanks. If we don't stop them from wrecking our lines, we won't be able to hold our positions here," Slater said.

The lieutenant nodded and spoke into the handset of the radio he was carrying.

A minute later, Ian saw several flashes of light that were magnified by the bright white of the snow falling and realized those must have been antitank missiles. They flew at lightning speed towards the enemy tanks, obliterating six of them outright. Ian still couldn't see where the Warthog was coming in from as the snow continued to swirl all around them. Visibility had gone from roughly three kilometers to maybe a kilometer at best.

Then everyone heard the familiar sound of the Warthog's 30mm chain guns firing, which sounded like strips of linen being ripped over and over. The 30mm anti-armor rounds tore through the remaining three tanks on the ridge, exploding them in spectacular fashion.

Strings of enemy anti-aircraft fire reached up into the snow-filled clouds, searching for the A-10 that had just destroyed the tanks they were supposed to be protecting. A few more burps from the Warthog's tank-busting gun blared over all of the other noise, and a couple more secondary explosions blasted on the enemy lines.

The lieutenant gave Ian a thumbs-up and yelled, "We should have some more artillery fire shortly! The Paladins should be arriving at their next firing position!"

Sergeant Slater nodded and yelled back, "Try and see if you can get some more reinforcements up to the trenches!"

Then Slater resumed firing at the gaggle of enemy soldiers still trying to advance up their hill. The ground was covered in dead Chinese soldiers. Just as Ian thought they might repel this assault after all, he heard the unmistakable sound of jet engines flying low and fast overhead.

Looking up instinctively, Ian saw a series of objects fall from the sky and headed right for their positions. One scored a direct hit on the other bunker that Ian's platoon was manning, roughly 100 meters away. The bunker exploded into a million pieces as shrapnel and debris flew in all directions. Then a second bomb exploded on top of the roof of the trench not more than 50 meters away from Ian's bunker, throwing not just wood planks from the roof and walls of the trench, but sandbags, bodies and parts of bodies in all directions.

A third bomb hit deadly close to Ian's bunker, throwing him and nearly everyone else inside to the ground. The flames from the explosion briefly entered the bunker, lighting those soldiers who had not gotten out of the way fast enough on fire. The entire structure of the bunker shifted from the explosion, causing part of the ceiling to collapse, and destroying one of the M2 heavy machine gun positions.

Ian was suddenly surrounded by agonizing screams from the wounded, men and women crying out for their mothers, loved ones, or anyone who could help them. As Ian pulled himself up to his knees, he saw the lieutenant who had been calling in support for them on the radio, his entire face missing. A chunk of something had smashed into his head, and all that was left was a gaping four-inch hole where his mouth and nose had once been, with blood and brain matter oozing out of it. The man's fingers were still twitching and so was his leg. Ian had to snap out of it and turn away before he threw up.

The roar of thousands of enemy soldiers suddenly boomed above all the other noises going on around him. Ian pushed aside part of the collapsed ceiling so that he could see out of the partially destroyed bunker. What he saw horrified him more than the lieutenant's gruesome dead body. The ground below their positions near the river bank was suddenly moving. It had come alive with enemy soldiers. While the visibility had continued to deteriorate from the swirling snow, the Chinese had moved thousands of additional soldiers across the river.

I don't see how we're going to make it out of this alive, Ian thought.

He brought his rifle to bear, taking aim at the enemy soldiers and quickly firing off one three-round burst after another at the men who were desperately trying to kill him and his comrades. Soldier after soldier dropped to the ground, but more just kept taking their place. In a matter of minutes, Ian had gone through four full magazines of ammo and was down to just three left.

He desperately called out, "I need more ammo! Can anyone bring me more ammo?" He hoped someone might hear him above all the racket of the shooting.

When Ian was changing out to his last full magazine, a soldier threw him a bandolier that contained ten more magazines. While Ian was not in the trench, his little position in the blown-out bunker provided him with an exceptional spot to pour fire into the charging enemy soldiers. The Chinese infantry were focused on the Americans in the trench in front of them, but they seemed to have no idea that a single soldier to their right was picking them off one at a time.

Ian swapped out yet another magazine for a new one and continued to fire. The Chinese had reached the trench at that point, and many of the men simply jumped in when they got near it, tackling the American soldiers to the ground so more of their comrades could jump in.

As one enemy soldier crested the top of the trench, Ian shot him three times in the chest; he collapsed, only to be replaced by two more of his comrades who made it into the trench. Despite his best efforts, Ian just couldn't kill enough of them to stop them from getting into their lines. Slowly at first, then very quickly, dozens upon dozens of enemy soldiers were getting into the trenches and silencing its defenders. Ian knew it was only a matter of minutes before they reached his bunker and he had nowhere to go.

I'm either going to die, right here and now, or I'm going to be taken prisoner, he realized.

A couple of the soldiers still left alive in the bunker with Ian turned to him, almost pleading with him to tell them what to do. They were now trapped, and it was only a matter of time before the Chinese made their way to their bunker.

In a moment of courage, he yelled to his comrades, "Listen up, guys, we're going to kill any enemy soldier who tries to come through that door! You hear me?"

They all nodded. The frightened looks on their faces turned to anger and determination. If they were going to die in this bunker, then they were going to take as many of their adversaries with them as possible.

Outside the bunker, they suddenly heard voices and a lot of yelling. A couple of machine guns opened fire and a few explosions shook the air. A few bullets and shrapnel suddenly hit the bunker door. The men knew it wouldn't be long now. The enemy was about to burst right through that door and try to kill them all.

There was more yelling in Chinese, and then a thunderous explosion burst into the bunker. Seconds later, two loud blasts rang out inside the bunker, punctuated by screams in English and Chinese, and even more rifle fire.

Ian was lying on his back at this point, his rifle having skittered across the floor not more than five feet away from him when he had been knocked to the ground from the most recent explosion. He knew he wasn't going to be able to get to his rifle before more enemy soldiers busted through the doorway, so he reached down and grabbed his SIG Sauer P320 pistol and aimed it at the door. He fired three rounds, hitting the first enemy soldier who came through the door.

Slater fired another two more rounds at the next soldier before something hit him multiple times in his front armor plate and his world went fuzzy. Suddenly Ian couldn't feel much or move anything, but he heard more screams in both Chinese and English, along with a few desperate struggles and a plea for mercy by one of his soldiers.

Just as he began to regain feeling in his arms and legs and the ability to move, a figure was standing over Ian looking down at him. An older-looking Chinese man smiled briefly, saying in broken English, "You are coming with us."

Then he hit Ian in the head with the butt of his rifle, knocking him out cold.

From the Authors

Miranda and I hope you've enjoyed this book. We always have more books in production; we are currently working on another riveting military thriller series, The Monroe Doctrine. If you'd like to order Volume One of this action-packed page-turner, please visit Amazon to purchase your copy.

If you would like to stay up to date on new releases and receive emails about any special pricing deals we may make available, please sign up for our email distribution list. Simply go to https://www.frontlinepublishinginc.com/ and sign up.

If you enjoy audiobooks, we have a great selection that has been created for your listening pleasure. Our entire Red Storm series and our Falling Empire series have been recorded, and several books in our Rise of the Republic series and our Monroe Doctrine series are now available. Please see below for a complete listing.

As independent authors, reviews are very important to us and make a huge difference to other prospective readers. If you enjoyed this book, we humbly ask you to write up a positive review on Amazon and Goodreads. We sincerely appreciate each person that takes the time to write one.

We have really valued connecting with our readers via social media, especially on our Facebook page https://www.facebook.com/RosoneandWatson/. Sometimes we ask for help from our readers as we write future books—we love to draw upon all your different areas of expertise. We also have a group of beta readers who get to look at the books before they are officially published and help us fine-tune last-minute adjustments. If you would like to be a part of this team, please go to our author website, and send us a message through the "Contact" tab.

You may also enjoy some of our other works. A full list can be found below:

Nonfiction:
Iraq Memoir 2006–2007 Troop Surge
Interview with a Terrorist (audiobook available)

Fiction:

The Monroe Doctrine Series
Volume One (audiobook available)
Volume Two (audiobook available)
Volume Three (audiobook available)
Volume Four (audiobook still in production)
Volume Five (available for preorder)

Rise of the Republic Series
Into the Stars (audiobook available)
Into the Battle (audiobook available)
Into the War (audiobook available)
Into the Chaos (audiobook available)
Into the Fire (audiobook still in production)
Into the Calm (available for preorder)

Apollo's Arrows Series (co-authored with T.C. Manning)
Cherubim's Call (available for preorder)

Crisis in the Desert Series (co-authored with Matt Jackson)
Project 19 (audiobook available)
Desert Shield
Desert Storm

Falling Empires Series
Rigged (audiobook available)
Peacekeepers (audiobook available)
Invasion (audiobook available)
Vengeance (audiobook available)
Retribution (audiobook available)

Red Storm Series
Battlefield Ukraine (audiobook available)
Battlefield Korea (audiobook available)
Battlefield Taiwan (audiobook available)
Battlefield Pacific (audiobook available)
Battlefield Russia (audiobook available)
Battlefield China (audiobook available)

Michael Stone Series

Traitors Within (audiobook available)

World War III Series

Prelude to World War III: The Rise of the Islamic Republic and the Rebirth of America (audiobook available)

Operation Red Dragon and the Unthinkable (audiobook available)

Operation Red Dawn and the Siege of Europe (audiobook available)

Cyber Warfare and the New World Order (audiobook available)

Children's Books:

My Daddy has PTSD
My Mommy has PTSD

Acronym Key

ASAP	As Soon As Possible
ASW	Anti-Submarine Warfare
BND	German Federal Intelligence Service
C3	Command, Control and Communications
CG	Commanding General
CIC	Combat Information Center
CIWS	Close-in Weapons System
CMC	Central Military Commission
CW4	Chief Warrant Officer Four
DIA	Defense Intelligence Agency
DPRK	Democratic People's Republic of Korea
FO	Forward Observer
FSB	Modern Russian KGB
G2	Intelligence Chief
G3	Operations Officer
HE	High-Explosive
HEAT	High-Explosive Anti-Tank
HVI	High-Value Individual
J3	Operations Officer
JDF	Japanese Defense Force
LNO	Liaison Officer
LST	Land Ship Tanks
LT	Lieutenant
LTC	Lieutenant Colonel
NATO	North Atlantic Treaty Organization
NDA	Non-Disclosure Agreement
NSA	National Security Advisor OR National Security Agency
ODA	Operational Detachment Alpha
PC	Politically Correct
PLA	People's Liberation Army (Chinese Army)
PLAAF	People's Liberation Army Air Force (Chinese Air Force)
PLAM	People's Liberation Army Militia (Chinese Reserves)
PLAN	People's Liberation Army Navy (Chinese Navy)
PM	Prime Minister

PRC	People's Republic of China
QRF	Quick Reaction Force
ROK	Republic of Korea (South Korea)
RPG	Rocket Propelled Grenade
RSO	Regional Security Officer
SAM	Surface-to-Air Missile
SDG	Sensory Deprivation Google
SecDef	Secretary of Defense
TOW	Tube-Launched Optically Tracked, Wire-Guided
WP	White Phosphorus
XO	Executive Officer

Made in United States
North Haven, CT
27 August 2022